LADY WITH A GUN

A chair exploded through the window of the office. *"Robbers!"* Stuart bellowed from inside. *"Police!"*

"Halt!" McDonald commanded. "Drop your guns!"

In an instant, McDonald and Masterson drew their pistols.

Lea opened fire. She held her horse steady, pistol at arm's length, and thumbed off five shots in a staccato roar. A slug pocked the sleeve of McDonald's coat, and another sent Masterson's hat spinning in the air. The third buzzed past Masterson and the fourth nicked McDonald high on his right arm. Even as the last shot was fired, they dove for cover and flattened themselves on the ground.

As Lea spun around, her hat flew off and her long, flaxen hair tumbled down over her shoulders. For a moment, her face framed in the noonday sun, there was no mistaking her features. Then she switched hands, winging a final shot with her other pistol, and gigged her horse after Stovall and Taylor.

McDonald and Masterson slowly got to their feet. They stared after the retreating horses in dumb silence.

"Tell me," McDonald said, "wasn't that your lady friend?"

Masterson rolled his eyes. "I wouldn't believe it if she hadn't almost killed me," he said.

ST. MARTIN'S PAPERBACKS TITLES

BY MATT BRAUN

BLOODSPORT

MATT BRAUN

St. Martin's Paperbacks

BLOODSPORT

ISBN: 0-312-97176-1

Printed in the United States of America

St. Martin's Paperbacks edition/ November 1999

St. Martin's Paperbacks are published by St. Martin's Press, 175 Fifth Avenue, New York, N.Y. 10010.

10 9 8 7 6 5 4 3 2 1

TO

BETTIANE

EVERY MAN SHOULD BE SO LUCKY

AUTHOR'S NOTE

Bloodsport is based on a true story.

Dan Stuart was a professional gambler, renowned throughout the Old West. By happenstance, late in 1894, he became involved in the sport of prizefighting. At the time, prizefights were illegal, universally condemned by the clergy and lawmakers as a barbaric spectacle. Yet the public was clamoring for a match between heavyweight champion Gentleman Jim Corbett and the leading challenger, Bob Fitzsimmons. Even then, fighters were the idols of millions of people.

How Dan Stuart overcame all obstacles represents one of the most bizarre stories to emerge from the Old West. His adversaries included the United States government and the state of Texas, the dictator of Mexico and the governor of New Mexico Territory, and a strange alliance of the Texas Rangers and the Mexican Rurales. Stuart defiantly led them on a chase that ended in 1896 along the banks of the Rio Grande.

And he achieved what remains the most daring feat in ring history.

Unknown until later, a gang of robbers were vitally interested in what was touted as "the fight of the century." Stuart was a showman of the first order, and his championship match promised to draw gate receipts in excess of a million dollars. The robbers, led by the boldest outlaw chieftain in the Old West, organized a plan to take down the largest haul in the annals of crime. Their final confrontation with Dan Stuart was a piece of history in itself.

The story of fistic exploits and bold robbers is grounded in fact. As with any fictional account, literary license has been taken in the telling. Yet the tale itself is true to the times.

Bloodsport depicts the saga of a man who laid it all on the line—including his life.

ONE

The horsemen rode into Round Rock from the south. The main street was all but deserted on a Wednesday afternoon, somnolent beneath a warm November sun. A dog lay sprawled in sleep on the sidewalk outside the hardware store.

The town was small but prosperous, located some fifteen miles north of Austin, the state capital. Shops and stores lined the street, serving the farmers and ranchers from the surrounding countryside. For the merchants, Saturday was the big day of the week, the street jammed with wagons and buckboards. By Wednesday, a cannon could have been fired down the main thoroughfare without hitting anyone.

All of which accounted for the three strangers on horseback. Their business was better conducted without crowds, and quickly. One was tall and lean, with a handlebar mustache and weathered features. The second man was clean-shaven, darkly handsome, broad through the shoulders and quilted with muscle. The third was short and lithe, wearing a lightweight duster and a low-crowned hat. They rode along the street in a cone of silence.

Opposite the hardware store, they reined their horses in before the Mercantile Bank. There was a military precision to their movements as they dismounted and looped their reins over the hitch rack. The one in the duster waited with the horses, subjecting the whole of the business district to a slow, careful scrutiny. The other two crossed the sidewalk without hesitation and marched into the bank. They went through the door with their guns drawn.

The cashier's window was to the rear of the room. Beyond that stood a massive safe, the steel doors closed. To the immediate left, seated behind a desk, the bank president was engaged in conversation with a man dressed in a business suit. A teller at the cashier's cage squawked a strangled warning, his eyes fastened on the robbers. Off to the side, another teller who was bent over an accounting ledger snapped his head around. The bank president started out of his chair.

"Sit tight!" the stocky robber ordered, motioning with his pistol. "Don't cause any commotion and you won't get hurt."

The lanky one held his position at the door. "Gents, that's damn good advice," he said equably. "No need gettin' yourself killed over money."

There was a moment of turgid silence. At the desk, the president stared at them with bewilderment, and the businessman swiveled around in his chair. The cashier seemed paralyzed, watching them intently, and the other teller sat frozen with his pen dipped in an inkwell. Their mouths were agape.

None of them could quite believe it. No one had attempted to rob the bank since 1878, when Sam Bass tried and was killed for his efforts. There were ballads about the daring young bandit and the shootout on the street that ended in his death. But that was seventeen years ago, and a fearful superstition had spread among those who rode the owlhoot trail. Robbers simply steered clear of Round Rock.

"You'll never get away with it," the bank president grumbled. "I'll have the Rangers on your trail before dark."

"That a fact?" The handsome robber grinned, his teeth square as tombstones and pearly white. "We cut the telegraph wires on the way into town. I doubt you'll raise any Rangers."

"You still won't get away!"

"What's your name, friend?"

"Homer Winslow."

"Well, it's like this, Mr. Winslow. That safe back there looks to be locked. And I'll bet you're the only one that knows the combination. Am I right so far?"

Winslow nodded. "That is correct."

"Thought so." The robber again flashed his mouthful of teeth. "Guess you know what that means, Homer. You're gonna have to open'er up for me."

"Never!"

"Or else I'm gonna have to make your wife a widow. You are married, aren't you, Homer?"

"You're not going to kill me. You're bluffing."

The robber thumbed the hammer on his Colt six-gun. "Your wife will be some pissed if you get yourself shot. Sure you don't want to change your mind?"

Everyone in the room stared at Winslow. A bead of sweat popped out on his forehead and he swallowed hard around something lodged in his throat. His eyes were fixed on the dark hole in the snout of the pistol, and his thoughts were on eternity. He bobbed his head.

"I'll open the safe."

"Wise decision, Homer."

Winslow led the way to the rear of the bank. A nudge from the pistol in his backbone focused his attention, and he spun the combination knob on the safe. After three rotations, he turned the handles with an audible *thunk* and swung open the doors. A shelf on the inside was virtually bare, thinly lined with stacks of cash.

"What the hell?" the robber said in a disgruntled voice. "Where's all the money?"

"In Austin," Winslow said with a smug look. "Saturday's the only time we need a large reserve of cash. We transfer funds up here on Friday."

"Wouldn't you goddamn know it! I'll bet there's not ten thousand in there."

"You're off by about five thousand."

"Kiss my ass, Homer."

The robber pulled a folded gunnysack from inside his coat. He handed it to the banker and stood watching while the shelf was quickly emptied of cash. When Winslow finished, he grabbed the sack with a sour expression. He turned toward the front of the room.

"You're a real sport, Homer. Thanks for nothing."

Winslow waited until he went through the gate beside the cashier's cage. The banker's hand dipped into a recess inside the safe and reappeared with a stubby revolver. As he brought the gun to bear, the robber standing at the door fired a quick snap shot. The slug struck Winslow in the shoulder and the bulldog revolver dropped from his hand. He collapsed backward into the maw of the safe.

"Goddammit!" the stocky robber howled. "Why'd he pull a fool stunt like that?"

"Got me," the other one said, equally baffled. "Maybe he don't have no sense of humor."

"You can bet that put the whole town on notice. Let's get while the getting's good."

A roar of gunfire sounded from outside. As they went through the door, the third gang member was already mounted, reins clenched in his teeth and a pistol in each hand. All along the street merchants appeared in their doorways and he peppered them with a scathing barrage. Windows in the storefronts shattered as they ducked for cover.

Across the way, the town marshal rushed from his office. He stopped on the sidewalk, shouldering a double-barrel shotgun as the other two robbers got mounted. When he tripped the triggers, a hail of buckshot fried the air around their ears. The one in the flapping duster holstered a pistol, grabbing the reins with his free hand, and fought his horse to a halt. He extended his other pistol at arm's length, sighting carefully, and fired. The lawman went down with a slug through the leg.

"Let's ride!" the robber yelled, whirling his horse. "Make tracks!"

The gang thundered north, out of Round Rock.

The sun dropped lower on the horizon. A last flare of light painted the sky in hues of gold tinged with vermilion. Dusk lurked not far behind.

The robbers reined to a halt along the banks of the Llano River. All afternoon they had pushed their horses at a ground-eating lope, and they were now some twenty miles west of Round Rock. There was no sign of pursuit by the law.

Stony Taylor, the tall one, stepped out of the saddle. As the others dismounted, he stretched the kinks out of his gangly legs. He jerked a thumb along their back trail. "Think we've outrun 'em?"

"Nobody to outrun," Earl Stovall said with a wide grin. "The Rangers probably still haven't gotten the word. We caught 'em with their pants down."

"So why'd we push our horses so hard?"

"Well, like Lea says, better safe than sorry."

Lea Osburn removed her hat. Her hair, tawny as flaxen wheat, cascaded down over her shoulders. She was an attractive woman, with a pert nose and vivid blue eyes, her cheeks lightly sprinkled with freckles. When she shrugged out of her duster, her shapely figure was revealed, a brace of pistols strapped around her waist. She looked at the men.

"Let's camp for the night," she said, more a statement than a request. "The law won't be on our trail till sometime in the morning. We'll be long gone by then."

"You're a corker, Lea," Taylor beamed. "You got 'em scratchin' their heads tonight."

Stovall laughed out loud. "Did you see ol' Homer's face when we waltzed in there? Just couldn't believe anybody would rob his bank!"

"Lea plumb had 'em pegged," Taylor remarked. "Never figured anybody'd pull a holdup in Round Rock again. Not after they plugged Sam Bass."

"It'll be dark soon," Lea said, ignoring their banter. "Suppose we get a fire started."

Their chores on the trail were by now routine. Taylor went off into the trees bordering the river to collect wood. Stovall unsaddled the horses, securing them with hobbles, and put them out to graze. Lea gathered a small coffeepot from the saddlebags, along with hardtack and jerky wrapped in oilcloth. Whenever they pulled a job, they traveled light and ate sparingly. The time to celebrate would come later.

Before long, the blaze of a fire lit the quickening

darkness. The nights turned chilly when the sun went down, and the outlaws gathered around the warmth of the fire. Stovall sat closest to Lea, and casually draped an arm over her shoulders. Their affection was evident, for they were lovers, and Taylor had long ago accepted the fact that he was the odd man out of the bunch. After the coffee boiled, they tore into their meager supper with considerable hunger. None of them had eaten since early that morning.

There was a quiet camaraderie among the three robbers. Yet they were a study in contrasts, hardly birds of a feather. Stonewall Jackson Taylor, originally a native of Tennessee, had drifted west and worked for years as a cowhand. He naturally came by the nickname "Stony," and though far from dumb, he was the slowest of the three. Earl Stovall, on the other hand, was bright and articulate, so handsome that it often got him into trouble. A native Texan, he had met Jackson while they were working on the same cattle spread. After a saloon gunfight, in which they killed a couple of tinhorn gamblers, they'd gone on the owlhoot. From there, it was a short step to the life of robbers.

Some two years ago they had met Lea in Fort Worth. At the time, she was working as a saloon girl in the town's infamous Hell's Half Acre. She enjoyed their company, and she was particularly attracted to Stovall. They were quick to brag about their exploits, and she was gradually drawn into their schemes. A saloon girl lived a hand-to-mouth existence, and the chance at big money, not to mention the excitement and danger, appealed to her as a way out. Until then, with haphazard planning, the men had robbed several banks, and barely managed to stay ahead of the law. She convinced them that there was a smarter way.

Lea was not an educated woman. But she possessed an innate intelligence, and at the age of twenty-five, she was mature beyond her years. She was able to subtly dominate the men, Stovall through their emotional attachment, and Taylor through underplayed mental agility. She taught them to scout a job in advance, plan every step in detail, and concentrate on unprotected, small-town banks. The risk of a shootout was greatly reduced, and escape into the back country enabled them to easily outdistance the law. For two years, by gently exerting her leadership, she had kept the men out of jail and in the money. Their string of holdups had left the Rangers stumped at every turn.

The men were no less impressed by Lea's extraordinary skill with firearms. A country girl, raised on a farm and taught to shoot at an early age, she had a natural gift. Whether a pistol or a rifle, she had an unerring sense of aim, and the uncanny ability to sling lead at rapid-fire and still hit the mark. She was quicker and more accurate than either Stovall or Taylor, and easily outshot them whenever they held a practice drill. During a robbery, her job was to safeguard the horses and hold off anyone who attempted to interfere or block their escape. She disguised herself as a man, bunching her hair inside her hat, and usually wore a duster to hide her figure. The disguise had served well enough to fool even the Texas Rangers.

"You two surprise me," she said when they'd finished their meal. "You always want to count the take the minute we stop. Something wrong?"

"Chickenfeed, that's what's wrong," Taylor grumped. "We was the ones that got robbed."

Stovall reached back to his saddle, which lay on the ground. The gunnysack was tied to the saddlehorn, and he pulled it loose. He rolled his eyes after a quick count of the loot.

"Four thousand six hundred," he said. "Not much of a payday."

Taylor muttered a curse. "We should've already had a million from that fight. Tell you, it's a helluva note."

A heavyweight championship fight was scheduled to take place in Texas. The gate receipts were projected at a million dollars, and Lea saw it as the haul of a lifetime. But the fight had been delayed for over a year by legal maneuvering, and the location of the match was still in doubt. She was nonetheless determined to pull off the robbery of the century. She believed in dreaming big.

"Have a little patience," she said to Taylor. "Some things are worth waiting for."

"Jesus H. Christmas, Lea! You've been saying that for a year now. And we're still pullin' jobs for small potatoes."

"No, she's right, Stony," Stovall chimed in. "We just got to sit tight and wait it out. Meantime, we need ourselves a stake here and there. That's what we got today."

"I dunno." Taylor looked skeptical. "Seems like we're chasin' some sort of rainbow. Goldurn fight is on again and off again and on again. Who knows if it'll ever happen?"

"Quit your worrying," Stovall said. "We'll get that million yet, won't we, Lea?"

Lea nodded with an enigmatic smile. "Yes, I'm sure we will."

"Why?" Taylor demanded. "Why are you so sure?"

"Because I have faith in Dan Stuart."

TWO

"Goddamn Jim Corbett!"

"What is it, Dan?"

"This!"

Stuart handed her the telegram, delivered only a moment ago by a bellboy. Julie was seated on the sofa in their suite at the Vendome Hotel. She quickly scanned the message on the telegram form, dated November 14, 1895. The words brought a puzzled expression over her features.

> *You are hereby advised that I have retired from the prizefight ring. I have awarded the championship belt to Peter Maher and will pursue my career on the stage. Time waits on no man. Not even you.*
>
> > *James J. Corbett*

"I don't understand," Julie said, looking up. "How can he award the championship belt to someone else?"

"Gentleman Jim believes he's the god of the prize ring. He thinks he can do whatever he chooses."

Stuart stalked to the window, staring down at the

street. He rocked back and forth on his heels, hands clasped behind his back. His jaw muscles flexed in a tight knot, and a vagrant thought passed through his mind. He wondered if El Paso was the last stop.

Julie rattled the telegram. "Who is this Peter Maher?"

"The Irish champion," Stuart said gruffly. "Wouldn't you know, Corbett gave it to one of his own. The Irish, to put it charitably, stick together."

"Yes, but is it legal? Can he simply hand over the championship—like it was a box of candy?"

"Unfortunately, the appearance of things is all that counts. Corbett's noblesse oblige effectively bestows the crown on Maher."

"Appearances or not . . ." Julie wrinkled her nose. "I must say, it all sounds very shoddy."

Stuart turned from the window. "Corbett should have been a ballerina, not a fighter. He's a prima donna right down to his socks."

"Oh, how delicious!" Her laughter was like warm brandy. "I can just picture him in toe shoes and a tutu. Is he really much of an actor?"

Gentleman Jim Corbett was appearing in the Broadway stage play *The Naval Cadet*. The press had dubbed him "America's Matinee Idol," and he reveled in the attention. So much so that he hadn't defended his heavyweight title in almost two years.

"Corbett's no more an actor than I am." Stuart lit a cigar, puffed a thick wad of blue smoke. "He likes to see his picture in the paper and hear the applause. Not to mention the money."

"Does he make a great deal on the stage?"

"Enough to give him a large measure of independence. He'd rather emote than fight."

"Yes, but that places you in a terrible position. What will you do?"

"You mark my word." Stuart grabbed the telegram from her hand, waved it overhead like a battle flag. "Corbett and Fitzsimmons will fight. No two ways about it!"

One of the things Julie loved about him was his great passion. There were no half-measures in his lexicon; he undertook any endeavor with all stops out, or he didn't undertake it at all. He played to win.

Stuart was a gambler by profession. In Dallas, where they made their home, he was acknowledged as a high roller without equal. His game was poker, and for twenty years, he'd been known to bet a fortune on the single turn of a card. He looked upon the prizefight venture as merely another wager.

A stout man, Stuart was a solid six-footer, built like a bull. His chiseled features were set off by a neatly trimmed mustache and a shock of dark hair flecked gray at the temples. He was forty-two, though he looked a decade younger, and an impeccable dresser. His customary attire was a conservative three-piece suit, with a gold watch chain stretched across the expanse of his vest. His ramrod bearing gave him a commanding presence.

Julie Gibson was proof that opposites do attract. She was dainty, with upswept auburn hair and exquisite oval features. Her flashing green eyes sparkled with spirit and vivacity, and her quick humor played in counterpoint to his wry, somewhat amiable manner. They had been together seven years, and she despaired that she would ever lead him to the altar. Yet she was no less devoted to him for want of a wedding ring. She felt secure in their unspoken vows.

"How will you force him to fight?" she asked now.

"A contract apparently means little or nothing to Mr. Corbett. His telegram makes that quite clear."

"I'll think of something," Stuart said, puffing his cigar. "Dammit, I have to, Julie! My reputation is at stake."

"I know, and I'm just miserable. But it all seems such a shambles. Where do you start?"

"Well, for openers, I have to talk with Judge Townsend and his fight committee. Telegraph operators are the worst gossips in the world. Half of El Paso probably already knows about Corbett's telegram."

"Is there any chance the committee would withdraw their guarantee?"

"Without Corbett in the ring, there's every possibility they would. Twenty-five thousand isn't peanuts."

"How will you reassure them?"

"I'll have to talk fast."

"And convincingly."

"That, too."

Stuart brushed her lips with a kiss. She watched him hurry out the door, trailing behind a cloud of cigar smoke. For a moment, she worried that he'd at last been presented with an insurmountable obstacle. But then, on second thought, she told herself it wasn't so.

He was at his best in a crisis.

Outside the hotel, Stuart turned upstreet at a brisk stride. The weather was fair, with a warm afternoon sun lodged in the sky, particularly pleasant for the middle of November. He thought there was something to be said for holding the fight on the border.

El Paso was spread along the banks of the Rio Grande. The locals were fond of quipping that the river was a mile wide and a foot deep, too thin to plow and too thick to drink. On the opposite shore stood Juarez, the northernmost outpost of Mexico. Looming westward were the snowcapped peaks of the Franklin Mountains.

Until 1881, El Paso had been little more than a way station on the trail from Santa Fe to Mexico City. But then, within a matter of months, the Southern Pacific and the Texas & Pacific laid tracks to the border and transformed it into a railroad boomtown. By 1883, it was a burgeoning city, with electricity and telephones, a center of commerce and trade. Civic boosters were quick to point out the cosmopolitan airs brought on by prosperity, complete with an opera house.

Yet, even in 1895, the sordid still existed alongside the cosmopolitan. Downtown, on Utah Street, a tenderloin of gaming dives, whorehouses, and dance halls operated around the clock. Detractors, most noteworthy the clergy, argued that El Paso's vice district rivaled those of Frisco's Barbary Coast and New Orleans's fabled Storyville. Nor was the Wild West of yesterday altogether a dim and faded memory. Not three months ago, John Wesley Hardin, the deadliest gunfighter of frontier times, had been brought down by an assassin's bullet. A victim of his own fame, he had been shot in the back of the head.

To Stuart, the shooting merely reaffirmed the vagaries of life. As he walked along the street, a cigar wedged in the corner of his mouth, he was reminded that a decision made today often altered a man's course all the days ahead. A year ago, he was the king of gamblers among the Dallas sporting crowd. Men traveled from distant places to test their luck at his table, and he invariably sent them home sadder for the experience. He was respected, comfortable if not wealthy, and generally at peace with his lot. Then, almost by a fluke, he got himself involved in the prizefight game. It all started with a vision too tempting to resist.

In 1894, the public was demanding that Gentleman Jim Corbett defend his title against a worthy challenger. A former bank teller, with a taste for fancy clothes, Corbett was a scientific boxer rather than a toe-to-toe slugger. Two years earlier, he had whipped the mythical John L. Sullivan and captured the heavyweight crown, winning by a knockout in the twenty-first round. His victory was all the more impressive since it was conducted under the Marquis of Queensberry Rules, with boxing gloves. The bare-knuckle brawls of Sullivan's day were by then a thing of the past.

Corbett defended his title only once in the next fifteen months. He devoted himself instead to Broadway and the stage, glorying in the spotlight as a matinee idol. But the fight crowd was not to be denied, and the challenger universally favored was Bob Fitzsimmons, noted for his sledgehammer punch and a long string of knockouts. On October 1, 1894, Corbett and Fitzsimmons were signed to fight at the Olympic Athletic Club in New Orleans. A month later, the state of Louisiana filed an injunction, declaring the bout contrary to the law "prohibiting assault and battery." The championship match was off.

In Texas, watching the charade play out in the newspapers, Stuart saw the chance of a lifetime. He seized on the opportunity, offering to hold the fight in Dallas for a $25,000 winner-take-all purse. Corbett and Fitzsimmons were agreeable, and on November 10, 1894, he signed them for the match. To show the world he was serious, Stuart then set about building a fifty-thousand-seat coliseum as a monument to the sport of pugilism. He announced that his "palace of sports" would produce gate receipts of $1,250,000 from the fight. The press ballyhooed it all across the nation.

Stuart was nothing if not an optimist. In 1894, prizefighting was illegal throughout most of the country. The statutes varied, but in many states it was a felony that carried a prison sentence. Clergymen righteously condemned the sport, labeling it a barbaric spectacle, and lawmakers across the nation endorsed the church's view. Yet fighters were idolized by the public and fights were still held, sponsored by local athletic clubs. To circumvent the law, the fights were billed as exhibitions of physical culture, or the manly art of self-defense. Even then, fighters were routinely arrested and subjected to heavy fines.

Under the banner of the Dallas Athletic Club, Stuart declared that no Texas statute would be violated by the championship match. He and his lawyers argued that the law, which made prizefights a felony with a misdemeanor fine, was so vague that it was unenforceable. The Dallas Pastors' Association promptly issued an outraged condemnation, roundly scorching the contest as a symbol of decadence and moral rot. Still, there was widespread public support for the fight, and Dallas businessmen urged state officials to ignore the clergy. The religious community retaliated with a strident demand for Governor Charles Culberson to call a special session of the legislature.

The governor, warily testing the political winds, allowed the debate to drag on for eleven months. Finally, besieged by a statewide assault from church leaders, Culberson convened the legislature in special session on October 15, 1895. He blasted prizefighting as an "insult to public decency" and warned that the bout would bring "ignominy and shame" on the Lone Star State. The lawmakers agreed, and swiftly moved on legislation that made prizefights a criminal offense, with a ten-year prison sentence. Passage of the bill took less than two hours, and there were only six dissenting votes. The championship match was now outlawed in Texas.

The rumor immediately surfaced that Stuart would take the fight across the Red River into Indian Territory. A day later the secretary of the interior ordered the War Department to alert the troops at Fort Sill and apprehend anyone involved with the fight. Ever a step ahead, Stuart fooled everyone by moving his headquarters to Hot Springs, Arkansas. Prizefights were a misdemeanor in Arkansas, with a fine that amounted to little more than a slap on the wrist. The sporting crowd laughingly joked that Stuart had at last outfoxed the law.

But the law was sometimes a nebulous thing. Governor James Clarke of Arkansas invoked an 1838 felony statute prohibiting unlawful assemblies and riots. The mayor of Hot Springs denounced the governor, and his defiance was widely supported by the town's business leaders. Their interest was in the estimated $500,000 that crowds drawn to the fight would leave behind in the community. Within days, two hundred workmen were laboring on a mammoth arena in a neighborhood park. Hot Springs welcomed Stuart into its midst.

A week later Jim Corbett arrived with his entourage and set up training camp on the outskirts of town. The next day authorities arrested Corbett on charges of "conspiracy to commit unlawful assault," and he was forced to post a $10,000 bond. Shortly afterward, when Fitzsimmons crossed the state line, he was taken into custody and similarly charged. The law had put the fighters, and Stuart, down for the ten count.

Governor Clarke, exercising the power of clemency, offered a solution. The charges would be dropped if Corbett and Fitzsimmons voluntarily deported themselves from Arkansas. Stuart accepted on behalf of the fighters and everyone readily hopped the next train out of town. The championship match, harried relentlessly by lawmakers and the courts, was again in limbo. Then, like divine intervention, came an invitation from a group of El Paso businessmen, guaranteeing the purse and the site. The fight would be held across the border, in Juarez, Mexico.

A long, grueling year had passed since Corbett and Fitzsimmons were signed for the fight. Stuart had taken on the governors of two states and spent upwards of $20,000 attempting to stage the bout. With the new match now set for February 14 of next year, he would have invested fourteen months of his life in what once seemed a straightforward business proposition. But he was confident this time out, no longer concerned about irate preachers and the laws of the Lone Star State. He had a plan that was little short of foolproof A lock.

Or so it had seemed until an hour ago. Corbett's telegram threatened to pour sand in the gears of all he'd put in place. Stuart cursed to himself, furiously puffing his cigar, hurrying along the street absorbed in thought. The more he weighed it, the more he realized that Julie was right. Fast talk alone would not persuade the El Paso fight committee.

He had to convince them that he could deliver Gentleman Jim Corbett.

THREE

A mule-drawn streetcar trundled along San Antonio Street. The driver clanged the bell as Stuart strode into a three-story office building. He mounted the stairs to the second floor.

Upstairs, Stuart entered the law offices of Judge Arthur Townsend. A secretary looked up from her typewriter, and by the expression on her face, he knew he was expected. She ushered him into a private office that overlooked the street.

Judge Townsend was a slender stalk of a man. His angular features and leonine head of gray hair gave him a distinguished appearance. With him was another member of the committee, Karl "Doc" Albers, who owned the town's leading pharmacy. Albers was heavyset and bald as a bullet.

"There you are, Daniel," Townsend said, rising from behind his massive walnut desk. "We were just talking about you."

Stuart laughed. "Bad news travels fast. I take it you got a phone call from the telegraph operator."

"Well, as you can imagine, he thought I might be interested. He considered it his civic duty."

"Word's probably all over town," Albers added, shifting his bulk in a leather armchair. "We'll have a panic on our hands before nightfall."

Albers was the ex-mayor of El Paso and the man responsible for forming the fight committee. He had convinced Townsend, a retired judge who had returned to the practice of law, to act as the nominal head of their group. The other member of the committee, not present today, was Juan Daguerra, organizer of an annual festival held in Juarez. Through their efforts, a syndicate of businessmen had donated funds to guarantee the purse for the fight. They estimated that the bout would generate at least a quarter of a million dollars in added revenue for the local business community.

"No need for panic," Stuart said, seating himself in an armchair opposite Albers. "I'm catching the evening train, and I'll be in New York by the end of the month. I feel confident Corbett can be persuaded to change his mind."

"Do you?" Townsend asked. "His telegram sounded rather final."

"Judge, I've dealt with Corbett for more than a year now. Believe me, I know how to bring him around."

"I appreciate your assurances. But as of today, we're faced with a monumental loss of business without the fight. How do we reassure our investors?"

"That's the question!" Albers chimed in. "What happens if you can't change Corbett's mind? We're left holding the bag."

"Not necessarily," Stuart said smoothly. "I'm a betting man, and I'll wager Corbett sees the light. But as a last resort, we can always go with Maher."

Albers scowled. "Fitzsimmons beat Maher three years ago. A rematch wouldn't draw flies."

In 1892, Fitzsimmons and Maher fought a non-title match, shortly after the Irish champion emigrated to America. It was a slugfest from the opening bell, Fitzsimmons flattening Maher in the first round, only to be decked himself moments later. The match went twelve rounds before Maher was forced to retire with a broken nose. The record books carried it as a technical knockout.

"That bout was a fluke," Stuart remarked. "Every sportswriter in the country said Fitz was on the verge of being knocked out. He got lucky and broke Maher's nose."

"Hardly the point," Townsend interjected. "The public wants to see Gentleman Jim Corbett in action. They still consider him to be the champion."

"No doubt about it," Albers said. "The fact that Corbett surrendered the belt to Maher means nothing. Corbett's the drawing card in this mix."

Stuart wagged his hand. "I think you're selling Maher short. He certainly got everyone's attention with the O'Donnell fight."

On November 11, just three days earlier, Maher had fought Steve O'Donnell in New York. O'Donnell was ranked among the top heavyweight contenders, and Maher demolished him in sixty-three seconds of the first round. The impressive victory was one reason cited by Corbett when he handed over the championship belt. The other, as everyone knew, was that Maher was Irish.

"Yes, but it still begs the point," Townsend insisted. "Insofar as the public is concerned, Corbett is the champion."

"Then let's talk about insurance," Stuart replied. "Suppose for a moment that Corbett won't listen to reason. Are you willing to let all our work slip by the boards?"

"What is this?" Albers demanded. "You just got through saying you could bring Corbett around. Now you're saying what—maybe not?"

"I'm saying we have too much invested not to consider the options. Maher could be our ace in the hole."

Judge Townsend leaned forward, elbows on the desk, his fingers interlaced. He stared at Stuart for a long moment, then nodded slowly to Albers. "I believe Daniel speaks to the heart of the matter," he said. "We've come much too far to allow anything to disrupt our plans. Fitzsimmons and Maher is better than no fight at all."

Albers looked resigned. "I don't like it, not even a little bit." His gaze shifted to Stuart. "Have we got your word you'll do your damnedest with Corbett?"

"You have my solemn oath, nothing less."

Stuart and Julie boarded the eastbound train that evening. He was still congratulating himself at having won over Townsend and Albers, and he was no less confident about Corbett. Yet he was reminded of the adage that no gambler lightly ignored.

A wise man always hedged his bet.

The train chuffed to a halt in San Antonio two days later. Stuart gave Julie a hand onto the platform, and waited for a porter to collect their luggage. From the depot, they took a hansom cab to the hotel.

On the way uptown, Stuart was unusually quiet, lost in thought. His next step was to hedge the bet with Fitzsimmons, who had elected to train for the fight in San Antonio. He silently marshaled his arguments, for there was more riding on a championship bout than anyone might imagine. He couldn't afford to lose.

Stuart planned to film the first motion picture in history of an actual prizefight. Three months earlier, he had entered into a partnership with Enoch J. Rector, a pioneer in the budding industry of motion pictures. Last July, in Thomas Edison's studio in New York, Rector had proved there was a market for fight films. He had staged an exhibition bout between Gentleman Jim Corbett and a down-at-the-heels heavyweight, Pete Cortney. He'd captured on film six one-minute rounds, with the champion winning by a knockout.

The Kinetoscope motion picture was then shown in peepshow arcades throughout the northeast. The film created a sensation, and people stood in line for hours, gladly paying admission to watch the exhibition. A month later, Rector approached Stuart with a deal to film the Corbett–Fitzsimmons championship match. Stuart immediately grasped the potential of the project, for there were millions of people who would never see a championship prizefight except on motion pictures. He and Rector signed a contract the same day.

By conservative estimate, Stuart calculated they would clear a million dollars. He envisioned the film being shown in vaudeville theaters across the country, and at least ten million people eagerly paying fifteen cents apiece to see the bout. From the day he signed the contract, he ceased to worry about where the fight would be held, or the gate receipts. The motion picture became the driving wheel behind his dogged efforts to stage the fight. He knew it would make him rich.

But first, he had to have a fight. Which meant two

fighters, preferably Corbett and Fitzsimmons. On the other hand, Fitzsimmons and Maher could work just as well. For the novelty of motion pictures was such that the public would pay to see any championship match. All he had to do was convince Fitzsimmons that the opponent was immaterial. The purse and the championship belt were what mattered.

Fitzsimmons was quartered at a spacious old hotel with his entourage. His manager and brother-in-law, Martin Julian, welcomed Stuart and Julie when they entered the suite. His wife, Rose, who had recently given birth, hurried in to display her baby boy. Across the room Fitzsimmons was playfully sparring with his pet lion, Nero, a four-hundred-pound bundle of claws and fangs. No one thought it unusual that the fighter traveled with a lion, and allowed it to share his quarters. He was considered something of an eccentric.

"Well, if it's not Dan Stuart." Fitzsimmons left his lion chained to the bathroom doorframe. "I don't have to ask why you're here. The newspapers are full of it."

Julie and Rose took a seat on a sofa, cooing over the baby. Stuart exchanged a handshake with the fighter. "I'm on my way to New York," he said. "I hope to convince Corbett to honor his contract."

"And if he refuses?" Julian asked, trying to sound like a hard-nosed manager. "What are your plans then?"

"That's actually why I'm here. I want Bob's agreement to fight Maher."

Julian frowned. "Bob should be the one to claim the championship belt. He's already whipped Maher."

"Damned if it's not so," Fitzsimmons agreed hotly. "I'm after teaching pretty-boy Corbett a lesson. I've bloody well whipped everybody else."

There was no disputing the statement. Robert Prometheus Fitzsimmons began his career in New Zealand, and went on to win the Australian championship. After emigrating to America in 1890, he took on all comers, racking up a string of eleven knockouts and three technical knockouts in just four years. His last fight, in which his opponent died from head injuries, resulted in a trial on manslaughter charges. A jury acquitted him after deliberating for less than an hour, and he walked out of court a free man. But he was now known as the fighter with a "lethal" punch.

Sportswriters had dubbed him "Ruby Rob." His red hair narrowed in a widow's peak, and he was the most unlikely looking fighter ever to enter the ring. He was knock-kneed, with spindly legs and a shambling gait, ungainly in appearance. But he'd started life as a blacksmith, and from the waist up he was a fearsome specimen, his arms and shoulders corded with muscle. John L. Sullivan jokingly referred to him as "a fighting machine on stilts." His opponents seldom lasted long enough to appreciate the joke.

"Listen to me, Bob," Stuart said earnestly. "Do you want the belt handed to you on a silver platter? Or do you want to win it like a true champion?"

"Well—" Fitzsimmons hesitated, suddenly flustered. "I'm not one to make cheap claims. I'd sooner win it."

"Then it doesn't matter if you fight Corbett or Maher—does it?"

"But I've just told you, I already whipped Maher."

Stuart smiled. "So you'll whip him again. You've no doubt of that, do you?"

"None at all!" Fitzsimmons retorted. "But I'd still prefer Corbett."

"I'll do my level best to make it happen. You have my word on it."

Stuart mentally patted himself on the back. He had his fight.

The gang paused to water their horses at the Brazos River. For the past four days, setting a leisurely pace, they had covered slightly more than thirty miles a day. They were now some twenty miles south of Fort Worth.

Their escape, much as Lea had predicted, went off without incident. From the Llano River, west of Round Rock, they turned northeast and traveled overland. Lea knew the Rangers would spread the alert by telegraph, and she had avoided towns for the first three days. But last night she had agreed to stop in Walnut Springs, for a hot meal and a couple of drinks. She now regretted the decision.

In the town's only café, she'd come across a two-day-old newspaper. A headline on the front page caught her eye, and all but took her breath. The article related that Gentleman Jim Corbett had retired from the ring, abdicating the championship. There was speculation that his hand-chosen successor, Peter Maher, would now fight Ruby Rob Fitzsimmons for the heavyweight crown. Yet there had been no announcement to that effect, and it was all conjecture. No one knew anything for certain.

Stony Taylor promptly got drunk at the town's only saloon. She and Stovall had to pour him on his horse, and they'd camped a few miles north of Walnut Springs. From the time they awoke to a chilly sunrise until now, watering their horses on the Brazos, they weren't altogether sure he wouldn't shoot himself. His eyes were bloodshot, his features stamped with gloom, and he seemed mired in a slough of despondency. Lea thought he looked as bad as she felt.

"Cheer up," she said. "You act like the world's come to an end."

"Well, hell's bells," Taylor groaned blearily. "Hadn't it?"

"Things are always darkest before the dawn. My mom told me that when I was a kid, and I still believe it."

"Nothin' against your ma, but she never saw a dawn this dark. We've just lost ourselves a million simoleons."

Stovall pulled out the makings. On the trail they always carried roll-your-owns rather than cart along the new tailor-made cigarettes. He sprinkled tobacco into a paper, licked the seal tight, and handed it to Lea. After repeating the process for himself, he struck a match on his thumbnail and they lit up in glum silence. He finally spoke around spurts of smoke.

"Have to tell you, I'm rowin' the same boat as Stony. I never felt so goddamn miserable in my whole life."

"Just stop it!" Lea snapped. "We haven't cashed our chips in this game yet. Not by a long shot."

"Yeah?" Stovall said dubiously. "What's got you so sparky all of a sudden?"

"I'll tell you what, sugarpie. You think Dan Stuart would work his butt off for a year and let it slip away? Do you? Huh?"

"So what's he gonna do? Bring John L. Sullivan out of retirement?"

"Maybe," Lea said, exhaling a streamer of smoke. "Or maybe he'll match Fitzsimmons against this Maher. Stranger things have happened."

"You're both cracked," Taylor muttered. "You

might as well wish he'd shanghai Corbett out to El Paso."

Stovall nodded. "Not goddamn likely."

"Anything's likely," Lea said defiantly. "One way or another, Dan Stuart will pull it off. He won't let us down."

"Hah!" Taylor grunted. "And bird dogs fly, too."

"You just wait and see—both of you!"

They forded the Brazos and rode north toward Fort Worth.

FOUR

Stuart arrived in New York on the afternoon of December 2. He took a cab to the Plaza Hotel, located across from Central Park, and engaged a suite. A quick glance at his pocket watch told him there was barely time for a bath and a change of clothes. He had an appointment with James Corbett at four o'clock.

After leaving San Antonio, Stuart and Julie had traveled on to Dallas. There, he'd met with Edward Bates, president of the Dallas Athletic Club and his associate in the prizefight venture. Bates was of a similar opinion with respect to the matter of Corbett and Maher. Corbett was the better draw, but Maher would do nicely. A motion picture of any fight would still play to packed crowds.

There were times when Stuart felt like a juggler with one too many balls in the air. Between negotiating for the site, and playing diplomat with the fighters, he constantly had one eye on the finances and the other on the calendar. The date for the fight was rapidly approaching, and instead of fewer problems, he was faced with putting yet another ball in the air. His trip would determine whether it was Corbett or Maher.

On November 27, he'd left Julie in Dallas and entrained for St. Louis. There, after an overnight stay, he boarded another train for Chicago, where he connected with the final leg of his journey to New York. He was frazzled from traveling from the Mexico border to the Atlantic Ocean, but a steamy bath and fresh clothes left him revitalized and ready for yet another contest. He set out to collar Gentleman Jim.

New York always invigorated Stuart. The streets teemed with carriages and some of the new motorcars, and the frenetic energy of the people made it unlike any other city in America. He took a cab downtown to the Savoy Hotel, where Corbett had maintained a penthouse suite for several years. The elevator whisked him to the sixth floor, and a butler, with a refined English accent, admitted him at the door. Last week, he had wired ahead for an appointment, and he found Corbett awaiting his arrival in the sitting room. The champion greeted him with an effusive handshake.

"How good to see you again, Dan. You're looking well."

"Thank you, Jim." Stuart was waved to a plush easy chair, and took a seat. "You're looking fit yourself."

"I must tell you, the theater is more demanding than the ring. One can never disappoint his audience."

Corbett struck a pose by the fireplace mantel. He was attired in a velvet smoking jacket, belted at the waist, with a royal-blue ascot fluffed at his throat. Stuart thought it appropriate for a man who considered himself one of the new aristocracy. He decided to bypass the amenities.

"You know why I'm here," he said. "We had a contract and you've left me in the lurch. I expected more of you, Jim."

"Did you, indeed?" Corbett said in an eloquent voice. "Perhaps you've forgotten I devoted a year of my life to your grandiose scheme. How easy to overlook that I was arrested like a common criminal." He paused, flicked his hand with a dramatic air. "I believe any legal obligation expired long ago."

"Not true," Stuart countered. "There was no time limit on our contract. But apart from that, don't you think you owe your public something? They genuinely want to see you defend your title."

"I meant exactly what I said in my telegram. I have retired from the ring. The theater is my life now."

Stuart was reminded of the old saying about a man who never saw a mirror he didn't like. Corbett was inordinately vain about his looks, and in many ways, he was never meant to be a fighter. A native of San Francisco, educated and well spoken, he was a bank teller who had taken to amateur boxing as a way of staying fit. His natural gift for the sport, and the lure of big money, led him almost accidentally to the professional ring. His polished manner, and his penchant for natty attire, led to the sobriquet "Gentleman Jim." He was twenty-nine, the heavyweight champion of the world, and unbeaten in nineteen fights. Yet he was still more at ease on a theater stage.

The matter of a contract now seemed a moot point. Stuart decided to try another tack. "You know, Jim, you might want to reconsider for the good of your reputation. Sportswriters are saying you're . . . reluctant to fight Fitzsimmons."

"Indeed?" Corbett drew himself up to his full height. "You pronounce that as though it were a dirty word. By 'reluctant,' are you saying I'm afraid?"

"Not me," Stuart said with an idle gesture. "I'm merely repeating what's become open speculation. Some people think you'd rather retire than lose the title in the ring."

"Fitzsimmons is an oaf!" Corbett said adamantly. "I've never seen a man so clumsy and uncoordinated. I could beat him with one hand. Easily!"

"Prove it," Stuart said. "Show the world you're the better man. Defend your title."

Corbett stared off into space. His face in profile was somehow lordly, and he might have been Caesar contemplating the Rubicon. Then, as though wakened to a revelation, a slow smile appeared at the corner of his mouth. He turned back to Stuart.

"You're a smooth one," he said with a trace of admiration. "You had me going there, for a minute."

Stuart feigned confusion. "I don't follow you."

"Well, in any event, a challenge to my manhood won't get me into the ring. I have nothing to prove by fighting Fitzsimmons."

The statement somehow rang false, bravado more than conviction. Stuart sensed the sportswriters had got it right, their cynicism underscoring an ugly truth. Corbett, given a year to assess his chances, was now unwilling to test himself against Ruby Rob's heralded knockout punch. He would take his chances instead as a thespian. "Too bad," Stuart said, rising to his feet. "It would have been a great fight."

"Try Peter Maher," Corbett advised with a jocular grin. "After all, I did give him the belt. He's the champion now."

"Not until he's won it."

"All the more reason to fight."

Corbett walked him to the door. They shook hands,

and Stuart turned toward the elevator with a profound feeling of loss. Not for the bout itself, but rather for the man.

Gentleman Jim Corbett was the loser without having thrown a blow.

The next day Stuart met with Peter Maher. He sent a messenger around that morning, and invited the Irish champion to his hotel suite. He fully expected the invitation to be accepted, for he knew Maher had a score to settle with Fitzsimmons. The messenger returned with an affirmative reply.

Maher arrived promptly at two that afternoon. He was accompanied by his manager, Jack Quinn, a stolid Irishman with shifty eyes. At twenty-six, Maher was burly, with a thick neck and oxlike shoulders, and a face that showed the ravages of his profession. His flattened nose gave him a pugnacious look, and there was a welt of scar tissue over his left eye. He appeared to be a fighter who got hit a lot.

Stuart offered them a drink. Maher declined, and Quinn gave it a moment's thought before shaking his head. When they were seated on the sofa, Stuart took a chair opposite them, crossing his legs. He lit a cigar.

"Well, now," he said, snuffing the match. "I'm delighted you could drop around. I thought we might explore doing business together."

"Forget the soft soap," Quinn said with the kind of smug look that invites, and often excuses, an act of violence. "You want my boy to fight Fitz. Why else would we be here?"

Stuart puffed his cigar, sent an eddy of smoke curling toward the ceiling. "Let's say it's a possibility. I'm also considering other fighters."

"Yeah, like who?"

"John L. Sullivan."

Quinn blinked. "You're full of it."

Given the need, particularly in business negotia-
tions, Stuart had a marvelous talent for duplicity. He'd
developed the knack long ago at the poker tables,
when running a stiff bluff. For the most part, he believed every lie he told.

"You're wrong, Mr. Quinn," he said, casually tap-
ping an ash off his cigar. "The Great John L. would
like nothing better than to come out of retirement.
He's itching to get back in harness."

"That'll be the day!" Quinn barked. "He's practically pickled in alcohol. Nothing but a drunk."

"He's still John L. Sullivan. His name alone would
draw a tremendous gate."

"You think my boy wouldn't? Gentleman Jim Corbett presented him with the belt himself! Don't you
read the newspapers?"

"Jack," Maher said in a gravelly voice. "Shut up."

Quinn looked startled. "What's that?"

"I'm tellin' you to close your trap. Let's hear what
Mr. Stuart has to say."

Stuart thought there was more between Maher's
ears than a thick skull. He recalled being impressed
by newspaper accounts of the fighter's bulldog tenac-
ity. Two years earlier, in the bout with Fitzsimmons,
Maher suffered a broken nose in the twelfth round.
When he went back to his corner, he was choked with
blood, unable to breathe except with sharp, wheezing
gasps. Unnerved, his trainer threw in the towel without asking, and the enraged Irishman decked him with
a single punch. Despite his protests that he could continue, the referee declared it a technical knockout.
Maher had to be physically escorted from the ring.

"Correct me if I'm wrong," Stuart said, holding the

fighter's gaze. "I suspect you have a grudge to settle with Fitzsimmons. True or not?"

Maher's brow furrowed. "I was robbed, and nobody knows it better than Fitzsimmons. I had him on his last legs."

"So you think you could take him in a rematch?"

"Gimme the chance and I'll lay him out stiffer'n a log. You'll have to send him back to Australia in a box."

"Hold on now!" Quinn blurted. "There'll be no fight unless all our expenses are paid. And we'll have to have a guarantee—"

"Stay out of it," Maher cut him off. "Keep your flapper shut and that's my last word on it." He looked at Stuart. "You name the terms and I'll be there."

Stuart motioned with his cigar. "You put the championship belt on the line. Winner takes down twenty-five thousand and the loser walks. It's all or nothing."

"Don't trouble yourself about that, Mr. Stuart. I'll not be the loser."

Stuart played out his bluff about the Great John L. He already had a contract prepared, with the name left blank. He filled in the blank and Maher signed it without hesitation. After a round of handshakes, the fighter and his manager went on their way. Stuart saw them out, then closed the door with a beaming grin.

He thought Fitzsimmons was in for a hell of a fight.

The press conference was scheduled for ten the next morning. Every newspaper in New York was represented, for the public was keenly interested in the long-delayed fight. The reporters and their cameramen filled the ballroom.

On the stroke of ten, Stuart marched through the door. He was followed by Enoch Rector, the motion-picture producer. They walked to the front of the room and Stuart took a position behind a speaker's podium. He faced the assembled reporters.

"Good morning," he said in a clear voice. "I am Daniel Stuart, known to most of you as a sports promoter. I have an announcement regarding the forthcoming heavyweight championship fight."

The crowd waited expectantly. Stuart milked the moment for dramatic effect. "Today is an auspicious day on several counts," he finally said. "I have the pleasure to inform you that Peter Maher and Bob Fitzsimmons will fight for the heavyweight championship of the world. The match will take place on February 14."

The crowd erupted in a babble of questions. The sportswriter for the *New York World* managed to outshout the others. "Where's Gentleman Jim in all this? Why won't he fight?"

"You are all aware that Mr. Corbett has retired from the ring. His appointed successor, Peter Maher, will defend the crown."

"Fitzsimmons already beat Maher! That's yesterday's news."

"On the contrary," Stuart declared. "Mr. Maher defeated his last two opponents by knockout, both in the first round. Ruby Rob will have his hands full."

A reporter for the *New York Sun* pressed forward "Where will the fight be held?"

"Nothing has changed in that regard. The location is Juarez, Mexico."

"How does the Mexican government feel about that?"

"Absolutely delighted," Stuart observed. "We have the full cooperation of the Mexican authorities."

"Let's hope it lasts," a reporter yelled. "Especially

after you got chased out of Texas and Arkansas."

The crowd burst out in laughter. Stuart raised his hands overhead for silence. "Gentlemen, this is an historic occasion," he said. "Allow me to introduce Enoch J. Rector."

Rector moved to the podium. He was portly, with graying hair and steel-rimmed eyeglasses, and an elfin twinkle in his expression. Stuart turned back to the reporters "Mr. Rector is a colleague of Thomas Edison's, and a true pioneer in motion pictures. Some of you are no doubt familiar with his name."

"I am," the *New York World* sportswriter called out. "I saw his motion picture with Corbett. Had to stand in line two hours."

"Your next wait may be longer," Stuart told him. "I am proud to announce that Mr. Rector will film the Maher–Fitzsimmons match. The first motion picture *ever* of a championship fight!"

"For peepshows?" a reporter shouted. "Is that what you're saying?"

"No, no, no," Rector protested in a piping voice. "We will show it in vaudeville theaters. All across America."

"Think of it!" Stuart boomed. "Millions of people will at last see a championship prizefight. *Millions!*"

Reporters pushed forward and flash-pans popped on cameras. Rector smiled like a leprechaun, eyes bright. He looked positively jolly.

Stuart stared into the cameras with a nutcracker grin.

FIVE

Dallas lay along the banks of the Trinity River. Stuart arrived aboard the afternoon train on December 15. After the porter collected his luggage, he took a cab from the train station. He settled back in the seat with the sense that all was well in his world. He was eager to tell Julie the news.

For some twenty years, Stuart had made Dallas his home. In 1874, when he'd settled there, he was twenty-one and out to make his mark. He had learned his trade in the Kansas cowtowns, and he was generally able to hold his own at a poker table. Over the years, with maturity and experience, his reputation had spread to every corner of the West. He was a patrician among the sporting crowd.

In that time, Dallas had grown from a railroad boomtown to a metropolitan city. There were now several colleges, over forty churches, and a downtown district devoted to finance and banking. The population exceeded fifty thousand, and there were sixty-eight miles of electric streetcar tracks. The cultural scene included opera and theater, and five railroad lines made it the richest city in Texas. Winter or summer, there was a smell of money in the air.

Stuart's home was located in a residential enclave on the north side of town. The house was a two-story Victorian, with turrets and gables, and a wide veranda. A manicured lawn fronted the house, and wrought-iron gates opened onto a circular peastone driveway. His neighbors included bankers, lawyers, and wealthy businessmen, the upper strata of Dallas society. He was welcomed into their ranks, even though he was a gambler, and widely respected for his contributions to civic causes. They politely overlooked the fact that he and Julie were not married.

She met him at the door. After he dropped his bag, she threw her arms around his neck and kissed him full on the mouth. Her eyes danced with merriment. "I'm so happy you're back," she said, holding him tighter. "It seems like you were gone forever."

"Glad you missed me," Stuart said with a playful grin. "Maybe I should go away more often."

"Don't you dare!"

"I missed you, too."

"Did you, honestly?"

"I'll prove it to you later."

"Ummm, that sounds scrumptious."

Stuart hooked his hat and topcoat on a hall tree. They walked arm in arm to the parlor, where a cheery blaze crackled in the fireplace. She took a seat beside him on the sofa, her fingertips tracing the ridge of his jawline. Her touch was like gossamer, subtly conveying a promise that made his skin tingle. He chuffed a deep chuckle.

"Keep that up and we'll be in bed before the sun goes down. Aren't you interested in my news?"

"Oh, all right." She hugged herself with a pouty

look. "Business first and pleasure later. The story of my life."

"You probably read about it in the newspapers anyway. I guess it's old hat."

"No, no, really it's not. I want to hear all the gory details."

Stuart told her. She was his confidante, privy to his innermost thoughts, and he valued her judgment. She listened now with rapt attention, clearly relishing all the tidbits he'd withheld at the New York press conference. She clapped her hands in delight when he recounted the meeting with Peter Maher.

"You didn't!" she said with mischievous glee. "You actually made him believe Sullivan would come out of retirement?"

"I just shaded the truth," Stuart said, pleased with himself. "Maher wanted the fight so bad his mouth was watering. He would have believed anything."

"Do you think it was the prize purse, or something else?"

"Aren't you the shrewd one?"

"Why, whatever do you mean?"

"I knew you'd see the play. Maher would have paid me for the chance to fight Fitzsimmons. He's a man with a lot to prove."

She nodded to herself. "Corbett giving him the championship belt was a stigma of sorts. He has to prove he's worthy."

"That's part of it," Stuart agreed. "Then there's Fitz, the only man who ever beat him. He has to redeem himself in his own eyes."

"Yes, of course, you're right. He carries his own cross into the fight, doesn't he?"

"Which means he'll fight all the harder."

"You clever devil, you. I just love it!"

Julie reveled in the machinations of Stuart's business dealings. She was a former showgirl, and they'd met when her traveling musical troupe played Dallas. The attraction between them was instant, and after a week of intense courtship, she had agreed to become his paramour. He was struck as much by her intelligence as her beauty, and the twelve-year difference in their ages bothered her not at all. He was the most virile man she'd ever met, and the most intriguing. His visions were on a grand scale, and he thrived on the dare itself. His life was a constant challenge.

"To tell you the truth," he said, reflecting on his most recent challenge, "I'm almost grateful Corbett forced me to make a deal with Maher. I like a man who's hungry to prove himself."

"So do I," she said in a sultry voice. "Especially when he's been away from home so long."

"I warned you where that kind of talk would lead."

"Are you sure you're not too tired from your trip?"

Stuart reached for her. "Try me and find out."

She led him upstairs to their bedroom.

Edward Bates was the most respected stockbroker in Dallas. His firm, Bates & Company, had brought its clients through the Panic of '93 with only minor losses. Others had gone under during the Wall Street crash, suffering financial ruin. His clients emerged from the ashes with their portfolios intact.

A man of some intellect, he was looked upon as a wizard by the business community. He was short and square, built like a stump, with guileless brown eyes that disguised a will of iron. For three years running, his friends and colleagues had elected him president of the Dallas Athletic Club. He brought to the position the same drive and insight that made him so successful in the stock market. He saw opportunity where others all too often saw nothing.

The Dallas Athletic Club was a congenial meeting ground for men of wealth and influence. Bates, in his role as president, had been responsible for throwing the support of the club behind the heavyweight championship bout. When the fight was outlawed in Texas, the club was forced to withdraw its sponsorship. But Bates remained personally involved, for he recognized the windfall profits to be gained from the first motion picture of a championship prizefight. He bought a ten percent interest in the venture.

A close friendship had evolved between Bates and Stuart. They were both members of the Dallas Athletic Club, and they shared as well a fondness for poker. Whenever a game was held at the club, Stuart insisted on modest stakes, and often folded strong hands rather than win too consistently. As a professional, he held the advantage, and Bates and the other members appreciated the tips he gave them on the art of poker. In return, Bates gave him tips on the stock market, and Stuart became fascinated with the gyrations of Wall Street. His portfolio had doubled in value under Bates's management.

Stuart stopped by the brokerage the morning after his return to Dallas. He found Bates seated in his office, initialing a stack of buy and sell orders. As he came through the door, Bates looked up and his mouth curled with a loopy grin. They exchanged an energetic handshake.

"Hail the conquering hero," Bates said genially. "You pulled off quite a coup in New York."

Stuart took a chair before the desk. "I won't pretend false modesty. Suffice it to say, I saved our bacon."

"I take it Corbett was his usual arrogant self."

"That's a major understatement. I'm convinced the man gets chapped lips from kissing cold mirrors. He's a walking definition of narcissism."

Bates chortled appreciatively. "I suppose actors and fighters have a good deal in common. They are the center of their own attention."

"No question about it," Stuart said. "None of them ever want for conversation. They talk to their favorite people—themselves."

"Well, in any event, you've returned covered in laurels. What's the next step?"

"I plan on holding a press conference tomorrow. It's vital to the project that we boost Maher's stock with the public."

"I couldn't agree more," Bates said. "Although I thought you did an excellent job in New York. The *Morning News* carried the story here."

"I'm not surprised," Stuart commented. "When the Associated Press puts it on the wire, you know you've made the news. Every paper in the country probably carried it."

"Just don't let it go to your head."

"How so?"

"I guess you didn't see the headline here. They've christened you the 'Impresario of the Prizefight Ring.' "

Stuart looked pleased. "Not all that bad a moniker. I've been called worse things on occasion."

"By the governor, no less," Bates noted. "I'm still convinced he'll make trouble for us in Juarez. He sees himself as the avenging angel of the fight game."

"Judge Townsend and his group are some of the most influential men on the border. They'll protect our interests in Juarez."

"And if the Mexicans won't listen?"

Stuart smiled. "There's always Judge Bean."

"That old reprobate," Bates groaned. "He'll soak us for a fortune."

"Edward, we've agreed that only a fool goes to war without a contingency plan. I'll stop off and talk with him on my way to El Paso."

"Well, like they say, any port in a storm."

"Don't concern yourself," Stuart said confidently. "We'll still make a million."

Bates briskly rubbed his hands together. "Nothing gets my attention like filthy lucre. Whoever said it's the root of all evil?"

"I think it comes from the Bible."

"So does 'God helps those who help themselves.' I'm sure He would agree that a motion picture qualifies."

"One thing's certain," Stuart said. "Enoch Rector believes it's all but ordained."

Bates nodded. "That was a nice touch, including him in the New York press conference. The papers gave it good coverage."

"The more coverage the better. Publicity greases the wheels."

"Funny you'd use that phrase. I meant to talk with you about an investment."

"Stocks?"

"Oil stock," Bates amended. "The horse and buggy is on the way out. Motorcars are definitely the thing of the future. Oil is what makes *those* wheels go round."

"Oil?" Stuart repeated thoughtfully. "You think there's money to be made?"

"John D. Rockefeller thinks so. He's doing his

damnedest to put together a monopoly. Now's the time to get a piece of the pie."

"How much should I invest?"

"Ten percent of your portfolio," Bates said. "In round figures, thirty thousand."

"Well, where the stock market's concerned, you have a crystal ball. Go ahead and do it."

Stuart weighed the curious juxtaposition of motion pictures, motorcars, and oil. The world was changing more rapidly than he'd imagined, and he told himself it would be quite a ride. All the way into a new century.

The press conference was held at the Dallas Athletic Club. Stuart and Bates arrived shortly before eleven the next morning. A number of reporters were already congregated in a large room off the central foyer.

Bates took a position off to one side of the room. Stuart walked directly to the podium, waiting while the reporters seated themselves in rows of chairs. The cameramen jockeyed for position closer to the podium.

"Thank you for coming today," Stuart said. "By now, you know that Peter Maher will fight Bob Fitzsimmons for the heavyweight championship of the world. I'm here to answer any questions you may have."

A sportswriter for the *Dallas Morning News* got to his feet. "The odds already place Maher at a six-to-one underdog. Do you honestly think he can win the fight?"

"I certainly do," Stuart affirmed. "You have to remember that this is a grudge match. Maher believes he was robbed in their last outing."

"Yeah, but his corner threw in the towel. Why think it'll be any different this time?"

"Never underestimate a man who has a score to settle. I predict a knockout within three rounds."

"Hold on!" The reporter from the *Fort Worth Standard* jackknifed from his chair. "Are you saying Maher will put Fitz down for the count?"

"I'm saying one of them will be counted out by the third round. This will be a brawl from the opening bell."

The newshounds scribbled furiously in their notepads. A reporter from the *Dallas Herald* motioned to Bates. "Why are we meeting here? I thought the Athletic Club withdrew from the fight."

"Only as a sponsor," Bates replied. "The match still has the wholehearted support of the club and its members. You can quote me on that."

"Governor Culberson won't take that sitting down. The word's out he thinks Juarez is just a smoke screen. He's convinced you'll try to hold the fight in El Paso."

"I'll answer that," Stuart broke in. "Governor Culberson sees a bogeyman behind every bush. He also likes to see his name in the headlines. That's the end of that story."

The newsmen were all too aware of the animosity between Stuart and the governor. A bitter struggle, lasting eleven months and ending in the state legislature, had spoiled Stuart's plan to build a sports coliseum in Dallas. The reporter from the *Fort Worth Gazette* raised his hand.

"So you're telling us it's definitely on for Juarez?"

Stuart nodded with a cryptic smile. "Quote me as saying I personally invite the governor."

SIX

Lea stretched like a languorous cat. She shielded her eyes against sunlight streaming through the windows, and pulled the covers over her head. She snuggled deeper into the pillow.

From the bathroom, she heard Stovall whistling tunelessly to himself. A mental picture formed in her mind of him standing before the mirror, straight razor in hand, his face covered with lather. Whenever they were in town, he was usually the first to rise, and his morning ritual seldom varied. He got about the day with a burst of energy.

Lea was just the opposite. In Fort Worth, where they were safe from the law, she could literally let her hair down. Her disguise was packed away, and she treated herself to the luxury every woman deserved. She lazed around their suite, generally staying in bed until late morning, content to do nothing. She liked to think of herself as a lady of leisure.

Stovall emerged from the bathroom in a cloud of steam. He was shaved, a towel wrapped around his waist, his hair slicked back with pomade. He padded barefoot to the bed, lowering himself down beside her, and playfully peeled the covers away. One of the things she loved most about him was his clean, masculine smell when he came to wake her every morning. The mere scent of him stirred something deep inside her.

"C'mon, lazybones," he said softly. "Time to face another day."

She nestled herself in his arms. "Do I have to?" she purred. "Why don't you come back to bed?"

"You should've thought of that before now. I've already called down for breakfast."

"Who cares about food? A girl needs a little loving."

"You got all the loving you could handle last night. Way I remember it, you were the one that hollered 'uncle.' "

"Did not."

"Did too."

Stovall swatted her across the rump. She yelped, squirming around in the covers, as he moved to an armoire along the wall. He selected a dark gray suit, a starchy white shirt, and a colorful tie, and began dressing. She crawled out of bed, not wearing a stitch, and hurried into the bathroom. He watched her bare bottom disappear through the door, then grinned at himself in the mirror. He shrugged into his shirt.

Some while later Lea entered the sitting room. Her tawny hair shone from brushing and she was wearing a filmy pink peignoir. Stovall and Taylor were seated at a table near the windows, absorbed in a breakfast of bacon and eggs, and fluffy buttermilk biscuits. She took a chair, stifling a small yawn, and poured herself a cup of coffee. Neither of the men looked up from their plates.

"Mornin'," Taylor said around a mouthful of biscuit. "Better dig in before it's all gone."

"Coffee's fine," she said languidly. "I might have something later."

Stovall chuckled. "Don't let her kid you, Stony. She's watchin' her figure."

"Well, I'm not." Taylor helped himself to more eggs from a serving platter. "They got damn good grub in this place."

Their quarters were in The Mansion, widely regarded as one of the finest hotels in Fort Worth. They occupied a two-bedroom suite on the fourth floor, with private bathing facilities in each bedroom. The sitting room floor was covered by a lush Persian carpet, and grouped before the marble fireplace were several chairs and a chesterfield divan. A series of handsomely draped windows overlooked the city.

Lea and Stovall were registered as man and wife. She never used the name Osburn, and Taylor was known as their friend and business associate. The men posed as cattle buyers, whose occupation necessarily took them on frequent trips throughout the state. The Rangers had never tracked them north of the Brazos River, and no one in Fort Worth suspected their true occupation. Lea played the part of a dutiful wife.

Today, watching the men eat, she was reminded that they made a good team. She considered Stony Taylor a likable if slow-witted brute, easygoing unless he was riled. His principal character flaw was that he might, without a moment's thought, get himself and those around him killed. The concept of "back off" or "give up" was not in his lexicon; once the fight was entered, he went at it with a do-or-die fatality. She attributed his bravery not to courage, but rather to the bullheaded inability to comprehend the nature of death. Taylor simply didn't know when to quit and run.

She was no less pragmatic about the man who shared her bed. Earl Stovall was smart and personable, a slick talker who got by on his looks and a gift for gab. He would fight to the death, but only if cornered, and he was therefore a curious mixture of caution and courage. He was no intellect, and yet he could weigh the odds with a finely honed sense of survival. For him, discretion was the better part of valor, and given a choice, he would live to fight another day. He was sharp enough to know that any tomorrow was better than no tomorrow at all.

Which was one of the reasons Lea had taken him as her lover. She had the unique gift of standing back and assessing herself with an objective, impersonal eye. The life of a bank robber suited her, and she was able to lead the men with manipulation wrapped in a velvet glove. Yet she knew that there was no such thing as a charmed life, particularly for an outlaw who frequently went in harm's way. So the better chance for survival was to be sleeping with the man who had a sixth sense for when the axe was about to fall. She meant to live a long and extravagant life.

A folded newspaper, brought by the room service attendant, lay on the table. Lea took a sip of coffee and idly unfolded the paper. Her eyes popped open.

"I knew it!" she exclaimed. "He's done it!"

"What?" Taylor asked. "Who you talkin' about?"

She held up the *Fort Worth Standard*. A headline was bannered on the lower section of the front page.

FITZSIMMONS SET TO FIGHT MAHER FOR VACATED HEAVYWEIGHT TITLE

"I told you!" Her face was afire with excitement. "I told you Dan Stuart wouldn't let us down."

"Damned if you didn't," Stovall marveled, staring at the headline. "Are they still set for Juarez?"

Lea quickly scanned the article. "Yes," she said, nodding as she read. "Juarez on February 14. Valentine's Day! A girl couldn't ask for a lovelier present."

Taylor wagged his head. "Wonder how Stuart pulled it off. Son of a gun must be some talker."

"Hell, he's a magician," Stovall said with a toothy grin. "Just flat pulled the rabbit out of the hat."

"Oh, I love him to death," Lea bubbled. "Do you realize he's going to make us rich? And I mean *rich*."

"Wouldn't mind it a bit," Taylor allowed. "We should've listened to you all along, Lea. You was damn sure right."

Stovall slapped the table. "Godalmighty! Don't that take the cake? Juarez, here we come!"

"We have to celebrate," Lea said, hardly able to restrain herself. "I feel like kicking up my heels."

"We'll do it," Stovall agreed. "Where'd you like to go?"

"The Comique," she said gaily. "And I want champagne."

Stovall laughed. "We'll drink a toast to Dan Stuart."

"Yes! It's perfect. Absolutely perfect!"

She clapped her hands like an exuberant child.

The Comique was located at Third and Main. A variety theater, it was considered one of the more respectable night spots in Fort Worth. The clientele was drawn from the uptown crowd and polite society, a select group. The rowdier element was not allowed through the door.

Early that evening, escorted by Stovall and Taylor, Lea walked along Main Street toward the theater. She was dressed in a teal-blue gown, her hair upswept, with a fashionable cape thrown over her shoulders. She felt excited and alive, and she was aware that she had come a long way in a short period of time. She was no longer one of the downtown crowd.

Fort Worth was situated on a rolling plain, bordered on the north and west by the Trinity River. Originally an army outpost, established in 1849, it had provided a line of defense against warlike tribes who preyed on Texas settlers. But now, late in 1895, it was a bustling metropolis, rivaling Dallas, which lay some thirty miles to the east. The population was pushing forty thousand, and the community was served by two railroads, the Missouri Pacific and the Texas & Pacific. Town boosters fondly touted it as the "Queen of the Prairie."

The immediate area around Union Depot was known locally as Hell's Half Acre. Located at the south edge of town, it was the heart of the sporting district, operating wide open day and night. The streets were lined with saloons, gaming dives, dance halls, and whorehouses, devoted solely to vice and separating working men from their wages. Over the years, as Fort Worth had doubled and doubled again in size, the district had grown to encompass the entire southern part of town. Today, it was referred to simply as the Acre.

For all its growth, Fort Worth was one of the few wide-open cities left in the West. Though the county seat of Tarrant County, the community was still largely controlled by local politicians. The city government imposed so-called taxes on saloons, whorehouses, and gaming dives, and the revenues generated kept the town treasury afloat. The politicians placed a discount on morality and a premium on economic stability, and rarely tried to enforce the letter of the law. A truce was maintained with the sporting crowd, with occupation taxes acting as the buffer, and everyone benefited. So long as the Acre held violence to a minimum and confined immorality to the south end of town, the law was tolerant.

The corner of Main and Seventh established a boundary separating the sporting district from the rest of the town. Below Main and Seventh, where the Acre started, a blind eye was turned to virtually all forms of vice. Anything went.

Uptown, where the better class of people lived and conducted their business, nothing unseemly was tolerated. There were gambling clubs, and saloons, and variety theaters, but none of the depravity to be found in the Acre. As though the town fathers had drawn a line in the sand, everything above Main and Seventh was held to a different standard. There the streets were free of violence and whores, and anything that smacked of disorder. The law worked, and worked well, uptown.

Uptown and downtown were all but separate worlds. Downtown, with its fleshpots and the hurdy-gurdy atmosphere of the Acre, was home to the sporting crowd. The respectable people of Fort Worth lived west of Courthouse Square. A section to the northwest, overlooking the river, was a residential enclave for the wealthier class, far removed from the Acre. Unless the need arose to catch a train, some of the uptown crowd never ventured south of Seventh Street. There were nine churches and sixty saloons within the city limits, and for most people, it was a case of never the twain shall meet. They kept to their own kind.

Lea felt blessed to have escaped the sordid world of Hell's Half Acre. These days she avoided the area below Seventh and Main, and she conducted herself as a lady. Her former friends, the saloon girls and cardsharps, thought she had married a handsome cattle buyer. She kept Stovall and Taylor away from the Acre as well, and they confined their activities to the uptown district. Her life was one of good taste and comfort, and she mingled among respectable people. She sometimes managed to forget that she robbed banks for a living.

The Comique was mobbed. A throng of people, men and women attired in their finest, were filing through the archway to the theater. Off to one side of the main entryway, a steady stream of men climbed the stairs to the gaming club on the second floor. There, they found honest games with honest odds, and devoted their evening to faro, roulette, dice, and poker. The atmosphere was sedate and the clientele comported themselves as gentlemen. The club, like the theater, catered to the uptown crowd.

Taylor elected to forgo the variety theater. Lea was hardly surprised, for he was an inveterate gambler who constantly chased after Lady Luck. He left them at the street entrance, and hurried off toward the upstairs club. Stovall stopped at the admission booth, and then took the house manager aside. A twenty-dollar bill exchanged hands, with the assurance of the best seats in the house. The manager personally led them through the archway.

The theater was a large room with tables and chairs neatly aligned in geometric rows. A proscenium stage occupied the far wall, with an orchestra pit for the musicians. Waiters scurried back and forth taking drink orders from a crowd of some three hundred people. The first show of the evening was virtually sold out.

The house lights dimmed as the manager got Lea and Stovall seated. Their table was in the front row, directly opposite center stage, with the most commanding view in the theater. A waiter appeared with a bottle of champagne, nestled in a standing ice bucket. As he poured, the footlights came up and the orchestra broke out in a rousing dance number. The curtain swished open.

A line of chorus girls exploded out of the wings and went high-stepping across the stage. The star of the show, Dolly Love, raised her skirts, revealing a shapely leg, and joined them in a prancing cakewalk. The girls squealed and Dolly flashed her bloomers and the tempo of the music quickened. The crowd roared with delight and Lea clapped her hands in time to the music. Stovall thought he'd never seen her so happy.

The number went on for several minutes. The girls swirled around the stage, kicking high in the air, their underdrawers bright in the footlights. Then the orchestra thumped into the finale with a blare of trumpets and a clash of cymbals. The chorus line, in a twirl of raised skirts and jiggling breasts, went cavorting into the wings. Dolly Love blew the crowd a kiss, dazzling them with a smile, and followed the girls offstage. The audience went wild with cheers.

"Weren't they wonderful!" Lea cried. "I wish they would do it all over again!"

Her excitement was infectious, and Stovall laughed. "Think they might need a breather. That was some show."

The chorus line was followed by a team of jugglers, who were entertaining if not sensational. The next act was a comic with a song-and-dance patter, and then a midget who performed death-defying stunts on roller skates. The crowd broke out in applause as he flipped high in the air, rolled through a headlong somersault, and landed upright. Lea clapped all the louder as he whizzed off into the wings balanced on one skate. She clutched Stovall's arm in a tight hug.

"I'm so happy I'm about to burst. Don't you feel the same way?"

Stovall grinned. "Honey, I'm tickled pink. Have been, ever since we saw the newspaper this morning."

"Oh, I almost forgot!"

"Forgot what?"

"Our toast." Lea raised her champagne glass. "To Dan Stuart, my hero."

"Yeah," Stovall agreed heartily. "I'll drink to that."

"Of course you will, sugar. He's our road to riches."

They clinked their glasses with a secret smile.

SEVEN

On December 24, Stuart met with the El Paso fight committee. The conference was held in Judge Arthur Townsend's office at one that afternoon. The purpose was to finalize logistics for the fight.

Apart from Judge Townsend and Doc Albers, they were joined by Juan Daguerra. The third member of the committee, Daguerra was also the manager of the annual fiesta held in Juarez. His responsibility was to guarantee that the bout came off as scheduled, with no intervention by the Mexican government. All of which made him essential to their planning session.

Judge Townsend opened the meeting. "Gentlemen, I must say I am most pleased with the response to date. We've received telegrams from the press all across the country. New York, Chicago, St. Louis, and on and on."

"Well, that's good news," Albers said. "Do they plan to cover the fight?"

"Indeed they do. Every paper of any merit intends to send a correspondent. Their inquiries have to do mainly with hotel accommodations."

"That's one of the items on my agenda," Stuart

observed. "I have every reason to believe that the fight will attract upward of thirty thousand spectators. Where are we going to lodge them?"

"Thirty thousand!" Albers parroted. "Are you serious?"

"Never more serious in my life."

Albers exchanged a dazed glance with Townsend. The judge steepled his fingers. "Daniel, that is an astounding number," he said. "In past discussions, you always estimated the figure at ten thousand. Why triple it now?"

"I have my own contacts with the press," Stuart noted. "From all I hear, there's a groundswell of interest in the Fitzsimmons–Maher match." He lifted his hands in a shrug. "With Corbett retired, the public wants to see a new champion crowned. And a great many of them want to see it in person."

Townsend looked bewildered. "I'm delighted by the prospects for our local business concerns. But where will all those people stay?"

"I suggest you work on it," Stuart said. "I've already been in touch with the railroads in Dallas and Los Angeles. They plan to lay on special trains to handle the overload."

"Madre de Dios," Daguerra murmured. "How will we seat so many people at the fight?"

Juan Daguerra was short and paunchy, with heavy jowls and a pencil-thin mustache. Every year he staged the Our Lady of Guadelupe fiesta, a month-long affair extending through Christmas and into the New Year. The fiesta drew thousands from along the border, attracted by daily bullfights, gambling booths crowding the plaza, and a nightly fandango complete with fireworks. His experience with the annual event was critical to holding the prizefight in Juarez.

"You raise a good point," Stuart said. "I know we planned to hold the fight in your bullring. But that won't work any longer. Not with this many spectators."

Daguerra looked perplexed. "What are we to do, Señor Stuart?"

"I'm exploring the possibility of using a tent. Something on the order of what's used for a traveling circus."

Albers grunted. "That would have to be one hell of a tent."

"I'm told it's possible," Stuart replied. "Actually, it would be several circus tents joined to form one large enclosure. We could probably seat twenty-five thousand people."

"A splendid solution," Judge Townsend announced. "Assuming, of course, a location can be found in Juarez. Do you envision any problem, Mr. Daguerra?"

"No, no," Daguerra said quickly. "There is much open ground outside the village. We will find a way."

"Speaking of problems," Stuart said. "All's well with the authorities in Juarez? We don't want any last-minute hitches."

"Have no fear," Daguerra assured him. "The *alcalde* and I are like brothers. There will be no difficulty."

The bureaucrats in Mexico operated on the premise that public office was a steppingstone to personal wealth. Stuart had agreed to pay Daguerra five thousand dollars, half when the fighters climbed into the ring and half when the fight ended. He thought the arrangement ensured that the bout would come off without interference from the authorities. He was confident that a substantial portion of the bribe would go to the *alcalde*, the mayor of Juarez.

"One last thing," Stuart went on. "Fitzsimmons arrives tomorrow morning. Are his quarters prepared?"

"All is in order," Daguerra acknowledged. "I have secured a fine home for him, *muy bueno*. He will be pleased."

"What about a reception at the train station? We want him greeted with the appropriate fanfare."

"Señor Fitzsimmons will receive a warm welcome from the people of Juarez. I have attended to it personally."

Judge Townsend made a grand gesture. "El Paso will be represented as well. I've arranged for Mayor Campbell to be there."

"Damned strange," Albers said pointedly. "Why would Fitzsimmons come into town on Christmas morning? Doesn't he realize it's a holiday?"

"Nothing strange about it," Stuart commented. "Bob Fitzsimmons wrote the book when it comes to eccentricity. Wait till you meet his lion."

"Lion?" Albers blurted. "A live lion?"

"A genuine African specimen. His name is Nero."

A large crowd was gathered outside the depot. The train pulled into the station shortly before noon on Christmas Day. The engine hissed, rocking to a halt, and belched a cloud of steam. The engineer tooted his whistle with a sportive blast.

Fitzsimmons stepped off the lead passenger coach. He was followed by Rose, carrying baby Rob, and his manager, Martin Julian. Farther down the tracks, his trainer, Charlie White, emerged from the caboose, with Nero attached to a heavy chain. The lion roared ferociously at the startled crowd.

A Mexican band, as though on cue, broke out in a festive air. The El Paso Fire Brigade, resplendent in their red shirts and domed helmets, stood at attention beside the depot. Several local dignitaries, including the fight committee, the police chief, and Mayor Robert Campbell, waited on the platform. Stuart walked forward with his hand outstretched.

"Welcome to El Paso," he said, careful of Fitzsimmons's granite handshake. "I see you arrived in good order."

Fitzsimmons nodded, eyeing the crowd. "You should've brought me by camel. We've just crossed a bloody desert."

"Well, you've found the oasis now, Bob. I think you'll like it here."

"Who are all these people?"

"Your welcoming committee," Stuart said. "They turned out to greet you in proper fashion."

"That's decent of them," Fitzsimmons observed. "I'd not expected anything so grand."

"You have to remember, you're a celebrity."

Stuart performed the introductions. Townsend, Albers, and Daguerra were particularly effusive in their greetings. The mayor, primed to make a speech, was treated to a rough handshake that left him wincing and at a loss for words. A reporter from the *El Paso Tribune* shoved through the crowd, trailed by a cameraman. He planted himself in front of Fitzsimmons, grinning like a frog.

"Mr. Fitzsimmons," he said boldly. "Would you care to make a statement about your chances in the upcoming fight? Will you win the crown?"

"You're looking at the next champion." Fitzsimmons raised his balled fist and the camera flashed. "Peter Maher will fold when he gets a taste of what

I have to offer. You can quote me on that."

"Do you have any comment on Gentleman Jim Corbett?"

"That bag of hot air!" Fitzsimmons scoffed. "I ran him out of the ring and onto a theater stage. Good riddance!"

The crowd roared approval. Juan Daguerra, bustling about in a frenzy, quickly orchestrated what amounted to a parade. Fitzsimmons and Rose, along with Stuart and Julian, were shown to an open carriage. Charlie White and Nero, with a load of luggage and training equipment, were consigned to a freight wagon. The band fell in behind, and the fire brigade, smartly arrayed in their uniforms, brought up the rear. The caravan, trumpets blaring, crossed the bridge over the Rio Grande.

On the opposite side of the river, throngs of people cheered as they marched into Juarez. The parade circled the plaza and came to a halt before a palatial adobe structure off the westward corner. Manuel Ortega, the mayor of Juarez, stepped forward to greet Fitzsimmons with lavish praise. By one o'clock, the fighter and his entourage were settled into the house, complete with a staff of servants. An hour later, with the band leading the way, Ortega escorted them to the local bullring. The amphitheater was packed with a holiday crowd, and they gave Fitzsimmons a rousing ovation. He modestly took a bow.

There were three *corridas* over the course of the afternoon, with all the pomp and circumstance derived from generations of tradition. Fitzsimmons, with Stuart and Rose and the others, were accorded the honor of being seated in the judges' stand. None of them had ever seen a bullfight, and they were impressed as much by the ceremony as the drama of man pitted against beast. They watched a picador get tossed high in the air during the first *corrida,* and a matador, gored through the thigh, fall in the second. The crowd buzzed with concern as he was carried from the ring.

"Rugged lot, these matadors," Fitzsimmons commented. "So far, the bulls have got the best of it."

"I think that's the exception," Stuart said. "The bulls usually end up in the butcher shop."

Rose shuddered with repugnance. "I've never seen anything quite so horrible in my life. I mean, honestly, sticking swords in animals. It's shameful!"

Stuart darted a glance at their hosts. Ortega and Daguerra were engaged in conversation, and failed to overhear the remark. He thought it was just as well.

Fitzsimmons smiled indulgently. "You're a soft one," he said, nudging his wife with an elbow. "You'd best stay home when I fight Peter Maher. Before I'm done, he'll wish for the butcher's block."

"I should hope so," Rose said, impervious to the irony. "What with an all-or-nothing purse, you'd best win. Otherwise, you'll be sleeping alone."

By the end of the third *corrida,* Fitzsimmons was as engrossed as the crowd. He watched, fascinated, as the bull charged and the matador deftly avoided the horns with a swirl of the cape. Hardly realizing it, he'd learned the proper response for artistry in the bullring. He jumped to his feet and joined in the chant.

"¡Ole! ¡Ole!"

The next day, Stuart got an earful from Townsend and Albers. Some of their investors felt slighted because Fitzsimmons had been whisked off to Juarez. There was a natural rivalry between the Anglos and the Mexicans, and the investors thought El Paso had been pushed out of the limelight. Something had to be done.

After considerable argument, Stuart persuaded Fitzsimmons to make a public appearance. Fitzsimmons declared that he was a fighter, not a showman, and stubbornly refused to make a spectacle of himself. But Stuart prevailed, and through Judge Townsend an engagement was arranged at the opera house that night. Hastily printed circulars were plastered all over town.

The opera house was the center of culture in El Paso. Throughout the year, touring opera companies and theatrical productions were presented on a regular basis. Four years ago, the renowned Shakespearean actor Edwin Booth had appeared there in *Julius Caesar*. But a prizefighter was unique, all the more so if he was Australian and widely touted to be the next heavyweight champion of the world. By seven that evening, every seat in the house was filled.

Stuart and Julie were seated in the orchestra section, directly before the stage. Townsend and Albers, and their group of investors, all accompanied by their wives, occupied the entire front row. Owen McKie, who owned the opera house, appeared from behind the curtains and made a brief introduction. Then the curtains were drawn, and a boxing ring, revealed by the glare of the footlights, stood positioned on the stage. The audience applauded politely.

Fitzsimmons and his trainer, Charlie White, conducted a sparring session. Never one to pull a punch, Fitzsimmons went at it with methodical precision. White bobbed and weaved, wary of the stinging jabs, and backpedaled to avoid any damaging blows. Finally, with a sizzling left-right combination, Fitzsimmons dropped him to the canvas. The audience applauded all the more loudly when White gamely struggled to his feet. But he'd clearly had it for the night, and switched roles, acting as a moderator. He talked the audience through a daily training session.

A punching bag, suspended from the rafters, was stationed at the edge of the stage. Fitzsimmons lumbered around the bag, feinting and jabbing, then delivering his sledgehammer right cross. The exhibition went on for several minutes before he set himself and walloped the bag with a murderous blow. The bag arced upward, snapped off its hinges, and sailed across the footlights into the front row. The crowd cheered the seemingly herculean feat.

Fitzsimmons took a bow, waiting until the applause dropped off. "That's what Maher will get the day we fight," he said in a booming voice. "I predict a knockout within six rounds. Thank you very much."

The audience gave him a standing ovation. Julie bounced with excitement, glancing at Stuart. "Did you see that?" she trilled. "He's strong as an ox!"

"Not quite," Stuart whispered in her ear. "His trainer rigged it before the exhibition."

"How could that be?"

"Simplest thing in the world. He loosened the hinge so the bag would fly off."

"The scoundrel!" she said, thoroughly amused. "Fitzsimmons may have a career on the stage, after all. He's more the showman than he admits."

Stuart laughed, watching Fitzsimmons parade around the stage. He saw the fighter basking in the applause, not yet willing to surrender the spotlight. He thought Julie might have a point.

Ruby Rob had a touch of greasepaint in his blood.

EIGHT

The press began gathering in El Paso after the New Year. Peter Maher was scheduled to arrive on January 10, and there was quickening interest in the fight. The public was eager for any news.

Judge Townsend had personally arranged accommodations. The Lindell Hotel, located in the downtown area, became headquarters for the press corps. Among the newspapers already represented were the *New York Times*, the *New York World*, the *Chicago Record*, the *Chicago Tribune*, the *Dallas Morning News*, and a correspondent from the Associated Press. Some fifty newsmen from around the country were expected before the fight.

The reporters filed daily stories by telegraph. Until the arrival of Maher, their primary focus was on Bob Fitzsimmons. Ruby Rob was always good for a quote, and the public never tired of his eccentric behavior. His pet lion was by now a national celebrity, and often the subject of a humorous feature. Nero terrorized the servants assigned to the fighter, but was docile as a tabby cat with Fitzsimmons and Rose. Hardly a day went by without some mention of Nero's latest escapade.

Yet the lion was a mere sidelight to his owner. A large room in the adobe home had been converted into a training gym. There, Fitzsimmons spent the afternoon whaling his sparring partners and the punching bag, and occasionally squared off against Nero. His roadwork, conducted in the morning, was grist for added coverage on his quirky idiosyncrasy. Unlike other fighters, who ran at a shuffling pace to improve their stamina and wind, he added a personal twist. His trainer drove a buckboard, whipping the horse into a trot, and Fitzsimmons pounded along behind for ten or twelve miles. The journalists loved it.

On January 9, Stuart called a press conference. He timed it for the conclusion of Fitzsimmons's afternoon training session. The reporters began congregating in the gym as the last sparring match got under way. They assumed some announcement was to be made about Maher's arrival in El Paso tomorrow. Gathered outside the ring, they watched as Fitzsimmons decked his sparring partner with a clubbing right to the jaw. Some of them made notes, while others looked on with idle interest. A sparring partner beng flattened was by now old news.

A short time after three, Stuart crossed the plaza and approached the house. He saw Nero in a vacant lot beside the adobe, chained to a metal stake driven into the ground. The lion was still a curiosity, and several children stood watching him from a distance. He lay with his forepaws crossed, staring back at them with yellow eyes, his mane like a bristly thatch of wheat. The children knew the outside limit of his chain, and so far, none of them had dared to cross the line into his territory. Nero seemed content to wait.

Rose, with baby Rob in her arms, met Stuart at the door. He jerked a thumb back outside. "Aren't you afraid Nero will eat one of those kids?"

"Heavens no," she said with some conviction. "Bob keeps him stuffed with goat meat and tortillas. You'd think he was a Mexican lion."

"How's Robby?" Stuart asked, tickling the baby under the chin. "Looks like you keep him stuffed, too."

"Oh, he's a greedy little bugger. He does like his tit."

Rose Fitzsimmons was a plain woman, her features sharp and angular. Her speech was often coarse, but oddly enough, she was never crude. She was pleasant, with an earthy wit, and more than a match for her husband. To Stuart's amusement, she even intimidated the lion. Nero kept his distance.

"Everyone here?" Stuart said. "I told them about three."

Rose nodded. "You've got them all atwitter. They're hoping for a story."

"Then they'll get their wish."

Stuart walked back through the house. The gym was in a large room at the rear of the building. He found the reporters waiting, engaged in conversation with Martin Julian. Across the way, he saw Fitzsimmons's trainer squatted down in the ring, reviving the groggy sparring partner. He halted before the small crowd of newsmen.

"Good afternoon," he said. "Thank you for coming today."

"Anything for a story," one of them replied. "Is this about Maher?"

"Peter Maher arrives on the noon train tomorrow.

But aside from that, I have even more momentous news."

That got their interest. Stuart went on with a broad smile. "I have decided to expand the scope of our event. We will now have five championship fights— in five days."

"Five!" echoed the sportswriter from the *Chicago Record.* "Who's fighting?"

Stuart quickly briefed them on the details. The event would now begin on February 10, with a fight a day for five days. On the first day, Jimmy Barry and Johnny Murphy would contest for the bantamweight title. George Dixon and Jake Marshall would tangle the following day for the featherweight championship. The third day Jack Everhart and Horace Leeds would meet for the lightweight crown. Joe Walcott and Scott Collins would battle the next day for the welterweight belt. The last day, the culmination of it all, would be Bob Fitzsimmons against Peter Maher.

"Holy Hannah!" yelled the *New York Times* reporter. "How the hell'd you pull that off?"

"I invited them to the prizefight extravaganza of all time. And, needless to say, I put up the purse."

Some two weeks ago Stuart had awakened with a brainstorm. A quick trip to Dallas had secured the approval of his partner, Edward Bates. They agreed that the added fights, with a five-thousand-dollar purse for each match, would create newspaper headlines throughout the country. For an extra twenty thousand dollars, they would reap a million dollars in publicity for their motion picture. The investment now would guarantee packed vaudeville theaters for the next year.

A flurry of telegrams went out to the fighters and their managers. The response was instantaneous, and wildly positive, though some tried to negotiate a better deal. Over the course of the next week, three of the champions accepted the terms, and agreed to arrive in El Paso the first week in February. The single holdout was Joe Walcott, the welterweight champion and one of the few popular black fighters in America. Only that morning, presented with an ultimatum to cancel the match, Walcott had accepted by telegram. Stuart immediately called the press conference.

The reporters were furiously scribbling in their notepads. Fitzsimmons, with Martin Julian at his side, moved forward through the crowd. Julian gave Stuart a dirty look.

"You're just full of surprises," he said. "Why weren't we told of this before now?"

"We have to be fair to the press," Stuart said, gesturing to the newsmen. "They all deserved to hear it at the same time. No one likes to be scooped."

Fitzsimmons was dripping sweat from his workout. "What's this about the purse?" he demanded. "I'll not fight for less than you've offered the others."

"Nor should you," Stuart said crisply. "Your purse is five times theirs, and rightly so. You're still the star attraction."

"Well, all right, then," Fitzsimmons conceded. "I'm not one to begrudge any man a payday. Just so it's held to five thousand."

"You have my word on it, Fitz."

"Mr. Stuart!" the reporter from the *Dallas Morning News* called out. "Governor Culberson will have a conniption fit when he hears about this. Won't he try to queer the whole thing with the Mexicans?"

"You may quote me," Stuart said confidently. "Nothing short of lightning will stop these matches from taking place. Nothing!"

"You're positive?"

"We will stage the grandest event ever witnessed in the United States. A carnival of the sport!"

The press giddily dubbed it "The Fistic Carnival."

Early the next afternoon, the train was over an hour late. Stuart waited on the depot platform with Judge Townsend and the fight committee, and Mayor Campbell. The Mexican band and the El Paso Fire Brigade were positioned at the end of the platform. The press corps stood talking among themselves by the stationhouse door.

Shortly after one o'clock the train appeared along the eastbound tracks. The engineer throttled down some distance from the station, then set the brakes with a screech of wheels. The cars shuddered to a halt before the platform, and the engine hissed a final burst of steam. The band, on cue from Juan Daguerra, trumpeted into a lively tune. The members of the fire brigade snapped to attention.

Peter Maher stepped off the center passenger coach. He was followed by his manager, Jack Quinn, then his trainer, Tommy Burns, and finally his sparring partner, Jim Hall. They stopped in a tight knot, startled by the large crowd and the thumping blare from the band. Stuart, trailed by the coterie of officials and the press corps, walked forward on the platform. He clasped Maher's hand in a firm grip.

"Good to see you, Peter," he said. "We're delighted to have you in El Paso."

"Glad to be here," Maher said, glancing about the crowd. "I wasn't expectin' a reception committee."

"The people of El Paso and Juarez wanted to welcome you in style. I'd like you to meet some of our supporters."

Stuart performed the introductions. Everyone

shook Maher's hand, greeting him with warmth, and the mayor made a short speech. The cameras recorded it with the pop of flash-pans and the newsmen surged forward. A reporter for the *Chicago Tribune* out-shouted the others.

"Ruby Rob says you won't last six rounds, Mr. Maher. What's your comment on that?"

Maher bristled, his fists clenched. "Fitzsimmons is a blowhard and full of clabber. I'll knock him off his pins. You can mark it down!"

"Last time he took you out," declared the sports-writer for the *New York World*. "Why do you think this time's any different?"

"I was robbed," Maher said angrily. "This time, Fitzsimmons won't steal it like before. He'll get the drubbing of his life."

"What about Corbett?" demanded the reporter from the *Dallas Morning News*. "How do you explain him giving you the championship belt?"

"I'm the best man in the ring today. There's your goddamn explanation."

"That's all!" Quinn stepped in front of his fighter. "No more questions. Save it for another day."

A murmur of protest erupted from the newsmen. Stuart quickly interceded, promising them more inter-views in the days ahead. With a tactful smile, he herded them toward the telegraph office, where they could file their reports. Then he turned back to Maher.

"Don't take it personally," he said with an apolo-getic shrug. "They're just after a story."

"To hell with 'em," Quinn said sullenly. "I won't have my man badgered, story or no story."

"Water under the bridge," Stuart assured him. "We've arranged an excellent training facility for Pe-ter on the edge of town. A nice house and a barn you can use for a gym. Perfect to set up a ring—"

"Forget it," Quinn interrupted. "I've made our own arrangements. We'll train in Las Cruces."

"Las Cruces?" Stuart said blankly. "New Mexico?"

Las Cruces was a small town some fifty miles to the north, in New Mexico Territory. Stuart had planned to quarter Maher in El Paso, readily available for press interviews and publicity. Jack Quinn was clearly of a different opinion.

"You heard me right," he said curtly. "I'll not have Peter distracted by your press circus. There's a train for Las Cruces tomorrow morning. We intend to be on it."

Stuart looked stumped. "Who do you know in Las Cruces?"

"Nobody, and that's the whole point. I picked it off a map and wired the mayor of the town. He's been most obliging."

"You're quite an industrious man, Mr. Quinn."

"You shouldn't blame Jack," Maher broke in. "I told him to find someplace quiet and out of the way. The less people the better."

"Well, Peter, you've certainly found it in Las Cruces."

Stuart suggested they spend the night at the Vendome Hotel. He started toward a line of carriages at the side of the depot when someone called his name. On the far end of the platform, he saw Walter Wheelock, one of his associates from Dallas, waiting with valise in hand. He sent Maher and his entourage ahead with Judge Townsend and the fight committee.

"Walt," he said, crossing the platform. "I almost forgot you were on this train. I've got a slight problem with Maher."

"Yes, I know," Wheelock said, returning his handshake. "I overheard them talking on the train. We won't get much publicity out of Maher."

Wheelock was a slight man, with deep-set eyes and narrow shoulders. A bookkeeper by profession, he'd been hired by Stuart to oversee administrative matters dealing with the fight. Stuart had rented an office in the Sheldon Building, near the hotel, to serve as their headquarters. Three days ago, he had wired Wheelock to come on to El Paso.

"We'll set up shop this afternoon," Stuart said. "I've been swamped with letters and telegrams asking about tickets for the fight. That's why I sent for you."

Wheelock nodded. "From the sound of it, you were right all along. We'll draw a big gate."

"Not the million I originally thought. But I believe we'll easily top four hundred thousand. That's nothing to sneeze at."

"By any gauge, that is a considerable sum of money. Have you given any thought to security?"

"I've hired Bat Masterson," Stuart said with a quick grin. "His name alone ought to put the fear of God into anybody with funny ideas. He's reputed to have killed twenty-six men."

"I see," Wheelock said, considering a moment. "Will he be operating by himself?"

"Not on your life! I authorized him to hire five men. Or perhaps I should say gunmen. They'll be here two weeks before the fight."

"Well, I must say that gives me a certain peace of mind. I'm sure there's *someone* who has his eye on all that money."

"Walt, the world's full of crooks."

Stuart led Wheelock to the waiting carriages. He joined Maher and Quinn at the head of the column, while Wheelock and the others clambered aboard carriages farther down the line. The band broke out in a rousing tune, with the fire brigade directly behind, and the parade marched off toward the center of town. All along the street people stopped to cheer the Irish champion.

Though tempted, Stuart said nothing more about Las Cruces. He chuckled instead to himself, for it was, quite literally, in the middle of nowhere. A land of sand, and scorpions, and harsh desert winds. Hardly the emerald isle so beloved by Irishmen.

He thought Peter Maher was in for a shock.

NINE

Julie poured herself another cup of coffee. The breakfast dishes were stacked on a room-service cart, and she was waiting for Stuart to finish in the bathroom. She took a seat in a tufted wing chair, still dressed in her peignoir. A bright morning sun spilled through the windows overlooking the street.

Stuart came through the door from the bedroom. His cheeks were rosy from a close shave and his mustache was neatly trimmed. He was attired in a navy blue suit, tailored with a matching vest, set off by an oxford shirt and a maroon tie. His cordovan half-boots shone like mirrors, and a gold watch chain gleamed across the breadth of his vest. He smelled faintly of cologne.

"How dashing," Julie said, setting her coffee cup aside. "You look very much the fashion plate."

Stuart smiled. "A man has to look the part."

"What's on your agenda today?"

"Well, first, I have a meeting with Fitz and Maher. We have to select a referee."

"Oh, that ought to be scads of fun. How long since they've seen each other?"

"Nearly three years," Stuart said. "I hope we can keep the meeting civil. There's no love lost between them."

Peter Maher had come in on the train from Las Cruces last night. A week had passed since his brief stopover in El Paso, and Stuart had communicated with him several times by telegraph. The wires were routinely answered by his manager, Jack Quinn.

"Will I see you at noon?" Julie said, her tone gently mocking. "Or is that too much for a girl to ask?"

Stuart moved to a table near the windows. He opened a humidor, removing several cigars, and stuffed them in his inside coat pocket. He was all too aware that he left her alone too much, and her understanding attitude did little to relieve his concern. He turned back to her with no suitable answer.

"Let's see how it goes," he said evasively. "After the meeting, I have the press coming in for a photograph session. The two gladiators squaring off for battle, that sort of thing."

"Another full day," she said, unable to hide her disappointment. "But you needn't worry. I'll amuse myself somehow. Maybe I'll go shopping."

"Good idea," Stuart encouraged her. "Buy yourself a new dress for tonight. All things considered, it's quite an occasion."

"I'm still amazed you got him to agree."

"I suppose every man has his weak spot."

Maher was to perform an exhibition at the opera house that evening. Stuart's pretext for bringing him to El Paso was the selection of a referee. But he'd goaded the Irish champion with several references to the success of Fitzsimmons's previous exhibition. Not to be outdone, and a victim of his own pride, Maher had finally agreed. The opera house sold out within an hour of posting the notice.

One reason was the steady influx of fight enthusiasts from around the country. The publicity on the "Fistic Carnival" had created a sensation from coast to coast. Though the event was almost a month away, half the hotels in El Paso were already full. The railroads were advertising special fares on Pullman cars, with sleeping berths, from distant points such as Boston and San Francisco. Those who made the trip were treating it as an extended holiday, much like the thousands drawn to Mardi Gras every year. They were there to celebrate the fight spectacular of the century.

"I think you're right," Julie said. "Tonight simply demands that I buy a new dress. An expensive one!"

Stuart chuckled. "You're a little vixen, aren't you? Just don't bankrupt me."

"Oh, perish the thought, sweetie. I'll settle for any old rag."

"I can't wait to see the bill."

"A girl has to be outfitted in style."

Stuart cupped her chin in his hand. "I'll make it up to you the minute the fight's over." He kissed her tenderly on the mouth. "You've always wanted to take an ocean voyage. How about a trip to Paris?"

She tugged his mustache. "Now you're trying to bribe me."

"Well, I wouldn't want you to think I'm entirely a rascal. Let's make it London."

"Go on," she said, pushing him away with a laugh. "Go to work."

Stuart grinned, moving across the room. He collected his hat, tilting it at a rakish angle, and looked back at her with a sly wink. When the door closed, she sat for a moment staring off into space. Business was business, she told herself, and she shouldn't be too hard on him. But once he'd made his million . . .

A naughty smile touched the corner of her mouth. She decided it would have to be Paris.

Outside the hotel, Stuart crossed the street. The stores were busy with Saturday-morning shoppers, the sidewalks unusually crowded. He suspected many of them were people he'd brought to town for the fight. Halfway down the block, he turned into the Sheldon Building.

The office was on the ground floor, with a plate-glass window fronting the street. He'd rented it furnished, unmindful of impressing anyone; it was merely a headquarters for the growing demands of the fight. A telephone and a typewriter, along with a massive steel safe, were the only things he had added to transform it into a working office. He found Wheelock seated behind a sturdy walnut desk.

"Good morning, Walt," he said in a chipper voice. "How's the world of pugilism today?"

"Never better." Wheelock leaned back in his squeaky swivel chair. "Every time I go to the post office, there's another slew of requests for tickets. It's a regular barn-burner."

"Wait till it gets closer to fight time. They'll be breaking down the door."

"I don't doubt it for a minute. Incidentally, a telegram came in for you last night. I found it under the door this morning."

Stuart tore open the envelope. He scanned what seemed a cryptic, and all too brief, message. The origin designation was marked Mexico City.

Arrive El Paso afternoon January 17.
Will report on affairs then.
                                        Edward Bates

"It's from Ed," Stuart said, tucking the telegram in his pocket. "He'll be here this afternoon."

Wheelock arched an eyebrow. "Does he say what happened?"

"Nothing one way or another. I guess we wait and see."

A week ago, the newspapers had reported a disturbing development. Texas Governor Charles Culberson had lodged a formal protest regarding the Fistic Carnival with Porfirio Diaz, the president of Mexico. Stuart was wary of anything that smacked of politics, and he sensed the need for action. Yet the demands of the impending fight made it impossible for him to leave El Paso.

Stuart wired Edward Bates, in Dallas. The stockbroker was the perfect emissary, a respected businessman, and his stake in the motion picture provided the incentive. He agreed to represent their interests, and caught a train the same day for Mexico City. Whether or not he had obtained an audience with Porfirio Diaz remained to be seen. His telegram revealed nothing.

"By the way," Wheelock said, shifting forward in his chair. "The bids came in on the lumber. Prices aren't too bad."

Stuart appeared distracted. "Who's the lowest bidder?"

"Acme Lumber Company."

"Go ahead and give them the order. I want it delivered to the railroad yards on February eighth."

Wheelock rolled his eyes. "When the word gets

out, the whole town will go bats. I can hear it now."

"Confusion is the best of all allies, Walt."

Earlier in the week, Stuart had let out bids on seven thousand feet of lumber. The purpose, considering the nature of his business, was clearly to construct a prizefight arena. Yet a circus tent in Juarez was the advertised site, and clearly required no additional seating. Questions would be raised as to what Stuart intended to do with all that lumber. But his contingency plan was a closely guarded secret, and he meant to keep it that way. His last resort would be triggered only by that—a last resort.

The reporters began crowding into the office. A few minutes later Fitzsimmons arrived, decked out in a checkered suit, with Martin Julian in tow. Hardly had the door closed than Maher walked in, accompanied by Jack Quinn. A chill settled over the room as the fighters glowered at each other, and the reporters waited expectantly to see who would break first. Stuart finally intervened, motioning them forward, and the two men grudgingly exchanged a handshake. Their managers merely exchanged curt nods.

Stuart moved on to the business of selecting a referee. By long-standing custom, the fighters were required to agree on the third man in the ring. The purpose was to eliminate bias, and ensure that neither fighter received an unfair call during the match. Julian and Quinn placed several names in contention, and then proceeded to wrangle themselves into a stalemate. In the end, they settled on George Siler, editor of the *El Paso Evening News* and a man with no ties to either camp. A telephone call to the newspaper confirmed that Siler would accept the assignment.

The next order of business was a photograph. Stuart asked both fighters to strip to the waist, and they obligingly peeled off their clothes. He got them positioned against the back wall, squared off in a fighting stance opposite one another. There was no need to request a pugnacious attitude, for their faces were already set in a hard scowl. They stood frozen in a mutual glare, their fists cocked, and the cameras recorded it for posterity. Within the week, the picture would appear in newspapers from Maine to California, and no one would doubt that it was a grudge match. The men looked ready to trade blows without the benefit of a referee.

While they were getting dressed, the reporters barraged them with questions. Stuart moved to the rear, allowing the newsmen to provoke a verbal sparring match. He felt reasonably certain that one or both of the fighters would spout off, delivering a quote that would further publicize the bout. A reporter from the *San Francisco Chronicle* struck lightning.

"Mr. Fitzsimmons," he yelled. "Mr. Maher says he'll give you the drubbing of your life. How do you feel about that?"

Fitzsimmons colored to his receding hairline. "I say he's all wind and no whistle. I'll put him on his Irish arse by the sixth round. You can bet on it."

"Mr. Maher!" the sportswriter from the *St. Louis Post Dispatch* clamored. "What's your response to that?"

Maher drilled Fitzsimmons with a look. "Your day's comin', boyo. I'm gonna drop you like a rock."

Fitzsimmons started forward, but Martin Julian stepped into his path. A moment of leaden silence slipped past, then Maher brayed a loud, cocky laugh. He turned on his heel and went out the door, Jack Quinn in his wake. The reporters erupted in an excited buzz, and Stuart smothered a laugh of his own. He could almost visualize the headlines.

No holds barred for Fitzsimmons and Maher.

Later that afternoon, Edward Bates walked into the office. His suit was wrinkled, smudges of train soot on his face, and he looked exhausted. He dropped his valise on the floor.

"*Viva Mexico,*" he said in a parched voice. "I don't recommend the trip."

Stuart was alone in the office. He'd sent Wheelock to finalize arrangements for Maher's exhibition at the opera house, and he thought it just as well. He wasn't reassured by Bates's appearance.

"Ed, you look like hell," he said, as they shook hands. "What the devil happened?"

Bates wearily slumped into a chair. "I'm the bearer of sad tidings, Daniel. We're in deep trouble."

"I suspected as much from your telegram. Didn't you get to see President Diaz?"

"Oh, I saw him, all right. Not that I'm wiser for the experience. He's slick as an eel."

"Damn," Stuart growled. "He turned you down, didn't he?"

"Nooo," Bates said slowly. "*El Presidente* didn't commit himself one way or the other. He took the matter under advisement."

"What does that mean, exactly?"

"Tell you the truth, I'm not quite sure. I tried everything from cajolery to reason to flattery. All I got in return was the runaround."

Stuart frowned. "How did you leave it with him?"

"Dan, it's all politics," Bates sighed. "Governor Culberson has put the heat on him to stop the fight.

For the moment, he's not saying yea or nay. He's thinking about it."

"Thinking about what?"

"How to turn it to advantage. I got the impression he wants something from Culberson. A trade treaty or maybe another foot of the Rio Grande. Who the hell knows?"

Stuart appeared bemused. "So where does that leave us?"

"A man by the name of Miguel Ahumada is the governor of Chihuahua. Diaz informed me that Governor Ahumada will arrive in Juarez on February 11. His parting statement was that we will have our answer by then."

"That's only three days before the main fight."

"Like I said, it's all politics," Bates observed. "Diaz gave himself time to play us off against the state of Texas. He's a shrewd cookie."

Stuart knuckled his mustache. "How do you assess our chances?"

"I think Culberson will make a deal. He's told the churches that come hell or high water, he'll stop this fight. To fail now would be political suicide."

"Are you saying what I think you're saying?"

Bates wagged a hand back and forth. "I'm a stockbroker, not a swami. But if you want my frank opinion—we're dead in Juarez."

Stuart stared out the window. He was silent for a long while, his gaze fixed on the middle distance. He finally looked around. "We have to keep this to ourselves. No need to panic everyone in El Paso."

"Mum's the word," Bates agreed. "Where do we go from here?"

"On your way to Dallas, stop off in Langtry. Tell the judge we've got a deal whether the fight's held there or not. Give him half his fee—five thousand."

"That might set him to talking. You'll recall, he's the world's worst braggart."

"Tell him if word leaks out, he'll lose the other half. We'll take the fight elsewhere."

"Won't he know that's a bluff?"

"Ed, it's no bluff," Stuart said. "There are lots of whistle stops along the border. Tell him that, too."

Bates nodded soberly. "I'll leave in the morning."

"I'll need you back here by the end of the month. Plan on staying until the fight's over."

"I've already arranged things at the brokerage. One of my staff will manage the accounts while I'm gone."

"Speaking of the fight reminds me," Stuart said. "Peter Maher's giving an exhibition tonight. You're in for a treat."

"Good thing I got here today," Bates noted. "How do you think Maher compares to Fitzsimmons?"

"We'll get a preview tonight."

The exhibition played to a full house. Maher carried his sparring partner for five rounds, and then flattened him with a corking left hook. Stuart was impressed, but he found it somehow anticlimactic. A knockout seemed oddly eclipsed by the day's events.

He wondered if the greater blow wouldn't be delivered by Porfirio Diaz.

TEN

Breckenridge was located some ninety miles west of Fort Worth. A thriving community, it served as the trade center for farmers and cattlemen throughout much of the county. The business district was boxed around the small town square.

Lea rode into town from the south. She was dressed in men's clothes, her features obscured by a low-crowned hat and her figure concealed beneath a long duster. Across the way, she saw Stovall enter the square from the north, attired in range gear and a mackinaw. Off to her right, she spotted Taylor on the road from the east, similarly outfitted in the garb of a cowhand. They held their horses to an easy walk.

The town was situated in the heart of the Upper Cross Timbers. A forest belt of blackjack and post oak, the Cross Timbers extended south from the Red River far into the interior of Texas. The woods varied in width from a half-mile to ten miles, and to the east and west were rolling prairies of grass. Towns dotted the countryside in all directions; but fencing was a sporadic thing, and it was still largely open range. The terrain lent itself to overland travel on horseback.

Breckenridge was typical of the towns Lea selected for a holdup. Though small, it was prosperous and relatively distant from other settlements. Something over two months had passed since their last job, and they were in need of funds. Taylor had gambled away his share, and she and Stovall were almost as broke from high living and maintaining the hotel suite in Fort Worth. She intended that this would be their last robbery before they went on to El Paso, and she was determined to ride away with a substantial haul. She wanted the wherewithal to establish the proper front among the fight crowd.

The newspapers were filled with coverage of the Fistic Carnival. Editors and sportswriters across the country lauded the sheer audacity of holding five championship fights in as many days. Lea read every word, and she'd come to admire Dan Stuart as a visionary, a man who grabbed for the brass ring with both hands. Sometimes, thinking about it late at night, she almost hated to rob a man who dared so greatly in the face of all obstacles. But her reservations were fleeting and quickly shunted aside, for her eye was fixed on her own brass ring. She too dared greatly.

Today, three weeks before the fight, she took the next step in her overall plan. The bank was located on the northeast corner of the square, and she'd timed their arrival for the close of the workday. A late afternoon sun dropped westward, casting a bright reflection off the plate-glass window fronting the bank. She crossed the square as Stovall and Taylor dismounted and looped their reins around the hitch rack. Seemingly just another rider, she reined in beside their horses a moment before they went through the door. She stepped down out of the saddle.

The square was virtually deserted. Stores and shops

were preparing to close for the day, and there were few people on the sidewalks. Lea pretended to check her saddle rigging, all the while carefully scrutinizing those who were still on the street. The town marshal's office was on the southwest corner, diagonally across the square, and a full fifty yards from the bank. She saw no movement there, and barring any mishap, she thought they would be well away before the law discovered the bank had been robbed. Her eyes roved back and forth, alert to any danger.

The plan was simple yet deceptive. After robbing the bank, Lea intended to ride north some ten miles to the Brazos River. There, holding their horses to the water, they would turn east and travel a few miles downstream. By dark, they would be clear of the Cross Timbers and headed southeast toward Fort Worth. The law would lose their tracks at the Brazos, and after a futile search, quite probably leap to the wrong conclusion. The Red River lay seventy miles or so to the north, and beyond that, the wilds of Oklahoma Territory. A breeding ground for outlaws, most notably the Doolin Gang, the territory was overrun with desperadoes of every stripe. Given all that, the law would naturally assume they had made a run for the Red.

Lea saw the bank door open. Stovall stepped out, pistol in one hand and gunnysack in the other. Directly behind him was Taylor, quickly scanning the street, his mouth hooked in a wide grin. She swung into the saddle as they crossed the sidewalk, vaguely aware of the gunnysack, stuffed full with cash. The door suddenly burst open, and a man attired in a business suit and vest rushed outside, brandishing a revolver. He stopped, extending the gun at arm's length, and drew a bead on Taylor's back. Her reaction was one of pure reflex; she pulled her right-hand Colt and fired in the same motion. She knew he was dead even as she tripped the trigger.

A bright red dot appeared on the banker's vest. He staggered, his features frozen in an instant of surprise, and toppled face forward on the sidewalk. Lea thumbed off another shot through the plate-glass window, determined to drive anyone else inside to cover. As Stovall and Taylor scrambled into their saddles, she whirled her horse toward the southwest corner of the square. She saw a man emerge from the marshal's office, drawing his pistol on the run, and start in their direction. One hand gripping the reins, she steadied her horse and fired three aimed shots. The first kicked up dust at the lawman's feet, and the second shattered a store window directly to his rear. The third slug stopped him, pocking his shirtfront below the right shoulder. He fell sideways in the street.

Stovall and Taylor opened fire. All around the square, storekeepers caught in their doorways ducked for cover as windows exploded in shards of glass. Lea booted her horse in the ribs, yelling at the men, and rode north out of the business district. Quick to follow her lead, Stovall and Taylor spun their mounts and spurred into a lope. A minute or so later, they cleared the outskirts of town.

Lea was sick with disgust. She cursed the banker for being a fool, and she cursed herself for firing too fast. Even a moment's delay might have allowed her to place the shot and bring him down without killing him. But the alternative was for him to kill Stony Taylor, and she'd fired too fast, too well. She gigged her horse with savage anger.

They galloped north toward the Brazos.

*　　*　　*

Captain Bill McDonald rode into Breckenridge early the next afternoon. The sheriff had summoned him by wire from Abilene, where he'd been investigating another case. He had ridden through the night to reach the scene of the killing.

The town marshal was seriously wounded. A doctor had operated to remove the slug from his chest, and expressed confidence he would recover in time. But Waylan Tolbert, the banker, now lay at rest in the local funeral parlor. He had been killed instantly by a bullet through the heart.

Sheriff Ben Logan was stumped. Late yesterday, upon arriving in town, he had led a posse in pursuit of the robbers. The trail ended on the banks of the Brazos River, and he'd called off the search soon after nightfall. Afterward, with nothing to show for his efforts, he had wired McDonald. He thought it was a job for the Rangers.

"Goddamn bastards," Logan said, standing with McDonald outside the bank. "Waylan Tolbert was a fine man, one of the best you'd ever meet. They just shot him down like a dog."

"Well, he's with the Lord now," McDonald said in a measured voice. "Our job's to catch his killers."

"You've got your work cut out for you, Cap'n. They're a slick bunch."

"I've never yet seen one that was slick enough."

The statement was a summation of the man. Captain Bill McDonald was regarded as the most deadly Ranger of them all. He was reputed to have personally killed eleven men in gunfights, and his legend was that of a peace officer who would charge hell with a bucket of water. He commanded Company B of the Ranger Battalion, and his troop was responsible for the apprehension of over two hundred outlaws in the past three years. A good many of them had been brought in dead.

McDonald was whipcord lean, with slate-gray eyes and a soup-strainer mustache. At forty-three, he had been a lawman most of his life, working as a deputy sheriff and a deputy U.S. marshal before he became a Ranger. His calm demeanor belied the tough, no-nonsense attitude of a religious man who wore a badge and smote lawbreakers with something approaching the wrath of God. He was not a man to be crossed.

Late that afternoon, McDonald and the sheriff reined to a halt before the Brazos. Logan pointed to a trail that ended at the river. "I kept the posse off away from them tracks. You'll see there's three riders."

"Same as when we left town," McDonald said in a dry tone. "Guess three's all there was."

Logan accepted the rebuke in silence. The Ranger dismounted and walked forward along the riverbank. He positioned himself so that the westerly sun was on the far side of the tracks. The angle of the sun created a shadow in the hoofprints, and he dropped to one knee, studying the scuff marks on the ground. After a time, apparently satisfied, he got to his feet. He motioned back toward town.

"How many people witnessed the shooting?"

"The bank tellers," Logan said. "Four or five more that was on the square."

"The one watchin' the horses was short, built on the slight side. Probably wearing a duster."

"How'd you know that?"

McDonald ignored the question. "One of the others was tall and lanky, fair hair. The third one was stout, with a mouthful of teeth. Fit the description?"

Logan nodded. "You know who they are?"

"Just by reputation. They've robbed mebbe ten or twelve banks the last couple of years. Stick strictly to small towns."

"How is it the Rangers haven't caught 'em?"

McDonald looked at him like he was dense. "They're a will-o'-the-wisp bunch. Hit here and there, and get out fast."

"Dirty sonsabitches," Logan said harshly. "You think they're operatin' out of Oklahoma Territory?"

"I'd tend to doubt it."

"Why so?"

"They've knocked off banks all over the state. I'd just suspect they're home-growed *bandidos*."

Logan gestured across the river. "There's no tracks over there. They took to the water right where you're standin'. Got any ideas, Cap'n?"

"You check upstream," McDonald said. "I'll have a look downstream. They come out of the water somewheres."

"We rode the river in both directions yesterday. Didn't find nothin' a mile or so either way."

"So we'll try two miles today."

Logan knew better than to argue the point. He reined his horse around and rode upstream. McDonald stepped into the saddle, his eyes on the ground, and turned downriver. He thought the chances of finding sign were somewhere between slim and none. Whoever led the gang was tricky and smart, already a myth of sorts among the Rangers. A phantom robber.

Yet McDonald was not overly concerned. He told himself that today might be the day, and if not, then there was always the next time. For just as God made little green apples, there was one certainty in the larger scheme of things. Nobody outfoxed the Rangers forever.

He rode off down the banks of the Brazos.

The gang arrived in El Paso on January 26. Lea stepped off the train in a taffeta gown that accentuated her figure and a feathered hat perched atop her tawny hair. Stovall and Taylor wore three-piece suits, with pearl stickpins in their ties, and white Stetsons without a speck of dust. The three of them looked like they'd just foreclosed the mortgage on the federal mint.

The impression was one crafted by Lea. Their last job had netted them $23,000, and she'd spent part of it to create an illusion of casual wealth. The men were still operating in the guise of cattle buyers, one traveling with his wife, come all the way from Fort Worth to see the fight. Their spanking new steamer trunks were unloaded from the luggage car, and Stovall idly tipped the porter twenty dollars. The porter arranged a hired carriage to take them uptown.

The Grand Hotel was a block down from the Vendome. Lea, using Stovall's name, had wired ahead, requesting the finest accommodations available. The manager, upon being informed of their arrival, rushed from his office to extend a personal greeting. He escorted them to the third floor, where they were shown into a two-bedroom suite with separate bathrooms. The sitting room was lushly appointed in leather and tapestry, and the bedrooms were furnished in the Victorian style. The windows looked north onto the snowcapped mountains.

Their trunks were delivered and the manager bowed his way out of the suite. A few minutes later, a waiter appeared with a bottle of champagne, compliments of the management. He deftly popped the cork, pouring crystal glasses to the brim, and nestled the bottle in a bucket of ice. Stovall slipped him a twenty on his way out.

"Good times," Lea said, raising her glass. "And better days ahead!"

"You're damn tootin'," Taylor said with a loopy grin. "I gotta tell you, there were times when I figured it'd never happen. But by God, here we are!"

"Stony, you're all wet," Stovall informed him. "God didn't have nothing to do with it." He clinked glasses with Lea, flashing a smile. "We owe it all to the little lady with stardust in her eyes."

Lea took a delicate sip. The bubbles tickled her nose, and she laughed. "Let's not get carried away," she said gaily. "We still have a lot of work to do, you know."

"Work?" Taylor echoed. "What kind of work?"

"We're not robbing some backwater bank, Stony. We have to get the lay of things, and most especially, we have to find out all there is to know about Mr. Dan Stuart. He's our ticket to the land of milk and honey."

"Don't worry your head about that," Stovall said. "Stony and me will stick to him like glue. By fight time, we'll have it down pat."

"Bet your life we will," Taylor barked with high good humor. "We'll know him better'n his own damn shadow."

Lea again raised her glass. "I think we ought to wish him well."

"Yeah," Stovall agreed. "Good luck and good fortune."

"The other way around," Lea amended, her eyes wicked. "His good luck and our good fortune."

They drank a toast to Dan Stuart and his Fistic Carnival.

ELEVEN

Fitzsimmons reveled in the limelight. At Martin Julian's suggestion, he opened his training sessions to the public, and every day dozens of people trooped over the bridge from El Paso. They lined up outside the back door, and groups of ten or so were ushered in for a few minutes to watch the fighter in action. Ruby Rob's gym was the best ticket in town.

The press turned out in force as well. Fitzsimmons was readily available, and Maher's training camp was fifty miles away. Some of them occasionally took the train to Las Cruces, and caught the evening train back after interviewing the Irish champion. But for the most part, they took the easy way out, which entailed nothing more than a short stroll over to Juarez. They thought the eccentric Aussie made better copy anyway.

Fitzsimmons, given the opportunity, proved to be something of a showman. He mingled with the public, shaking hands and signing autographs, and generally went out of his way to entertain them. Rose enjoyed the attention herself, and usually wandered back to the gym every afternoon with baby Rob. Someone in the crowd invariably had one of the new Kodak cameras, which were rapidly transforming Americans into a country of shutterbugs. Their favorite picture was of Rose and the baby, posed beside the bare-chested fighter.

Yet the highlight of the day was Nero. Stuart walked into the gym shortly before three in the afternoon, just as the show got under way. Charlie White, whose duties as trainer included tending to the lion, stood at the rear of the room. He was holding Nero on a heavy chain, and struggling not to be pulled off balance as the lion paced back and forth. By now, Nero was accustomed to his daily workout and clearly had little patience with delay. Fitzsimmons moved forward, attired in boxing tights and lightweight leather shoes laced to the ankle. He addressed the crowd of spectators.

"Ladies and gentlemen," he said pleasantly. "Today you will see an African lion that I've personally trained for the prizefight ring. His name is Nero and he packs a lulu of a punch."

Stuart, who was watching the crowd, stood near the ring. His attention was drawn to a woman, a small blonde accompanied by two men dressed in business suits. Her features were animated by excitement, and he noted not for the first time that attractive women were often fascinated by the prize ring. She glanced at him, then quickly pulled her eyes away when she caught his stare. He saw the freckles beneath her makeup brighten with color.

Fitzsimmons moved to the speed bag. Suspended from a platform at head height, the lightweight leather bag was inflated with air and used to improve a fighter's coordination and reflexes. Charlie White approached, tugged forward by Nero, and took a tight grip on the chain. Fitzsimmons looked back at the crowd.

"Here's the only lion in captivity that fights on two feet."

Nero reared up on his hind legs. He swatted the speed bag with his left paw and grunted deep in his chest as it rebounded off the backboard. His yellow eyes glittered fiercely, and he hobbled around on his hind legs, whacking the bag with a thunderous right. His paws flashed in a blur and the bag rattled against the backboard in a steady, drumming tattoo. He pounded it a final time, fangs bared in a mighty growl, and settled back onto all fours. His eyes tracked the bag as it wobbled to a stop.

The crowd broke out in wild applause. Nero glanced at them with no great interest and accepted a hunk of goat meat from Charlie White as his reward. Fitzsimmons roughed the lion's mane, playfully dodging the swipe of a paw, and stepped away from the speed bag. He spread his arms to the spectators.

"There you have it," he said proudly. "Nero, the world cham-peen!"

"Hey, Fitz," one of the reporters yelled. "Why don't you let the lion fight Maher?"

"Nero or me, it makes no difference. Peter Maher will end up flat on his back."

"Any comment on Corbett's latest bout?" asked the sportswriter from the *New York World*. "Everybody says he got the worst of it."

The incident had been covered in the morning newspapers. Gentleman Jim Corbett had become involved in an argument with a New York fireman, who was inspecting the backstage area of the theater. Corbett tried to bar the fireman from his dressing room, and when the fireman resisted, Gentleman Jim punched him in the mouth. Unimpressed, the fireman delivered a punch himself, and in the ensuing wrestling match, he hurled Corbett to the floor. The newspapers jokingly called it a technical knockout.

"I thought you'd heard," Fitzsimmons said in a jocular tone. "Corbett's not a fighter anymore, he's an actor. Small wonder he got himself decked by a fireman."

"Think that's why he retired?" the sportswriter called back. "Was he afraid of your punch?"

"I would've put out his lights. You can quote me on it."

Nero roared as though in agreement. Stuart, pleased by the fighter's repartee with the press, got the odd sensation that he was being watched. He looked around and caught the pert blonde studying him with open interest. She again averted her gaze, linking arms with the overly handsome man at her side. Stuart was flattered, thinking perhaps she was attracted to older men. Then, before he could pursue the thought, his attention was diverted.

Fitzsimmons and Nero went into their wrestling act. The crowd gasped as Nero stood and locked his paws over the fighter's shoulders. Stuart mentally placed three to one on the lion.

Las Cruces lay in a desert valley. To the east were the Organ Mountains and farther west were the humpback slopes of the Potrillo range. The upper Rio Grande wound through town on its serpentine path northward.

The training camp was situated along the banks of the river. The house was a one-story adobe, with four rooms and an unimpeded view of the desert. There was a fireplace in the central room, which served as a kitchen and a living room. The rest of the house was heated only by the sun, and the furnishings were spartan. Not one bed in the sleeping quarters was softer than a board plank.

Outside, a heavy bag hung suspended from the limb of a tree. The ring, which was covered with a fine coating of dust, stood in forlorn desolation off to the rear of the house. Maher whacked the bag with a right cross, his oxlike shoulders knotted with muscle. He bobbed, feinting with his head, and hammered the bag with two left hooks delivered an instant apart. He let the bag slam hard into his belly as it swung back on a creaky rope.

Maher paused, breathing heavily, his torso slick with sweat. Not quite three weeks into the training program, and he thought he'd never been in better shape in his life. To no small degree, he credited the isolation of Las Cruces with his progress in so short a period of time. The town was scarcely more than a village, and there was little to do besides train. Yet, with the advantage of hindsight, he might have selected someplace other than a desert. He was still amazed at how cold it turned when the sun went down.

Quinn, slumped on a bench outside the house, sat talking with a reporter for the *San Francisco Chronicle.* All of the press considered Las Cruces the end of the earth, and they took the train north only when there was a paucity of news in El Paso. Their absence seemed to Maher a blessing in disguise, for he was there to prepare for the fight, and conversation was not high on his list. Tommy Burns, his trainer, who felt much the same way, motioned him over to the ring. The reporter, until now bored with what he'd seen, at last looked interested.

"No rest for the weary," Burns said. "Let's have a go at sparring."

Maher crawled into the ring. He felt the grit of dust under his feet, and again wondered about the desert. Then Burns whistled, sounding the start of a round, and he shuffled forward for another session with Jim Hall. A brute of a man, Hall seemed designed by the gods to absorb punishment and keep coming back for more. They met in the center of the ring, and Maher decided to try the tactic he'd just worked out on the heavy bag. He feinted with his head, cocking his right, and belted a double left hook to the jaw. Hall went down as though he'd been struck by a thunderbolt. He was out cold.

"Jee-zus," Burns groaned. "How're you gonna get any ring time if you keep knockin' him out? What's the matter with you, Pete?"

Maher looked abashed. "I was working on the left hook, Tommy. How was I to know?"

"You'll just have to start pullin' your punches, that's all. You're gonna kill the poor bastard."

Burns knelt down beside the fallen fighter. He lifted Hall's head off the mat and lightly patted his cheeks. "Are you all right, Jimmy? How're you feel-in'?"

Hall's eyes rolled open. He stared up at the trainer with a vacant expression. "Gimme a minute," he said blearily. "I'm ready to go again."

"Not today, you're not," Burns said, glancing around at Maher. "Go work out on the heavy bag some more. We're finished here."

Maher paused, still looking sheepish, then ducked through the ropes. The reporter from the *Chronicle* was waiting for him at ringside. "Very impressive, Mr. Maher. Ten seconds of the first round."

"I'll take your word for it."

"You've certainly perfected your left hook. Do you think it will work as well on Fitzsimmons?"

"Why wouldn't it?" Maher said gruffly. "I dumped him on his pants the last time we fought."

"So you did," the reporter acknowledged. "But I recall he didn't stay down. Do you honestly believe you can put him away this time?"

"I don't believe it, I know it. He'll go down for the count."

"How can you be so positive?"

"A fortune-teller told me so. Read it in my palm, she did."

"You're joking."

"The joke's gonna be on Bob Fitzsimmons."

Maher walked back to the heavy bag. He planted his feet, jabbing with a stiff left, wondering if the reporter would print what he'd said. Fortune-teller or not, he told himself, it was still true. A simple statement of fact.

Fitzsimmons wouldn't get up this time.

On February 1, Edward Bates returned to El Paso. He checked into the hotel and then walked over to the office. He found Stuart pacing the floor and Wheelock seated in glum silence. Their expressions were owlish, oddly solemn.

"Somebody die?" he asked. "You two look like pallbearers."

"You might say we're holding a wake," Stuart replied. "I've just come from a meeting with Juan Daguerra. We've lost Juarez for the fight."

"What happened?"

"President Diaz has issued what can only be termed

an edict. He has prohibited the fight from taking place on Mexican soil."

"Hate to say I was right," Bates said. "But you'll recall I predicted he would strike a deal with Governor Culberson. Wonder what the trade-off was?"

Stuart took out a cigar. "Whatever it was, they made a devil's bargain." He popped a match and lit up in a haze of smoke. "I'm informed by Daguerra that Governor Ahumada will arrive in Juarez in ten days. He'll command a force of five hundred Rurales."

The Rurales were the elite troops in the Mexican army. Their reputation for violence was known all along the border. Bates looked stunned. "Diaz apparently means business. Nobody in his right mind messes with the Rurales."

"Exactly," Stuart said, puffing on his cigar. "Unless Governor Ahumada would be amenable to a bribe. Any chance he'd look the other way—for the right amount?"

Bates considered a moment. "You never know with Mexican politicians. It's worth a try."

"Worth a try, but nothing to take to the bank. So in the meantime, we'll depend on our old ally, confusion."

"What have you got up your sleeve now, Dan?"

"A diversion," Stuart said, gesturing with his cigar. "Let them believe we've selected an alternative site—New Mexico."

New Mexico Territory had no statute on the books barring prizefights. By train, the border was hardly more than an hour from El Paso. Bates laughed, clearly intrigued with the idea. "You're a devious man," he said. "Turn their attention west, just in case we head east toward Langtry. I like it."

Stuart nodded to Wheelock. "Walt, drop a few hints around town. Nothing too open, just a word here and there about New Mexico." He paused, smiling at the thought. "Let's start the rumor-mill churning."

"I'll get on it tonight," Wheelock said, his face squinched in a grin. "The bartender at the Gem has a big mouth. He'll spread the word."

The door opened and William Barclay Masterson walked into the office. "Bat!" Stuart said, extending his hand. "I've been expecting you."

"Our train just got in," Masterson said. "I sent the boys on over to the hotel. Got you five good ones, Daniel. Handy with a gun."

"I knew you wouldn't let me down."

Stuart introduced him to Bates and Wheelock. A man of medium height, Masterson was in his early forties, built on the stocky side, with a thick mustache. By trade, he was a professional gambler, headquartered now in Denver, and he and Stuart had been friends for years. Yet he was best known as a frontier lawman, and his reputation as a gunfighter was all but legend. He sometimes hired out his reputation.

"The train stopped in Las Cruces," he said. "The conductor told us Peter Maher's got his training camp there. How'd he come to pick that burg?"

"Let's just say his manager's not too bright. A regular know-it-all."

"Anymore, seems like the world's full of them. So how's the fight going?"

Stuart chuckled mirthlessly. "As of today, we're locked out of Juarez. We may be headed elsewhere."

"I'll be dipped," Masterson said, amazed. "Damn Mexicans could screw up the recipe for ice water."

"Bat, I think I could say that's a fair assessment of our situation."

"When you talk about holding the fight elsewhere, where's elsewhere?"

Stuart exchanged a quick glance with Bates. Then, without reservation, he went on to explain their strategy in some detail. He considered Masterson essential to their plan, and he knew him to be a man of honor. Anything said here would not be repeated.

"Nothing's set in stone," he concluded. "We'll play it out as it goes along. Take it day by day."

Masterson wagged his head. "You've got more moves than a three-dollar whore. I'm impressed, Daniel."

"Tell me that when the fight's over."

"You think there's any chance at all for Juarez?"

"I'd say that depends on whether or not Governor Ahumada has larceny in his heart."

Masterson grinned. "Does a bear shit in the woods?"

Stuart thought it a point well taken. The crux of the matter, succinctly phrased.

TWELVE

Stuart avoided the El Paso fight committee for two days. Then, on the morning of February 3, he received a stiffly worded note from Judge Townsend, demanding a meeting. There was no way to skirt the issue any longer.

Shortly after ten o'clock, Stuart entered the judge's office. Townsend rose from behind his desk, and exchanged a brusque handshake. Doc Albers looked like a man on the verge of spitting nails, and offered his hand in a perfunctory manner. A tense moment passed as everyone got seated.

"We are most distressed," Townsend said without any preliminaries. "The newspapers reported that President Diaz has banned the fight from Juarez. Jaun Daguerra informs us that he advised you of this day before yesterday."

"That's correct," Stuart said. "Where is Daguerra, anyway? I expected to see him here."

"I prefer that Mr. Daguerra not be privy to our discussion. Given the situation, you might say he's now in the enemy camp."

"Judge, I suspect that's a reasonable assumption."

"Let's get down to it," Albers cut in. "There's rumors flying around town that you intend to move the fight to New Mexico. Any truth to it?"

Stuart shrugged. "New Mexico becomes an alternative only if we're barred from Juarez. I still have hopes that we can salvage the situation."

"Do you?" Townsend said abruptly. "Would you mind taking us into your confidence? The position of the Mexican government seems quite clear—and final."

"Not necessarily," Stuart remarked. "What we have here is a political charade, posturing for newspaper headlines. Things are never quite what they appear."

"Go on, we're listening."

"Governor Ahumada will be here in a week or so. I plan to approach him with some sort of . . . accommodation."

"That's rich!" Albers woofed. "You actually think you can bribe him?"

"Too strong a word," Stuart replied. "I'd rather think of it as a quid pro quo."

"Call it what you want," Albers said. "Why would Alhumada go against orders from President Diaz? They shoot people for that in Mexico."

"Consider a moment," Stuart said in a musing tone. "If the price were right, maybe the order would be rescinded. Maybe that was the scheme all along."

"You're saying Diaz rigged it to boost a payoff?"

"Why not?" Stuart suggested. "Stranger things have happened."

Townsend squinted at him. "You understand, we will not be a party to any of this. Whatever you do, you do on your own."

"I wouldn't compromise your reputation, Judge. Your name will never enter into the matter."

Albers cleared his throat. "I'm a damnsight more worried about the fight. What if Ahumada turns you down?"

"Don't concern yourself," Stuart said. "You have my word, the fight will come off."

"Yeah, but where?" Albers persisted. "We're not interested if you're talking about New Mexico."

Stuart warned himself to play it cautious. Neither of them could be trusted with the truth, not until the last moment. He decided that evasion was the best tactic. "No need to borrow trouble," he said. "Let's wait until Ahumada gets here."

"Allow me to be frank," Townsend said bluntly. "We guaranteed the purse for a fight in Juarez, not New Mexico. Take care you don't jeopardize our support."

"Judge, you won't lose money in any dealings with me. You have my word on it."

Stuart ended the meeting on that note. The least of his worries was the purse, and he'd told the truth. By rough estimate, there were at least five thousand people in town for the fight, and more arriving every day. El Paso would profit no matter what happened.

He thought he'd kept his end of the deal.

Joe Walcott arrived on the noon train. He stepped off the rear passenger coach, which was reserved for colored people, and stood for a moment surveying the depot. Then he headed toward the uptown business district at a brisk clip. There were no cabs for coloreds in El Paso.

A diminutive man, Walcott carried himself with the cocky assurance of a bantam rooster. He was an inch over five feet, weighing in at a solid one hundred forty pounds, and there was a decided strut to his walk. His bearing indicated that he was somebody, and those in the prizefight game were quick to agree. He was the welterweight champion of the world, known fondly as "Little Chocolate."

For all his small stature, Walcott attracted attention on the street. He was attired in a pearl-gray suit and a matching homburg hat, with a diamond stickpin in his tie. The diamond was the size of an acorn, and it glittered no less than the gold tooth that lit his smile. He tipped his hat to the ladies, but he gave way to no man on the sidewalk, white or black. All along the street, people stopped to stare as he breezed past.

A policeman, who couldn't take his eye off the gold tooth, directed Walcott to the fight headquarters. When he walked into the office, all conversation ceased and everyone stared as though struck mute. The pearl-gray suit and the stickpin, set off by the gold tooth, was a dazzlement beyond their experience. Before anyone could recover, Walcott did a fast shuffle and struck a fighting pose. He peered at them over his balled fists.

"Joe Walcott's the name," he said with a blinding smile. "Known to my friends and some that ain't as Little Chocolate. I'm lookin' for Mistuh Daniel Stuart."

Stuart moved forward. "Mr. Walcott," he said warmly, extending his hand. "Welcome to El Paso. I'm Dan Stuart."

"Just call me Joe." Walcott returned his handshake with a firm grip. "They only calls my daddy mistuh."

"And I insist that you call me Dan. All my friends do."

Stuart introduced him to Bates and Wheelock. Walcott shook their hands with a cordial smile. "Don't mean to take up your time," he said, turning back to

Stuart. "Just wanted to tell you I'm here and ready to fight. You heard from Scott Collins yet?"

"I got a wire this morning," Stuart said. "He'll be here day after tomorrow. Do you know Collins?"

"Not personal," Walcott said slyly. "But I'll take care of that when we fight. Get to know him real good, then."

Walcott was living proof that dynamite comes in small packages. His string of knockouts attested to the fact that he was the reigning welterweight of the day. Yet, like most black fighters, he seldom met his white opponents until they stepped into the ring. The color barrier was still strongly entrenched, even though he was the champion. The public accepted him simply because he was unbeatable.

"Are you alone?" Stuart asked. "I thought your manager would be with you."

"Left him back in New York," Walcott said. "Man likes to travel in style, and I foots the bill. I'll get along fine by myself."

"Have you made arrangements for training facilities?"

"Don't worry yourself about that. I'll find me somebody to spar with once I gets to colored town. El Paso do have a colored town, don't it?"

"Well, yes," Stuart said, suddenly embarrassed. "Down at the end of Utah Street. That's the sporting district."

"Ought to be right up my alley. Some folks say I'm a sporting man, myself."

"Let me know if you need anything, Joe."

"Mistuh Dan, you just get Collins in the ring. I'll take care of the rest."

Walcott flashed his gold tooth. After another round of handshakes, he waved and went out the door. Stuart watched him saunter down the street, drawing bemused stares from passersby. He wondered how the black man would fare in El Paso.

Texans had never seen anything like Little Chocolate.

Joe Walcott proved to be the catalyst. Until now the clergy had adopted a wait-and-see attitude toward the Fistic Carnival. But their parishioners were suddenly galvanized by a black man who casually strolled the streets of the uptown area. All the more so when he tipped his hat and boldly grinned at white women.

Late that afternoon the El Paso Ministers' Union convened in an emergency session. The members of their congregations, both men and women, had bombarded them with ugly calls. There was talk of the "uppity nigger" who didn't know his place, and the "coon fighter" in flashy clothes. The people were incensed that a New York Negro had been dropped into their midst, even though he'd taken quarters in colored town. They blamed Dan Stuart for importing the "trashy" element into their city.

The ministers deplored the prejudice. To a man, they were appalled that their flocks exhibited something less than a Christian attitude. Yet every preacher was obligated to voice the concerns of his people, for without the support of the people, he would have no pulpit. Still, wary of exposing bigotry, the ministers decided to cloak it beneath a broader cause, one that merited public condemnation. They denounced Dan Stuart, rather than an uppity black man, and attacked the Fistic Carnival. Their indignation took on a properly righteous note.

Early that evening there was a knock at the door of Stuart's hotel suite. When he opened it, he found

Ferris Johnson standing in the hallway. A spare man with a guileless face, Johnson was the telegrapher at the railroad depot. He handed over a telegram form.

"Evenin', Mr. Stuart," he said. "Judge Townsend asked me to bring that around. He's already seen it."

"Am I reading other people's messages, Ferris?"

"The judge figured you'd want to. It's a copy of a wire from the local Ministers' Union. Went out about an hour ago. Pretty much speaks for itself."

"You're certainly a good friend to the judge."

"Just doing my part, Mr. Stuart. I'd like to see your fight come off."

Johnson turned away with a courteous nod. Stuart closed the door, exchanging a glance with Julie, who was seated on the sofa. He unfolded the message as he moved back into the room. It was addressed to Thomas B. Catron, Congressional Delegate, Washington, D.C.

> *The undersigned strongly oppose prizefight venture by Daniel Stuart. We understand neither territorial nor federal law prohibits prizefights in New Mexico. Implore you to act immediately with legislation to reverse situation. Our congressman instructed to support your efforts.*
> *El Paso Ministers'*
> *Union*

Stuart gave the telegram to Julie. She read it through, then looked up. "Who is Thomas Catron?"

"Congressional delegate from New Mexico. Have you ever heard of the Santa Fe Ring?"

"Not that I recall."

"Catron's the ringleader," Stuart said. "He and his cronies control over a million acres of land in New

Mexico. Not to mention banks, and railroads, and anything else that smells of money. Their influence got him the appointment to Congress."

Julie looked confused. "I thought you weren't interested in holding the fight in New Mexico. Did I miss something?"

"New Mexico doesn't matter one way or the other. But I'm not keen on the idea of congressional legislation."

"What difference does it make?"

"I don't want the door closed to Juarez. Everyone jumping on the bandwagon against us makes it look bad. President Diaz might stick to his guns."

"Tell me honestly," Julie said, searching his eyes. "Do you have any hope for Juarez?"

"Well, like they say, it's never over until the fat lady sings. We'll know soon enough."

Stuart walked to the window. He stared out into the deepening night, wondering what had provoked the El Paso clergy. There seemed no rhyme or reason to their busybody telegram. But then, on second thought, he realized it didn't matter.

A prizefight was an easy target for politicians and preachers.

Thomas Benton Catron believed in seizing on opportunity. He was a staunch advocate of statehood for New Mexico, and since prizefighting was universally condemned, he saw it as a platform for his larger goal. A campaign to outlaw the sport would further garner allies in Congress for statehood. He got his colleagues' attention by labeling it a "bloodsport."

All within the last few days, Catron had seen a groundswell of opposition to the fight. William Thornton, governor of New Mexico Territory, had requested congressional action to amend the law. Fearing the fight was indeed headed their way, the New Mexico clergy had united in their support of the governor. The telegram from the El Paso Ministers' Union merely heaped coals on an already simmering fire.

On February 5, Catron introduced an anti-fight bill in the Congress. He took the floor in a rousing speech, and informed his fellow members that El Paso, the current fight headquarters, was only a short train ride from the New Mexico line. He went on to state that the law, as it now stood, left the territory helpless in the face of Dan Stuart and the troop of prizefighters ready to board the train. He proposed enactment of legislation similar to that adopted by the state of Texas. His voice rang out in a trumpeting battle cry.

"The Congress of the United States *alone* must control its territories!"

The legislation was directed at all territories, such as New Mexico and Oklahoma, which had not yet been granted statehood. Catron's proposed bill would make prizefighting a felony, with a penalty of one to five years in prison, at the discretion of the trial judge. The bill was sent to the Judiciary Committee, where it was unanimously approved early that afternoon and returned to the full House. Congressman David Henderson of Iowa tacked on an amendment that would also prohibit amateur boxing in colleges. He denounced the so-called sport in a strident voice.

"The sentiment of the entire country mandates us to outlaw this barbarous practice!"

The House passed the bill by unanimous vote. Late that afternoon the legislation was forwarded on to the Senate for consideration. The juggernaut of political expediency was thus set in motion.

No one in Washington would dare oppose the bill.

THIRTEEN

Enoch Rector arrived in El Paso on February 7. He waved from the coach window as the train rocked to a halt before the stationhouse. Stuart and Bates were waiting on the depot platform.

The motion picture producer was accompanied by five assistants. As he stepped off the train, he began issuing instructions, his hands fluttering madly, directing them toward the baggage car. They hurried off and he walked forward, his arms spread wide. His mouth crinkled in an elfin smile.

"Daniel!" he said, pulling Stuart into an affectionate hug. "How wonderful to see you again. I thought we would never get here."

Stuart pried himself loose from the older man's clasp. "I'm delighted you made it safely, Enoch. Any problems on the trip?"

"No, no," Rector said airily. "But so many trains to change, and all our equipment to be moved from one to the other." He gestured with palms outspread. "A trek to Africa would have been no worse."

"I can imagine." Stuart motioned Bates forward.

"Enoch, I'd like you to meet our partner in this enterprise—Edward Bates.

"A great pleasure," Bates said, pumping the producer's arm in a handshake. "I'm tremendously excited by our project. We're going to make a bit of history."

"Not to mention a lot of money," Rector cackled wryly. "A man of science should not sound so mercenary, huh? But I ask you, aren't we entitled to live well?"

"No question about it," Bates affirmed. "Money makes the world go round."

Rector pushed his wire-rimmed glasses to the bridge of his nose. He peered around at Stuart. "Does everything go well here, my friend?"

"Even better than I expected. Look for yourself."

Stuart directed his attention to the train. There were five passenger coaches, all crowded to capacity with fight enthusiasts. A swarm of people milled around the depot, waiting for their luggage to be unloaded, talking excitedly among themselves. A wide smile creased Stuart's features.

"The town's a madhouse," he said jovially. "A week before the fight and we've already drawn ten thousand people. And more arriving by the hour."

"Dan's right," Bates added. "There's not a hotel room to be had for love or money. People are sleeping in the streets."

"Good, good," Rector said, nodding his head. "But have you made any progress with the Mexican government? The newspapers all say there has been no change."

Stuart and Bates had anticipated Rector's concern. Before his arrival, they had agreed the less said the better. The film producer tended to tell everything he knew to anyone who would listen, and his loquacious manner was not be to trusted. Their strategy, for the moment, would remain a secret.

"You shouldn't concern yourself," Stuart said. "The Mexican governor will reach Juarez in four days. We plan to negotiate something with him at that time."

"Four days!" Rector repeated. "You've announced your Fistic Carnival will begin the day before, on February tenth. What about these extra fights?"

"We've already thought that out. We'll hold two fights a day instead of one."

"And what if this Mexican governor refuses to negotiate? What will we do then?"

"Enoch, listen to me," Stuart said evenly. "The one fight that matters is Fitzsimmons–Maher. Am I correct?"

"Yes, of course," Rector agreed. "Without that we have no motion picture!"

"You have my solemn assurance that it will happen. If nothing else, Fitzsimmons and Maher will fight."

"And I will make my motion picture? You swear it to me, Daniel?"

"You have my oath on it."

"Thank you, thank you." Rector seemed to heave a sigh of relief. "All the way here on the train, I could think of nothing else. I was at my wits' end. How can you be so calm?"

Stuart smiled. "I suppose it comes from twenty years at a poker table. The fight game's not all that different from cards."

"No?"

"Not really."

Rector gave him a crafty look. "Perhaps you have an ace up your sleeve. Something you haven't told me."

"Oh?" Stuart's expression betrayed nothing. "What's that?"

"I think you must have some secret arrangement. New Mexico, am I right? I know I am!"

Stuart lowered his voice. "Don't say that too loudly, Enoch. Especially in public."

"No, no." Rector placed a fingertip over his mouth. "We will not speak of it again. My lips are sealed."

"That's probably best all the way around."

"Your secrets are safe with me, Daniel."

Rector suddenly darted past them. He hurried along the platform, to where his assistants were unloading the baggage car. The motion picture apparatus was bulky yet fragile, secured for shipment in heavy wooden crates. He fidgeted around, fussing at the men, while they unloaded the crates onto a freight cart. His tone was that of a schoolteacher lecturing students.

"That was quite a performance," Bates said sardonically. "I'm surprised you could keep a straight face."

Stuart chuckled. "I've had lots of practice."

"I'll remember that the next time we play poker."

"Keep it in mind when you meet with Governor Ahumada."

"Just call me the Sphinx."

"Pull it off and I'll call you Mr. Sphinx."

They stood watching Enoch Rector scold his assistants.

Early that afternoon Stuart returned to the office. Wheelock was working over an accounting ledger, and Bates was talking on the telephone. He hung up as Stuart came through the door.

"That was Judge Townsend," he said. "Called to see if we had any news."

"What did you tell him?"

"No news is good news."

"Exactly right," Stuart observed. "You should have been a diplomat, Ed."

Bates got to his feet. "Everything squared away at the hotel?"

"Yes, I finally got Enoch and his wards settled in. He's still a bundle of nerves."

"Think he'll ever calm down?"

"Not in our lifetime," Stuart said. "A genius is somewhat like a clock. Tick-tick-tick, night and day."

"You really believe that?" Bates asked. "About Rector being a genius?"

"Anybody who keeps pace with Thomas Edison qualifies as a genius. You have to operate in a different sphere just to understand what makes the whirligig go around."

"Now that you mention it . . ." Bates paused, a quizzical expression on his face. "What makes a motion picture work?"

"You've got me," Stuart admitted. "I'm no genius."

"Guess that makes two of us."

The door swung open. Fred Martin, the sportswriter for the *New York Times,* walked into the office. His smile somehow reminded Stuart of a cat with a mouthful of feathers. He handed Stuart a telegram.

"Thought you'd want to see that," he said. "Just now came in from our Washington correspondent."

Senate passed Catron anti-fight bill by unanimous vote this morning. President Grover Cleve-

*land signed bill into law one hour later.
Prizefights now criminal offense in all U.S. territories.*

Stuart read the telegram aloud. He glanced at Bates,
who shrugged, and Wheelock, who simply nodded.
He handed the form back to Martin.

"Hardly a surprise," he said. "We expected passage
of the bill before now."

Martin looked disappointed. "That closes another
door on your fight. Aren't you getting worried?"

"There's a key to every door, Mr. Martin. I see no
reason for alarm."

"Which door are you talking about? Texas, New
Mexico, or Mexico?"

"All in good time," Stuart said with an offhand
gesture. "I'll have an announcement for the press
within the next few days."

"That's no answer," Martin insisted. "Thousands of
people are in town to see these fights. Don't you think
you owe them an explanation?"

"You may quote me as saying the Fistic Carnival
will take place as scheduled. Other than that, I have
no comment."

"No one will be satisfied with that, either. Why
keep us in the dark?"

"As I said, no further comment."

Martin left the office frustrated, with nothing news-
worthy to report. When he went out the door, Stuart
turned to Bates. "I think tonight's the night to start
everyone guessing. We'll let Bat Masterson handle
it."

"Why not?" Bates said with a smile. "Nothing like
muddy waters to confuse the issue."

"Exactly my thought."

Not quite an hour later, a man with a badge walked through the door. His features were weathered by wind and sun, and set in a sober cast. He introduced himself as Ralph Ascarate, sheriff of Dona Ana County, New Mexico.

"You've come a long way," Stuart said. "What can I do for you, Sheriff?"

Ascarate hooked his thumbs in his gun belt. "I'm here at the orders of Governor Thornton. He wants you put on notice that prizefights are now illegal in New Mexico Territory."

"The governor must have a pipeline into Washington. I only just got the news myself."

"President Cleveland wired the governor, and the governor wired me. I caught the next train out."

"Interesting," Stuart said. "Why did he pick you for the job?"

"Las Cruces is in my county," Ascarate informed him. "You've got Peter Maher training there, and the governor don't much like the idea. He thinks you might try shifting the fight up our way."

"Do I look like a man who would break the law?"

"I'm not here to bandy words with you, Mr. Stuart. But I'll tell you one thing, and it'll save you a world of grief. Stay the hell out of New Mexico."

"You've done your duty," Stuart said agreeably. "Will that be all, Sheriff?"

Ascarate stared at him. "What should I tell Governor Thornton?"

"Why, tell the governor I send my warmest personal regards."

"I'll be keepin' an eye on Peter Maher—and you."

"We're in good hands then, Sheriff. Have a pleasant trip home."

Ascarate slammed the door on his way out. There

was a moment of silence, and then Bates and Wheelock erupted in laughter. Bates wagged a finger at Stuart.

"Dan, you're a corker. Talk about leading a man
down the garden path! He thinks we're headed for
New Mexico."

"Muddy waters," Stuart said with a chuckle, "keep
them guessing."

"Tonight ought to do that up in high style."

"Nothing would please me more, Ed. Nothing."

A full moon hung suspended in the sky. The rail yards
south of the depot were lit by a brilliant, silvery glow.
The air was crisp, and the men huffed spurts of frost
as they worked. The stationmaster stood watching
from the depot platform.

Bat Masterson walked along the tracks. His crew
of gunmen were postioned as guards, while a force of
some twenty workmen labored beneath the moonlight.
A lone boxcar was positioned at the front of a siding,
isolated from the other freight traffic in the railyards.
The men were loading lumber from a wagon into the
boxcar.

Hands in his pockets, Masterson looked on as the
last of the lumber was unloaded. The foreman of the
work crew waved the wagon on, and another, drawn
by a team of horses, was rolled into place. The lumber, until now stored near the rail yards, was clearly
intended for the construction of a boxing arena and
spectator seating. The men scrambled onto the wagon
and went to work.

An hour or so later, the final lumber wagon pulled
away from the boxcar. Masterson spoke to the foreman, who then began shouting orders at his men.
They grabbed the tongue of the freight cart that held

the crates of motion picture equipment and jockeyed it into position. Four men to a crate, straining under the weight, they gingerly offloaded the three crates. The foreman secured them with lashing to cleats in the floor of the boxcar.

When he finished, he jumped down to the ground. Masterson walked forward, studying the interior of the boxcar a moment, then muscled the door shut. He pulled a heavy padlock from his coat pocket, hooked it into the door hasp, and snapped it tight. After pocketing the key, he peeled bills off a wad of greenbacks and paid the foreman for the work crew. The boxcar was left bathed in moonlight, positioned for linkage to a freight train on either the Southern Pacific or the Texas & Pacific. All that remained to be announced was the destination.

Masterson and his squad of gunmen marched off toward the depot. The stationmaster, plainly overcome with curiosity, waited at the end of the platform. "Late night's work," he called out as they went past. "Where's the boxcar headed?"

"Don't know," Masterson said in an equable tone. "We're just hired help."

"Who would know?"

"Ask Dan Stuart."

Uptown, Masterson stopped off at the Gem Variety Theater for a drink with his men. After downing a shot of rye, he slapped a twenty on the bar, and walked on to the Vendome Hotel. The clock in the lobby was ticking on toward midnight, and he took the stairs to the third floor. Stuart admitted him when he rapped on the door.

"All done," Masterson said, handing over the key to the boxcar. "Sealed tight and ready to roll."

Stuart nodded. "Anyone ask any questions?"

"The stationmaster finally got over his lockjaw and popped the question. I told him to ask you."

"Which means it'll be all over town by morning."

"You figure they'll think it's headed for New Mexico?"

"Bat, I'd lay odds on it."

"So what's your next move?"

"Say nothing and deny everything."

Masterson laughed. "You sure you never dealt three-card monte?"

"I deal in something far trickier."

"What's that?"

"Misdirection, the magician's art."

"When's the magic show?"

Stuart smiled. "Valentine's Day."

FOURTEEN

The next morning Stuart met with George Siler. The editor of the *El Paso Evening News,* Siler would act as the referee during the Fistic Carnival. As the third man in the ring, he would be the sole judge of the outcome in the event of a close call. His ruling might easily determine who won and who lost.

A spare man in his late thirties, Siler was a native of El Paso. He had begun his career in the press room, and eventually worked his way into the position of reporter. He was a man of unimpeachable character, and his reputation as an unbiased newsman was widely regarded throughout the community. Three years ago, he had been appointed editor of the *Evening News.*

Siler was still a reporter at heart. Though he was to referee the bouts, he was nonetheless interested in the story. After he was seated in the office, he went directly to the question on everyone's mind. "Any word on where the fights will be held?" he asked. "You've got everybody thoroughly bumfuzzled on that score."

Stuart was weary of dodging the question. Over the

past week, he'd been besieged by reporters as well as the general public. With the arrival of the fighters for the Fistic Carnival, the questioning had become even more intense. The federal law barring New Mexico as a site merely served to aggravate an already dicey situation. His one alternative was to yet again skirt the truth. He was forced to stall for time.

"George, you put me in an awkward position," he said. "I'm not at liberty to discuss the matter, simply because it's at a delicate stage. Just take my word for it, things will work out in the end."

Siler scrutinized him a moment. "A lot of people are counting on you to come through. I hope you don't let them down."

"I have no intention of letting them down. The matter will be resolved very shortly."

"The sooner the better for everyone concerned. I don't have to tell you that folks are downright jittery over this."

"Let's move on to the fight," Stuart said, changing the subject. "Have you read the pamphlet I gave you on the rules? Are you clear on the procedure?"

"I believe so," Siler replied. "Of course, there's a lot to remember. I'm still studying the material."

Stuart wanted him well versed in the conduct of a boxing match. Once a bout started, Siler would make all the calls, and there was no appeal to his decision. The rules that applied during the reign of John L. Sullivan were no longer standard. With the advent of Gentleman Jim Corbett, a far more complicated system had been adopted. There was still a good deal of confusion, even among those involved in the fight game.

During the bare-knuckle era, fights were governed by the long-standing London Prize Ring Rules. The rules, established in the seventeenth century, dictated that a fighter could not kick, gouge, or butt with his head. A round ended when either man was knocked down and there was a thirty-second break before the next round began. With bare knuckles, it was not uncommon for bouts to last a hundred rounds. The match went on until there was a knockout, or until one of the men could no longer continue. At the end of a thirty-second break, the fighters were required to "toe the line," an imaginary line drawn in the center of the ring. If a man was unable to toe the line, he lost the bout by default. Or in the worst case, he was counted out while on his back.

By the early 1890's, when the sport became more science than brute strength, the conduct of prizefights had been revamped. John Douglas, the Eighth Marquis of Queensberry and an influential figure in London sports circles, had devised revolutionary new rules for boxing. He declared that the rounds would be of three minutes' duration, with a one-minute break between rounds, effectively eliminating the rule that a round ended only when a fighter was knocked down. Another change was that a fighter knocked down must toe the line, unassisted, within ten seconds or be counted out. A limit of ten seconds all but ended bouts that lasted forty or fifty rounds.

Yet the greatest innovation was the requirement of padded boxing gloves. In bare-knuckle matches, fighters were routinely maimed for life, and all too frequently killed from massive head injury. These days, the Queensberry Rules were commonly followed throughout the world.

"For the most part, it's fairly clear," Siler said. "A knockout is a knockout, and a man can be disqualified for a foul. Hitting below the belt, head-butting, that sort of thing."

"Exactly right," Stuart said. "But remember, unless it's a blatant foul, you have to issue at least one warning before you disqualify a man. Otherwise we'll have a riot on our hands."

"There's one thing that's sort of a gray area. What constitutes a technical knockout?"

"Two situations apply. First, if a man can't continue after the minute break between rounds, it's a technical knockout. Second, if a man is hurt so badly that he can't defend himself, you have the discretion to stop the fight. We don't want anyone killed."

Siler appeared dubious. "You're saying it's my responsibility to stop the fight. What if the fighter who's losing objects?"

"George, it's a judgment call. No matter who objects—the fighter, his manager, the spectators—your decision is final. Your judgment alone rules in the ring."

"And if they don't agree with my judgment, what then? Things might go to hell in a hurry."

"You have nothing to worry about," Stuart said with some conviction. "Bat Masterson and his men will be stationed around the ring. They'll handle anyone who gets out of line."

"I'll hold you to it," Siler said with a lame smile. "I'd hate to wind up in a fight myself. I'm not much for fisticuffs."

"You'll do just fine. Everyone knows you're an honorable man, or they wouldn't have selected you as referee. There won't be any trouble."

"Tell you the truth, I wouldn't have missed it for all the tea in China. Not every newspaper editor gets to referee a championship fight."

"Five!" Stuart said vigorously. "Five championship fights."

"Dan, are you sure you were never a snake-oil salesman? I seem to buy whatever you're selling."

"Well, you're certainly not alone—I bought it myself."

Some while later, Martin Julian wandered into the office. He was not a physical man, and he made it a habit never to accompany Fitzsimmons on the morning ten-mile run. He preferred the sedentary life, a leisurely stroll at most.

"Good morning," he said, nodding to Bates and Wheelock. "How's the world treating you gents today?"

"Peachy keen," Wheelock said with unusual bonhomie. "How about yourself?"

"Never better," Julian responded, flipping Stuart a jester's salute. "You might say I'm in top form."

Stuart was forced to grin. "Well, you're certainly chipper. What's the occasion?"

"I've just had a walk through town. Do you realize the place is crawling with people?"

" 'Swamped' might be the better word. The mayor's office estimates fourteen thousand and climbing. Another thousand or so are arriving every day. The trains look like sardine cans on wheels."

"Well, anyway," Julian said cheerfully. "I stopped by to congratulate you on a superb job. You've drawn them from across the entire country."

"Congratulate Fitz," Stuart said. "He and Maher are the real draw."

"I agree with you about Fitz. As for Maher, I doubt he would have drawn flies. The bookmakers are of the same opinion."

"Sounds like there's heavy action."

"Throw a rock in any direction and you'll hit ten bookmakers. People are betting everything but their eyeteeth."

"What are the latest odds?"

"Hold on to your hats!" Julian crowed. "It's dropped to ten to seven on Fitz. No one believes Maher has a chance."

"I do," Wheelock said stoutly. "Nothing against your fighter, but Maher's a tough customer. He'll make a scrap of it."

"Pardon me if I laugh," Julian said with high good humor. "Fitz would have to drop dead in the ring for Maher to win. I almost feel sorry for the Irishman."

"Spoken like a true manager," Wheelock said dryly. "Not to mention a loyal brother-in-law."

Julian waved him off. "You forget, I saw them fight before. Fitz will slaughter him this time out."

Their jousting was interrupted as the door rattled open. Gabe Lawlor, the reporter for the *New York World,* walked into the office. His features were flushed, like a man who had sprinted some great distance. He looked at Stuart as though he were about to announce a death in the family.

"You ready for this?" he said incredulously. "I just got a wire from the New York office. The War Department has ordered a troop of cavalry to patrol the New Mexico border. The U.S. Cavalry, for chrissakes!"

Everyone in the room seemed struck speechless, their eyes fixed on Stuart. He shook his head with a sardonic smile. "Our government certainly knows how to waste money."

"Maybe so," Lawlor said. "But it sure upsets your applecart."

"Which applecart is that?"

"You've got a boxcar loaded for a quick getaway. I heard all about it down at the depot. How do you figure to get it past the cavalry?"

Stuart feigned surprise. "Who said I was going to New Mexico?"

"Aren't you?" Lawlor demanded. "Why else would you have Masterson and his boys load a boxcar in the middle of the night? You're sure as heck not going to Juarez."

"Don't believe everything you read in the newspapers . . . even if you write it yourself."

"Are you saying there's still a chance for Juarez?"

"Never discount anything," Stuart said with an enigmatic smile. "Where there's a will there's a way. I always finish what I start."

"So you're saying the fight will come off?"

"Gabe, no matter what, I guarantee it."

"Funny thing," Lawlor said in a baffled tone. "Newshounds like to think of themselves as cynics. But I listen to you, and damned if I don't go away convinced. We all do."

The crowds flocking to El Paso provided ample proof of Lawlor's statement. Despite all the obstacles, the press believed Stuart would somehow pull off the fight. Their belief was transmitted through their articles, and the public in turn was convinced by what they read. Fight enthusiasts continued to board trains all around the country.

"You're not a cynic," Stuart told the reporter. "A true cynic worships before the altar of pessimism. You still have your optimism intact."

"If I'm an optimist," Lawlor said jokingly, "what does that make you?"

Stuart laughed. "How about a cock-eyed optimist?"

"Are you saying it never rains on your parade?"

"I only work on sunny days."

"So what's the forecast for Valentine's Day?"

"Look for fair weather and blue skies."

"And I suppose you'll guarantee it?"

"Well, don't you see . . . I already have."

Lea stood looking out the window of their suite. She was fascinated by the swarms of people attracted to the fight. She saw dollar signs attached to every one of them.

Taylor was playing solitaire on a low table positioned before the sofa. Stovall sat slouched in an easy chair, reading the morning edition of the *El Paso Tribune*. The breakfast dishes were stacked on a room-service cart, and the men were not yet dressed for the day. Neither of them looked up as Lea turned away from the window.

"Talk about money on the hoof," she said, crossing the room. "I feel like a rancher counting cows. They're here in droves."

"Twenty thousand," Stovall noted, rattling the newspaper. "Says here the mayor expects at least that many by fight time. The railroads have laid on extra trains."

Lea took a pack of cigarettes off the fireplace mantel. She tapped one out and lit it with a match. "I can't sleep thinking of it," she said, exhaling smoke. "We're going to ride out of here filthy rich."

"Trouble is, where's here?" Stovall amended. "The paper says Stuart's got his eye on New Mexico. Nobody thinks that new law means a hill of beans."

"No, trust me, it's Juarez," Lea said. "The Mexicans are just holding out for a bigger piece of the pie. Stuart will make a deal, you'll see."

"She's right," Taylor said, placing a black six on a red seven. "Damn greasers have all got sticky fingers. Never seen one yet that wasn't a bandit."

Stovall folded the newspaper. "Well, don't matter how you cut it, we're still in the dark. Stuart's playin' it damn close to the vest."

The remark neatly pinpointed their problem. For the last two weeks, Stovall and Taylor had shadowed Stuart's movements. Their efforts were sporadic, alternating days and times, for they couldn't risk being spotted. From what they'd seen, they thought the proceeds from ticket sales were being stored in the office safe. Yet, given the irregular nature of their surveillance, it was possible that one of Stuart's men was depositing the money in a bank. They simply couldn't be certain.

There was even less certainty about the location of the fight. The newspaper reports were more conjecture than fact, what amounted to uninformed guesswork. Stuart apparently confided only in his closest associates, and none of them was talking. The public was waiting for the announcement as well, and at the last minute, there would be a rush on ticket sales. Lea planned to pull the robbery just before the fight, when gate receipts hit the maximum level. But for the moment, she had to admit that Stovall was right. They were operating in the dark.

"You know—" She hesitated, toying with a whole new approach. "I think maybe we're wasting our time with Stuart. There's somebody else that might be an easier touch."

"Yeah?" Taylor said, glancing up from his solitaire hand. "Who's that?"

"Bat Masterson," Lea said eagerly. "He's thick with Stuart, or he wouldn't have been hired to handle security. He'll have the inside dope on the fight and the money."

Taylor nodded. "Makes sense to me."

"Why didn't I think of it before?" Lea said, suddenly excited by the idea. "We have to get close to Masterson."

"When you say 'we,'" Stovall asked, "are you talkin' about the three of us?"

Lea smiled. "I've heard Masterson has an eye for the ladies."

"So you aim to play him yourself? Was that what you meant by get *close* to him?"

"Sugar, don't worry about it. All I have to do is flutter my lashes."

"Just make sure that's all you flutter."

"Aren't you the jealous one?"

Taylor listened to their bickering. He placed a black jack on a red queen, slowly studying the solitaire layout. He told himself that Earl Stovall had every right to be jealous. Not of another man, but a more threatening rival.

Lea would do anything to get close to the money.

FIFTEEN

The westbound train ground to a halt before the depot. A noonday sun hovered overhead, cottony clouds framed against an azure sky. The date was February 9.

Captain Bill McDonald stepped off the lead passenger coach. He was dressed in a dark suit and a somber tie, topped off by a wide-brimmed Stetson. A pistol was strapped around his waist, and he carried a Winchester in one hand and a warbag in the other. His eyes raked the stationhouse at a glance.

Adjutant General Woodford Mabry followed him off the train. A stout man, with florid features and a thick mustache, he was the head of the Texas Rangers. Directly behind him were Captain Jim Brooks, Captain John Hughes, Captain Hank Rogers, and a force of forty Rangers. The lawmen were armed with Colt pistols and Winchester rifles.

All around the depot everything came to a standstill. The stationmaster, a gaggle of porters, and other passengers deboarding the train watched as the heavily armed men formed ranks. Mabry took the lead, trailed by the four captains, with the Rangers stretched out behind in columns of twos. At a brisk clip, like a troop of soldiers, they crossed the platform and rounded the corner of the depot. They marched off along the street.

A week ago, at the direction of Governor Culberson, Mabry had ordered the Rangers to assemble in Austin. The captains commanded the four companies scattered across Texas, and they had each been instructed to select ten of their best men. The governor wanted a show of force on the border, and a contingent of forty-four Rangers was usually considered adequate to quell an insurrection. Night before last, they had entrained for El Paso.

The Rangers were unique to Texas. Unlike other law-enforcement officers, they served at the discretion of the governor and were empowered to operate anywhere within the state. Formed in 1836, the Rangers had played a vital role in the defense of the frontier against Mexican raiders and Commanche marauders. After statehood, in 1845, the regiment had fought with distinction under General Zachary Taylor in the war with Mexico. In 1865, following the Civil War, the Rangers had assumed the traditional duties of law enforcement, pursuing outlaws of every stripe. Their record for the past thirty years was one of rough justice.

Woodford Mabry was a man cut from the Ranger mold. A graduate of the Virginia Military Institute, he had been appointed adjutant general of Texas in 1891. His stiff bearing was that of a soldier, and three years ago, he had personally led a battalion against Mexican bandits along the border. Under his command, the Rangers practiced swift law enforcement, sometimes writing the rules as they went along. On occasion, he had been criticized for a ham-fisted approach to law and order, often at the expense of justice. Yet his methods, however harsh, got the job done. He made Texas a dangerous place for outlaws.

A block from the railroad station, he led the Rangers into the Pierson Hotel. The desk clerk snapped to attention as the phalanx of lawmen crowded into the lobby. Mabry gave him a curt nod.

"I am Woodford Mabry, adjutant general of the state of Texas. You received my wire?"

"Yessir," the clerk responded. "We're holding the rooms, just like you wanted. Gave you our best suite. No extra change."

"Thank you," Mabry said, as though he'd expected no less. "Our men will take all their meals in your dining room. I want them fed properly and on time. Alert your kitchen staff accordingly."

"Don't you worry about a thing, General. I'll take care of it personal."

Mabry turned to his four captains. "First things first," he said in a firm voice. "Let's get the men quartered and then gather in the dining room. I imagine they're ready for a hot meal."

The officers bobbed their heads in unison. Mabry was forty, their senior by only a few years, and a man of commanding presence. He was square-jawed, stern in manner, and he brooked no nonsense in the performance of their duties. He had long ago earned their respect.

"By your leave, General," Hughes spoke out. "After we have dinner, what's your orders for the day? We ought to let the men know."

"Today we reconnoiter the situation," Mabry said. "Captain Hughes, take your men over to Juarez. Give me a report on Fitzsimmons."

"Yessir."

"Captain Brooks, you and your men check out the business district, and make yourselves obvious. I want everyone in El Paso to know we're in town."

Brooks grinned. "We'll put 'em on notice, General."

"I trust you will," Mabry said. "Captain Rogers, you pay a courtesy call on the sheriff—what's his name again?"

"Frank Simmons."

"Tell Sheriff Simmons we expect his full cooperation."

"I'll relay the word," Rogers said. "He won't give us no problem."

"I daresay you're right," Mabry allowed. "Captain McDonald, send one of your men to Daniel Stuart's office. Inform him that I will be there at two o'clock sharp. I expect him to make himself available."

McDonald considered a moment. "You going by yourself, General?"

"I believe you should accompany me, Captain. As a matter of fact, I am assigning you as Mr. Stuart's— how shall I say it?—his guardian."

"Come again?"

"You'll be our watchdog," Mabry said. "Wherever he goes, whatever he does, you're to keep me apprised."

McDonald chuckled. "General, I'll stick to him like a mustard plaster."

"Exactly."

Word spread rapidly though town. Stuart heard of it a full half hour before the Ranger walked into his office. He listened with equanimity, masking his puzzlement, and readily agreed. He would be available at two o'clock.

The Ranger, laconic to a fault, merely nodded and turned toward the door. When he was gone, Bates let out his breath in a low whistle. "What the deuce?" he said, baffled. "Why would the adjutant general suddenly pop up?"

"Good question," Stuart said, equally at a loss. "Not to mention forty Rangers and every captain on the rolls. That is a *lot* of law."

"You'd think somebody declared war."

"Ed, I suspect it's been declared on us. But the bigger question is why—and to what purpose—at this late date."

Bates shook his head. "Maybe word leaked out somehow. You know, about our idea to bribe Governor Ahumada."

"Even so," Stuart said. "What does that have to do with Texas?"

"I haven't got the faintest notion. None of it makes any sense."

"Well, one thing's certain. The Rangers aren't here except by order of Governor Culberson. Our old nemesis has something in mind."

"Holy Christ!" Bates abruptly went pale. "Maybe they got wind of our contingency plan—Judge Bean."

Stuart grimaced. "I hope to God you're wrong. How could they know about Bean?"

"Dan, it beats me. Why would he talk, when he's only gotten half his money? Nothing makes any sense."

"I suppose we'll find out when Mabry gets here. I'm sure he's come to deliver a message."

"Yeah, that's what I'm afraid of."

Woodford Mabry came through the door on the stroke of two o'clock. With him was McDonald, a Ranger badge pinned to his vest. The introductions were short and perfunctory, conducted with an air of veiled hostility. Stuart offered them chairs, and Mabry seated himself before the desk. McDonald chose to remain standing.

Stuart took the swivel chair behind the desk. "What can I do for you gentlemen?" he said, lighting a cigar. "I presume you're not here for tickets to the fight."

"Let me be blunt," Mabry said sharply. "I consider you a scalawag and a man who holds himself above the law. I would like nothing more than to arrest you on the spot."

"Well, so much for the amenities. Is that your personal opinion, or do you speak for the governor?"

"We are here at the direct order of Governor Culberson. He has authorized the Rangers to take whatever measures necessary to enforce the law."

Stuart blew smoke at him. "You've made a long trip for nothing, Mr. Mabry. At last count, I haven't broken any laws."

"You will," Mabry said with certainty. "Unless you intend to cancel this prizefight."

"I assure you that won't happen."

"Then it will give me great pleasure to place you in irons."

"On what charge?"

Mabry fished a telegram from inside his coat. "Read that," he said, tossing it on the desk. "You will note it's from Leland Harmon, Attorney General of the United States."

Stuart unfolded the telegram, quickly scanned the contents. The message was terse and to the point.

A prizefight held in any territory of the United States will result in imprisonment of offenders.

This includes promoter, fighters, and all involved.

When Stuart looked up, he became aware of McDonald's stare. The Ranger's eyes were steady and cold, fixing him like a butterfly pinned to a board. He was reminded of the grizzled lawman's reputation as a mankiller. A moment passed before he glanced back at Mabry.

"This is old news," he said, dropping the telegram on the desk. "President Cleveland signed the bill into law two days ago."

"You miss the point," Mabry informed him. "Mexico has banned the fight, and now you're locked out of New Mexico. What does that leave?"

"You tell me."

"Texas."

"Texas?" Stuart repeated. "You think I plan to hold the fight in El Paso?"

"Indeed I do," Mabry said smugly. "All your other options have been foreclosed. It's here or nowhere."

"You've brought your Rangers on a wild-goose chase. I have no intention of holding the fight in Texas."

"Why don't I believe you, Mr. Stuart? If not here, then where?"

"That's for me to know and you to find out."

"Listen closely," Mabry said in a hard voice. "Hold your fight on Texas soil and I will personally escort you to prison. Do we understand one another?"

Stuart puffed his cigar. "I understand perfectly."

"Then understand as well that Captain McDonald has been assigned to watch your every movement. You will be under constant surveillance."

"Every man to his own job," Stuart said, nodding

to McDonald. "I won't be hard to find, Captain."

McDonald's eyes narrowed. "Never yet saw anybody that was."

Mabry rose from his chair. He gave Stuart a corrosive look, then turned toward the door. McDonald followed him out, leaving behind a vacuum of silence. Bates finally found his voice.

"What the devil do you make of that?"

Stuart grunted a laugh. "I think our smoke and mirrors worked."

"You really believe we fooled them?"

"I'd say they outsmarted themselves."

"How so?"

"The damn fools still believe it's Texas."

Late that evening Stuart came out of the bedroom. He wore a robe, belted at the waist, with his tie off and his shirt collar open. He poured himself a snifter of brandy from the liquor cabinet.

Julie was seated on the sofa. A merry blaze danced in the fireplace, warming the room. She patted the cushion as he crossed from the liquor cabinet, and he took a place beside her. He savored a sip of brandy, staring into the flames.

"I've been thinking," she said. "Your meeting with Mabry?"

"What about it?"

"You said he never mentioned Langtry, or Judge Bean."

"Not a word."

"Could it have been a ploy?" she suggested. "Perhaps he was feeling you out. Looking for a reaction."

"No, I think not," Stuart said. "He's convinced we'll try to hold it in El Paso."

"How can you be sure?"

"I read his cards."

Twenty years at a poker table had taught Stuart to trust his instincts. He read men by their mannerisms, an inflection in the voice, the telltale signs of over-confidence, or often as not, a bluff. He knew what he'd seen in Mabry.

"You and your instincts," Julie said, batting her eyelashes in mock reproach. "He might be more clever than you think."

"I suppose anything's possible," Stuart conceded. "But my hunches have never played me false. You've proved it a hundred times over."

"Me?"

"The first time I saw you, I got a hunch. Way down deep something told me."

"Oh?" She eyed him coyly. "Told you what?"

Stuart looked at her over the rim of his brandy glass. "You might say it was a revelation." He took a long sip, made her wait. "I knew then and there I was a goner. You'd clipped my wings."

"You're terrible!"

"Terrible good or terrible bad?"

"I'll take you either way."

"You already have."

She laughed a sultry little laugh. Scooting closer, she slipped beneath his arm and snuggled against his chest. She caressed his cheek with her fingers.

"Are your wings really clipped?"

"Must be," Stuart said with a chuckle. "I haven't flown the nest."

"I like that," she purred. "A nest for two."

"Give you any ideas?"

She took his brandy glass and set it aside. Then,

her eyes locked on his, she led him to the bedroom. A log snapped in the fireplace as they went through the door.

Neither of them saw any need to stir the embers.

SIXTEEN

A fierce wind blasted across the desert. Walls of dirt, blown skyward by the sandstorm, blotted out the sun. The distant mountains were obscured by a wailing vortex of dust.

Maher stood in the doorway of the house. He stared out at the ravaged landscape and wondered not for the first time what he was doing in New Mexico. The boxing ring, not twenty yards away, was barely visible through the swirling eddies. His heavy bag swayed violently beneath a stout tree limb.

The sandstorm raged unabated into its second day. All activity in the training camp had been suspended since yesterday morning, when the winds began to howl. The men stayed in the house, playing cards while the gale battered at the windows. Their tempers were frayed by the constant pounding, and they had slept fitfully through the night. Today, the storm had moderated only by degree.

For Maher, it was yet another assault on his nerves. Any day now he expected to be arrested, and thrown into the Las Cruces jail. Sheriff Ralph Ascarate, acting on orders from the New Mexico governor, had dropped by the training camp several times. He'd warned them that they were unwelcome in Dona Ana County, and generally badgered them with threats of arrest and incarceration. A deputy had been assigned to watch the house.

The barrens of New Mexico, worsened now by the blustery storm, seemed to Maher an inhospitable place. He longed for the verdant fields of Ireland, and cursed the day he'd sailed from the Emerald Isle. His one solace was the upcoming fight, and the chance to show the world that he was worthy of the championship belt. With his training regimen broken by the weather, he felt weighed down by idleness, fidgety with concern. He was determined not to lose his edge.

Jack Quinn, along with Burns and Hall, were seated at a table, playing cards. The keening moan of the wind grew louder, rattling the glass in the windowpanes. Maher turned from the door, abruptly overcome by impatience and the need to keep his reflexes sharp. He thought the least he could do was put in some roadwork.

"I'm going for a run," he said, interrupting the card game. "Anybody want to come along?"

"Are you mad?" Tommy Burns scolded him. "You'd swallow a bucket of dust in that squall. I'll not have it."

Maher ignored his trainer. "Maybe you've forgot the fight's only four days away. How am I to stay in shape?"

"Do your exercises, or shadowbox a few rounds. Another day won't make any difference."

"No, my mind's made up. I need a good run."

"Tommy's right," Quinn interceded. "You're as fit as you'll ever be, and no reason to push it. Tomorrow's soon enough."

"I'll be the judge of that." Maher glanced around at Hall. "Would you care to join me, Jim?"

Hall spread his hands. "We could clear the furniture away and spar a bit in here. You oughtn't be out in that stuff, Pete."

"Sweet Jesus, I'll run by myself, then!"

Before anyone could respond, Maher stepped outside and slammed the door. He was immediately buffeted by the force of the sandstorm, and he turned downwind. He took off at a steady pace, jogging south along a path that bordered the river. Dirt swirled in a blinding haze, and he pulled a handkerchief from his pocket, tying it over his mouth and nose. He pounded off with the wind at his back.

Not quite an hour later, Maher reappeared along the banks of the river. The storm still battered the countryside, and he was breathing heavily from a ten-mile run. For the last five miles, headed north upriver, he had been running into the wind. He tried to shield his eyes with his arm, but it was like swimming in a sea of dirt. The sheer velocity of the squall peppered his eyes with alkali dust, and the salty grit stung worse with every step. His vision was blurred when he stumbled into the house.

"Holy Christ!" Quinn exclaimed as he came through the door. "What happened to you?"

"Nothing." Maher knuckled his eyes and blinked rapidly. "I just got a little dust in my eyes."

"A little dust, he says! Your eyes are so bloodshot it's a wonder you don't bleed to death. You'd better lay down and rest those peepers a while."

"Yeah, maybe that's not a bad idea. I'll have myself a nap."

Quinn and Burns exchanged a glance as he wobbled toward the bedroom. "Mother of God," Quinn growled. "I wish this fight was behind us."

Burns nodded. "You and me both, Jack. Long behind us."

Throughout the afternoon, Maher's condition steadily became more acute. By early evening, his left eye was swollen shut, and rubbing only aggravated the pain. His right eye was open but inflamed, the blood vessels fanned outward in jagged red streaks. The sensation was like jellied fire poured over his eyeballs, and despite himself, he was unable to silence a string of muted groans. Tommy Burns finally took charge.

"Jimbo!" he ordered, motioning to Hall. "Fetch me a pan of water and some clean washcloths. Hop to it!"

The alkali dust was like a fine abrasive, and over the hours it had left Maher's eyes raw and puffy. Burns got him stretched out on the bed, waiting until Hall returned with a porcelain dishpan. He gently held the eyelids open, admonishing Maher to lie still, and squeezed droplets of water from a cloth over the inflamed eyeballs. At last, after repeating the process several times, he felt confident he'd flushed out the grit. He placed a wet compress across Maher's eyes.

"There now," he said, admiring his handiwork. "I'll wager that feels a good deal better."

Maher's voice was muffled. "Still stings like hell."

"Not to worry. You'll be fit as a fiddle come morning. Mark my word."

Jack Quinn watched silently from the doorway. Outside, the darkness like a witch's brew, the wind pebbled the house with flurries of sand. The sound, unrelenting in its ferocity, grated on his nerves.

He again wished they'd never heard of New Mexico.

*　　*　　*

The Gem Variety Theater was the most popular night-spot in El Paso's uptown district. The establishment was a combination saloon and gaming club, with a spacious theater at the rear of the building. The variety acts were imported from around the country, some from as far away as New York. There was rarely an empty seat in the house.

Lea was seated with Stovall and Bat Masterson at a table near the stage. Taylor, as usual, had elected to forgo the vaudeville show for a poker game. Stovall thought cards might have been the wiser choice, for he was the odd man out at the table tonight. Masterson was all but drooling over Lea.

Sy Ryan, owner of the Gem, had brought them together. Last night, like a moonstruck schoolgirl, Lea had approached him about an introduction to Masterson. She pretended to be smitten with admiration for the legendary frontier marshal, and Stovall dutifully played the role of an indulgent husband. Somewhat amused, Ryan had arranged for them to have a drink with Masterson.

One drink led to another, and Masterson was soon smitten himself. Lea worked on his vanity, feigning wonder at his exploits, and kept him talking about himself. With only slight prompting, he went on to regale them with tales of outlaws and gunfights, and how he'd tutored Wyatt Earp in the trade of law enforcement. Stovall thought it was all horse manure, and wrote Masterson off as a swellheaded braggart. But he pretended to listen with rapt attention, acting out his part in the charade.

Lea quickly captivated Masterson with flattery and looks of starry-eyed amazement. Her seductive manner was heightened by the fact that forty Texas Rangers and their captains had arrived in El Paso. The presence of the Rangers complicated matters, for they were certain to remain in town until after the fight. She knew that gulling Masterson was essential to pulling off the robbery and escaping with their lives intact. He was a direct link to the fight, and whatever he revealed would lessen the hazard posed by the Rangers. Her own plans would be revised accordingly.

Tonight, intent on bewitching Masterson, Lea was dressed for the role. She wore a green moiré gown, with daring décolletage, and her waist cinched tight. Her breasts heaved, threatening to spill out of her gown, and Masterson could scarcely contain himself from looking down her dress. He had readily accepted the story that Stovall was a cattle buyer, and her saucy manner convinced him that the marriage left something to be desired. His mind was focused on how he might separate man from wife, and somehow spirit her away to his hotel room. Her flirtatious eyes gave him hope.

Onstage, a song-and-dance man went into a shuffling soft-shoe routine. The sound of his light feet on the floor was like velvety sandpaper, backed by a sprightly tune from the orchestra. Halfway through the routine, he began singing a bawdy ballad that brought bursts of laughter from the audience. Then, walking back and forth, he delivered a rapid comedic patter that was at once risqué and hilarious. On the heels of a riotous joke, the orchestra blared to life and he nimbly cavorted about the stage in a madcap buck-and-wing number. At last, tipping his derby, he skipped offstage with a rubbery grin. A line of chorus girls, kicking and squealing, pranced out of the wings. The crowd greeted them with wild applause.

"Wasn't he wonderful!" Lea cried, her eyes bright

with excitement. "And those jokes. Wicked, wicked!"

Masterson, trying for a suave tone, chuckled softly. "Naughty but nice, that's the trick. He has the gift."

"Oh, I don't know," Lea said with a sultry smile. "Sometimes I prefer naughty to nice. It's certainly more fun."

"No question about it." Masterson paused, gave Stovall a sidewise glance. "Your wife has a fine sense of humor, Mr. Stovall. You're a fortunate man."

"Don't I know it," Stovall said with a lopsided grin. "Count my blessings once a day and twice on Sunday."

"Who cares about me?" Lea said vivaciously. "I want to hear more about you, Mr. Masterson. Honestly—"

Masterson stopped her with an upraised palm. "I think we're past all these formalities. All my friends call me Bat."

Stovall pretended not to notice the suggestive repartee. He appeared absorbed in the high-stepping chorus line, his eyes glued to the stage. Lea leaned forward, the fullness of her breasts straining the top of her gown. Masterson swallowed, his Adam's apple bobbing, darting a quick look at her cleavage. Her voice was like warm honey.

"I so admire a real man," she said softly. "Everyone in town is talking about you."

"Are they?" Masterson leaned closer. "What do they say?"

"Oh, how you were brought all the way from Colorado to oversee this prizefight. It must be a fearsome responsibility."

"Tell you a little secret. Dan Stuart doesn't make a move without asking me."

"Honestly?"

"Cross my heart."

Lea simply kept him talking. He was a prideful man, and his favorite topic was himself. She led him on, wide-eyed and breathless, seemingly awed. An occasional question was all the prompting needed.

He told her everything about the fight.

"Queens bet ten."

"Your ten and raise twenty."

Taylor studied the cards. The game was five-card stud, and the raiser, seated across from him, had a pair of nines on the board. The man's name was Calvin Lockhart, a fight enthusiast from San Francisco. Or so he claimed.

Lockhart and Taylor were the only players left in the hand. For the night, Taylor was down almost three hundred dollars, and he thought it had nothing to do with luck. He was convinced Lockhart was cheating; all the more so since the man invariably won whenever he dealt. Yet there was nothing to indicate crooked cards.

Until now. With the fifth card dealt, Lockhart set the deck aside. Taylor's gaze was somehow drawn to his hands, and a ring, an opal set in silver, on his right hand. All evening Lockhart's eyes had flicked down and up as he dealt the cards, a sort of nervous blink. Taylor suddenly felt like a blind man whose sight had been restored; he was amazed by his own stupidity. The gaff was a shiner.

"I'll just call," he said, tossing chips into the pot. "What've you got?"

Lockhart turned his hole card. "Three little nines."

"How'd you know I hadn't caught a third queen?"

"Get a hunch, bet a bunch, Mr. Taylor. That's poker."

"Bullshit!" Taylor said coarsely. "Let's have a look at that ring you're wearin'."

The other players exchanged startled glances, suddenly alert. "You're an odd one," Lockhart said stiffly. "What's your interest in my ring?"

"I think you're wearin' a shiner."

A shiner was a ring with a flat bottom that had been polished to a mirror surface. Any man with a quick eye and nimble hands could catch the reflection of the cards as he dealt. The trick was to hold back the card he needed, dealing seconds until it came his turn. A cardsharp with a shiner was an unbeatable combination.

Lockhart looked offended. "You've got some nerve, Mr. Taylor. I don't deal crooked cards."

"Then make me a liar," Taylor said. "Show us the bottom of that ring."

There was an instant of wooden silence. Lockhart abruptly jackknifed out of his chair, clawing at a revolver wedged in a shoulder holster beneath his coat. Taylor was a beat faster, leaning back and pulling a Colt pistol from his waistband. His arm extended, he thumbed off two shots across the table. The slugs stitched red dots on Lockhart's shirtfront, and he stumbled backward in a nerveless dance. His eyes went blank with shock and his legs buckled at the knees. He dropped dead on the floor.

On the street, Captain Bill McDonald stood talking with Sheriff Frank Simmons. Some while earlier, McDonald had trailed Stuart to the Vendome Hotel, and then decided to call it a night. As he turned back downtown, he'd happened across Simmons and paused to compare notes on the prizefight. The roar of shots from inside the Gem brought their conversation to a halt. They burst through the door, guns drawn.

Taylor wisely laid his pistol on the poker table. The sheriff demanded an explanation, and Taylor gave a straightforward account of the shooting. A check of the dead man's hand revealed that the opal ring was indeed a shiner, the underside flat and polished mirror bright. The other players verified Taylor's story, confirming that he had fired in self-defense. The sheriff agreed that it was a case of justifiable homicide.

McDonald was of the same opinion. Yet his curiosity was aroused when Taylor identified himself as a cattle buyer from Fort Worth. He thought it peculiar that a well-dressed businessman was so quick, and deadly, with a gun. His interest was further piqued when Lea and Stovall, accompanied by Bat Masterson, rushed in from the theater. Something struck him as odd.

Sheriff Simmons instructed Taylor to hold himself available for a coroner's inquest. Looking on, McDonald suddenly got the sense that everything was not as it appeared. There was a strange familiarity about Taylor and Stovall as they stood listening to the sheriff. Whatever it was eluded McDonald, for he'd never seen them before tonight. But a gut hunch, strong and visceral, was something a lawman never ignored. He felt he knew these men—from somewhere.

The woman was an unknown. She was clearly involved with the men, and they appeared to be friends with Masterson. When the sheriff sent someone to fetch the undertaker, McDonald excused himself and moved through the crowd onto the street. All the way downtown, the haunting familiarity of the men stuck with him, shadowed images in the corner of his mind. At the railroad depot, he awakened the night telegrapher and wrote out a message. The wire was directed to the sheriff of Tarrant County, in Fort Worth.

He requested a report on Stonewall Jackson Taylor and Earl Stovall.

SEVENTEEN

Governor Miguel Ahumada arrived in Juarez on February 11. He stepped off a private car of the Mexican Central Railroad at nine o'clock that morning. A large crowd was gathered at the depot, and his aides quickly cleared a path. He strode forward with the ramrod bearing of a conquering general.

Mayor Manuel Ortega greeted him with a fawning smile and a respectful bow. Waiting as well was Juan Daguerra and a clutch of local dignitaries, all attired in their finest. Ahumada moved among them with lordly hauteur, nodding like a priest dispensing blessings. His benign expression fooled no one.

A carriage waited beside the depot. Ortega led the way, bowing once again as the governor climbed aboard. To the rear, Daguerra cued a thirty-piece band and the morning resounded with a fanfare of trumpets. The procession got under way, passing along streets thronged with people, cheering and gaily waving their hats. Women tossed flowers in the path of the carriage.

On the plaza, a brigade of mounted Rurales waited in formation. Fully five hundred strong, the cavalrymen had arrived the night before and bivouacked on the edge of town. Their officers raised their sabers in salute, and masses of people arrayed around the plaza burst out in thunderous cheers. The carriage rolled to a halt in front of the cathedral, which was built by Spanish conquistadors in the seventeenth century. The bells in the cathedral tower tolled a booming welcome.

Miguel Ahumada made a brief speech from the steps of the cathedral. He was a man of imposing stature, straight and tall, somewhere in his late fifties. His features were angular, with deep-set, piercing eyes, and a sweeping mustache set off by a spiked goatee. The cathedral bells fell silent as his voice rang out over the plaza, eloquent and strong, crisp with command. He thanked the people of Juarez for their welcome, and commended the Rurales on their march north. His words carried all the way to the river.

A soldier by profession, Ahumada had been appointed governor of Chihuahua in 1892. As a young man, he had fought in the war against Emperor Maximilian, ending the threat of French domination in Mexico. Later, in the revolution against Benito Juarez, his valor in battle helped bring Porfirio Diaz to power. His stern measures as governor, and his ruthless employment of the Rurales, had effectively eliminated banditry and lawlessness from his province. He ruled Chihuahua with the iron fist of a tyrant.

After his speech, the crowd roared lustily. Then, the ceremonies at an end, the plaza quickly emptied and the Rurales returned to their bivouac. Mayor Ortega escorted him to a large table near the cathedral, already provisioned with a box of cigars and bottles of *aguardiente*. Several delegations of tradesmen and the *patrónes* of outlying ranches came forward to pay their respects as the sun rose higher in a cloudless sky. By late morning, with all the courtesies concluded, the reason for the governor's visit was broached. Edward Bates, following an introduction by Daguerra, took a seat before the table.

"I appreciate your consideration, Excellency," Bates said with an engaging smile. "I'm here on behalf of Daniel Stuart and the Fistic Carnival. He hoped we might discuss the matter."

Ahumada, who spoke fluent English, offered an elaborate shrug. "What is there to discuss, señor? I am here on the orders of President Diaz."

"I thought we might talk of related matters. Mexico has a proud tradition of bullfights, and your *toreros* are accorded great honor. Surely you understand that we Americans bestow similar honor on our prizefighters."

"I understand that the practice is permitted nowhere in the United States. Your own leaders denounce it as brutal and inhumane. Why should we allow it in Mexico?"

The question was phrased in such a way that it gave Bates an opening. He held the governor's gaze. "Perhaps we could speak in private, Excellency. Would that be possible?"

Ahumada stared at him for a long moment. Then, with a flip of his hand, he motioned to Ortega and Daguerra. "You may excuse yourselves," he said in an imperative tone. "I will call when I need you."

Ortega and Daguerra obediently bowed, and moved back toward the cathedral steps. Ahumada poured glasses of dark *aguardiente* and invited Bates to select a cigar. Bates struck a match, held it for the governor, then lit his own cigar. They puffed thick wads of smoke.

"Very well," Ahumada said at length. "We are alone, Señor Bates. Please continue."

"You are most gracious, Excellency," Bates said with a genuine smile. "We are both men of the world, and with your permission, I hope we might speak frankly . . . on a matter of business."

"Of course."

"I would like to propose an accommodation. One that will satisfy our mutual interests."

"Accommodation?" Ahumada repeated, as though testing the word. "You refer to this prizefight. Correct?"

"Yes, Excellency." Bates lowered his voice, his look conspiratorial. "We are prepared to offer you a generous sum, in exchange for your assistance. We ask only that the Fistic Carnival be allowed to proceed."

"And the extent of your generosity . . . ?"

"Fifty thousand dollars . . . in gold."

Ahumada puffed his cigar. "That is most generous, indeed. Far more than I expected."

"I—" Bates hesitated, momentarily taken aback. "You anticipated my proposal, Excellency?"

"But of course, Señor Bates. President Diaz was quite impressed when you spoke with him in Mexico City. He cautioned me that you would attempt a bribe."

"I ask you to think of it as an exchange."

"*El Presidente* is a man of some humor. He was curious as to the amount of your . . . offer."

"I don't understand," Bates said. "Does that mean he authorized you to accept?"

"No, no." Ahumada took a sip of brandy, rolled it around on his tongue. "I would stand before a firing squad if I accepted. President Diaz made that quite clear."

"You have me at a loss, Excellency. Given all this, why did you allow me to proceed?"

"As I said, *el Presidente* appreciates a jest. He will be entertained by the sincerity of your proposal."

Bates appeared bemused. "So there is no way for the event to be held in Juarez?"

"None." Ahumada tapped an ash off his cigar. "I suggest you look elsewhere, señor. The matter is closed."

"Too bad." Bates considered a moment. "I wonder if we might reach an accord of a different nature. Would you consider a location outside Juarez, somewhere along the banks of the Rio Grande?" He paused for emphasis. "Naturally, our offer of fifty thousand would still apply."

"And how would I explain that to President Diaz?"

"You would have complied with his orders, Excellency. No prizefight would take place in Juarez."

Ahumada stared out across the plaza. He puffed smoke, his expression one of calculated deliberation. Finally, with a heavy sigh, he shook his head.

"You are a persuasive man, Señor Bates. But I fear you would get me shot. I must decline."

"Perhaps you could think on it overnight."

"Let us be clear," Ahumada said firmly. "I will have Rurale patrols up and down the river. Ten miles, maybe twenty miles, on either side of Juarez. Do not risk being caught."

"And if we were?" Bates asked. "What penalty would be imposed?"

"*¡Madre de Dios!*" Ahumada gave him a hard look. "You would not care for Mexican justice, señor. Accept that as a profound truth."

Bates thought it was excellent advice. He too had no wish to be shot. "I regret we were unable to reach an accord."

"I wish you well, señor. *¡Buena suerte!*"

The audience was at an end. Bates rose, nodding politely, and walked off across the plaza. Governor Miguel Ahumada stared after him with a deep sense of loss.

Fifty thousand dollars was almost worth the risk. Almost.

Stuart and Walter Wheelock were seated in the office. A noonday sun stood at its zenith as Bates came through the door. The expression on his face told the story.

"Let me guess," Stuart said, rising to his feet. "The governor turned us down, right?"

"Not without a struggle," Bates replied. "Fifty thousand really got his attention. He was sorely tempted."

"But . . . ?"

"But he wasn't about to sign his own death warrant. Diaz threatened to stand him before a firing squad."

"Wait a minute," Stuart insisted. "Are you saying they expected a bribe?"

"What the hell, they're crooks," Bates observed. "Diaz just got a better deal from President Cleveland, that's all. We were never in the running."

"What about somewhere outside Juarez? Did you try that on him?"

"Governor Ahumada advised me to steer clear of the Rurales. He's ordering patrols along the river."

"Well, nothing ventured, nothing gained. It was worth a try."

The door banged open. Fred Martin, sportswriter

for the *New York Times,* walked into the office. His features were set in a wide, sardonic smile. He waved a telegraph form.

"You'll never believe it," he said. "Arizona has called out the militia!"

"Arizona?" Stuart said, astonished. "You're kidding."

"Got it hot off the wire." Martin dangled the telegram before them. "Governor Arnold Hughes has mobilized five militia companies. He says, and I quote, 'Arizona Territory will repel any attempt by Daniel Stuart's prizefight circus to cross our border.' How about them apples?"

"What's the point?" Stuart said. "We're not going to Arizona."

"Yeah, but you've got them worried. Everyone knows you have a boxcar loaded with fight gear and ready to travel. And the Arizona border is only four hours west by rail."

"I think it's just another politician grabbing for headlines. The whole thing is ridiculous."

"Daniel, old sport, they have you surrounded. Pick a point on the compass and there's somebody waiting with an army. Did you hear the Rurales are camped outside Juarez?"

"As a matter of fact, we got it first-hand," Bates said. "I met with Governor Ahumada this morning."

"You did!" Martin whipped out his pad and pencil. "Well, c'mon, give me the straight dope. Any change of plans?"

"I'm afraid not," Bates said grudgingly. "Juarez is still out of the picture."

"So where will you hold the fight?"

"I'd rather let Dan answer that."

"All right, give," Martin prompted, turning back to

Stuart. "Where's that boxcar headed? And don't tell me you're not surrounded."

Stuart laughed. "We'll let you know on Valentine's Day."

"That's the day of the fight!" Martin howled. "Have a heart, gimme a break."

"All in good time."

Stuart told himself it would make the boldest headline yet. A bombshell of a story, and one that would fool them all. The Texas Rangers included.

They only thought they had him surrounded.

Stony Taylor burst into the suite. His face was flushed and his eyes were round, and he seemed out of breath. He stopped before Lea, who was seated on the sofa beside Stovall. His brow furrowed in a knot.

"Word's all over town," he gulped. "That Mex governor turned 'em down flat. There won't be no fight in Juarez."

"Are you sure?" Lea said. "This town's full of rumors."

"Damn tootin', I'm sure," Taylor said loudly. "Stuart's partner, that Bates feller? He met with the headdog greaser this morning. Nobody's talkin' about nothin' else."

Stovall grunted. "Told you Masterson was full of hot air. No way they were gonna pull that off."

Lea was forced to concede the point. Last night she'd given a virtuoso performance, beguiling Masterson with unspoken promises. He believed it was only a matter of time before he got her in bed, and she had extracted one secret after another. The most important was that the proceeds from ticket sales were kept in the office safe. He had also revealed that an attempt would be made to bribe Governor Miguel Ahumada. But now, clearly, the attempt had failed.

"Not to worry," she said casually. "Stuart's not the type to put all his eggs in one basket. If not Juarez, then somewhere else . . . probably New Mexico. I'll coax it out of Bat."

"Bat!" Stovall said with a petulant scowl. "You and him got on a first-name basis mighty quick. Turned my stomach, him slobberin' all over you."

Lea patted his cheek. "Sweetie, it's all for a good cause. He's our ticket to the money."

"Maybe so," Stovall grumped. "But don't you carry it too far. He means to get in your britches."

"Of course he does," Lea said breezily. "I charmed his bird right out of the trees. That's the whole point."

"Just make damn sure it don't go no farther."

"Bat Masterson should be so lucky!"

"Oh," Taylor broke in hurriedly. "Got so wound up about Juarez I forgot to tell you. The sheriff caught me on the street just as I was headed into the hotel. They've set the coroner's inquest for tomorrow afternoon."

"Damn nuisance," Stovall said. "You shot the bastard in a fair fight. They already know everybody'll swear to it."

"Even so," Lea added, nodding to Taylor, "you have to be more careful from now on, Stony. We can't afford to draw attention to ourselves."

"What'd you want me to do?" Taylor protested. "The sorry son of a bitch was dealin' seconds!"

"I'm just saying we don't need trouble with the law. We've got too much at stake. Won't you try . . . for me?"

Taylor shuffled his feet. "Yeah, I'll manage somehow."

Lea smiled inwardly, somehow reminded of Masterson. She thought all men were like overgrown boys. Their strings were there to pull.

EIGHTEEN

The Chinese community was located near the railroad depot. The local newspapers often referred to them as the "Celestials," for they followed their own customs and kept to themselves. Their culture was as foreign to Texans as an Egyptian mummy.

Early that evening the Chinese began the celebration of their traditional New Year's Eve. The following day marked the Year of the Monkey on their calendar, and all of Chinatown turned out for the occasion. The streets were packed with sloe-eyed women and men in pigtails.

El Paso, like many Western towns, saw an influx of Orientals during the railroad boom. In 1881, the completion of the Southern Pacific and the Texas & Pacific left a thousand or more Chinese laborers marooned on the banks of the Rio Grande. Ever an industrious people, they opened laundries and cafés and all manner of business enterprises. Their numbers had multiplied manyfold in fifteen years.

The New Year's celebration was a fascinating oddity to the Anglos of El Paso. A parade formed in Chinatown, replete with firecrackers, and banging gongs, and men costumed in the guise of festive dragons. The column of Celestial merrymakers slowly wound its way uptown, where the streets were lined with thousands of spectators. Then, reversing course, the parade turned back toward Chinatown. The Year of the Monkey jubilee would last all night.

The Texas Rangers, no less than the general public, were drawn to the rollicking celebration. Captain John Hughes, who was charged with guarding the rail yards, left one man to keep an eye on things. With the rest of his detachment, he then joined Adjutant General Mabry and the other Rangers in the uptown district. They watched from the curb as the procession clanged along the street and set off strings of fireworks. All of them agreed that the dancing dragons were half the entertainment.

Absent from the festivities were Bat Masterson and his squad of gunmen. A starry indigo sky shone down on the rail yards, and their movements were cloaked in darkness. The noise from nearby Chinatown, with popping firecrackers and ear-splitting gongs, further obscured their stealthy mission. Their purpose was to spirit Enoch Rector and his film technicians out of El Paso. To that end, they set about hoodwinking the Rangers.

Masterson was assisted by a gang of some twenty robust workmen. He split the men into three groups, with his mercenaries supervising the operation. Not unlike a streetcorner grifter, he was playing an elaborate shell game with boxcars. There were three boxcars involved, two of which were empty and served merely to confuse matters. The third, loaded on their previous foray into the rail yards, held the lumber and the moving picture cameras. Deception was the ultimate goal.

A work crew was assigned to each of the boxcars. Their orders were to keep the boxcars in constant motion, shunted from siding to siding, and mixed among dozens of cars standing idle in the rail yards. Beneath the silty starlight, they muscled the cars here and there, halting momentarily, and then starting all over again. The action was uniformly sporadic, yet at once steady and thoroughly disorganized. It was hide-and-seek on a grand scale.

The hoax had been purposely staged to coincide with the Chinatown celebration. Stuart knew the Rangers would be distracted by the fireworks and parade, and he had instructed Masterson to employ sleight of hand with the boxcars. His assessment was proved correct when Captain Hughes left a single Ranger to watchdog the vast expanse of the rail yards. By eight o'clock the Ranger was dizzy trying to keep track of which boxcar was where, and he gave it up as a lost cause. He took off running for town.

Masterson went into action. He ordered the boxcar with the fight paraphernalia hooked onto an eastbound freight train scheduled to depart at nine o'clock. One of the empty boxcars was attached to a westbound due to get under way at about the same time. From the shadows, one of his men hustled forward with Rector and the five movie technicians. All of them but Rector were hurriedly loaded aboard the caboose on the eastbound freight. The producer stubbornly lagged behind, motioning to Masterson.

"Where are we going?" he said testily. "I demand to know our destination."

"Sorry, professor," Masterson replied. "I'm under orders from Dan Stuart on that score. Your destination's a secret."

"Then I will not board this train. I insist on being told."

"Look, we don't have a whole lot of time. Just be a good sport and go along with the plan."

"Absolutely not!" Rector bridled. "Who am I, not to be trusted with this big secret? I won't be treated like a nobody."

Masterson was momentarily stymied. At Stuart's direction, he had furtively brought Rector and the technical assistants to the rail yards. But Stuart had been adamant that the producer was to be told nothing. Not until the train was under way.

"Here's how it works," Masterson said, a hard edge to his voice. "You climb aboard on your own, or I'll have my men carry you on and tie you down. It's your choice, professor."

"You wouldn't dare use force!"

"Try me."

Rector's mouth ovaled in protest. But then, on the verge of speaking, he saw a cold glint in Masterson's eyes. He abruptly turned, muttering indignantly to himself, and stepped aboard the caboose. The gunman assigned to safeguard the train followed him through the door. Masterson quickly crossed the yards to the westbound freight.

Some ten minutes later Captain Hughes and his squad of Rangers appeared out of the darkness. As they rushed forward, they saw Masterson and his mercenaries boarding the caboose of the westbound freight. Hughes was all too aware that Governor Ahumada, only yesterday, had sealed off Juarez with a brigade of Rurales. He was surprised by Stuart's speedy reaction; but it confirmed what the Rangers had suspected all along. The fight was on the move.

The locomotive chuffed smoke, steel wheels gath-

ering purchase on the rails. Hughes gestured to one
of his men, who hopped aboard and ordered the engineer to shut down. With the other Rangers at his
heels, Hughes hurried along the tracks toward the end
of the train. A moment later he halted by the caboose,
where Masterson and his men stood on the rear deck.
He drilled Masterson with a stare.

"You gents step down," he said. "You're not
headed anywhere tonight."

"Who says so?" Masterson replied brusquely. "Last
I heard, it's still a free country."

"By God, the state of Texas says so! Haul your
butt off that train."

John Hughes was a dour man with flat eyes and a
bristly mustache. He commanded the Ranger troop
stationed at Ysleta, a small town some ten miles south
of El Paso. His years along the border, and his knowl-
edge of the far-flung Rio Grande, were the reasons
he'd been assigned to guard the rail yards. His reputation as the scourge of Mexican *bandidos* and as-
sorted desperadoes was yet another reason. He was
reported to have killed eight men in gunfights.

"You're in the wrong, Captain," Masterson said,
stepping off the caboose. "But I'm not one to take
these things personal. I always cooperate with the
law."

Hughes snorted. "You used to be a decent lawman,
yourself. How'd you get mixed up in this fight
game?"

"I confess to a weakness for the long green. The
job pays better than sporting a badge."

"Well, we're just gonna have a look at your train,
Mr. Masterson. You and your boys stand aside, and
don't give me any trouble. Savvy?"

"You won't have any problem with us, Captain."

Hughes ordered his men to search the train. As they spread out, the eastbound freight, on the opposite side of the rail yards, got under way. Masterson kept a straight face while the Rangers unlocked boxcars and began rummaging through tons of freight. The search was abruptly halted when they discovered an empty boxcar toward the end of the string. Hughes walked back to Masterson.

"What's the story here?" he barked. "Why'd you put an empty car on that train?"

"Did I?" Masterson said innocently. "Do you have any witnesses, Captain?"

Hughes knew that the railroads were in cahoots with the fight promoters. He sensed that Masterson was laughing at him. "You're real cute," he said shortly. "Keep us hoppin' around till we miss your next move. That the idea?"

"I don't know what you mean."

"Yeah, I'll just bet you don't. Why were you and your boys on this train?"

"No reason," Masterson said with a roguish smile. "We had nothing better to do."

"You mess with me and I'll slap your ass in jail. Don't think I won't, neither."

"Like I said, Captain, I always cooperate with the law."

Masterson suppressed a low chuckle. Far in the distance, he saw the taillight of the eastbound freight disappear into the night. A thought flashed through his mind, and he had to force back a laugh. Tonight was not his night to make friends.

Enoch Rector was no less pissed than Captain John Hughes.

*   *   *

The Gem Variety Theater was mobbed. After the Chinese New Year's parade, the crowds had jammed into nightspots in the uptown district. Men were standing three deep at the bar.

Lea sat with Stovall and Taylor at a table near the front door. A bottle of champagne was wedged in an ice bucket, though both of the men would have preferred whiskey. They were celebrating Taylor's day in court.

"Here's to you," Stovall said, lifting his glass. "You plumb popped their eyes with that story."

Taylor gulped champagne. "Whole truth and nothin' but the truth, that's what it was. Told it straight."

The coroner's inquest had been held that afternoon. The sheriff and Captain Bill McDonald had testified with regard to the scene of the killing. Taylor then recounted how he'd exposed the cardsharp; the other men in the game corroborated his testimony in every detail. A ruling of justifiable homicide was rendered in short order.

"Damnedest thing," Stovall said in a musing tone. "That Ranger captain, McDonald? You catch the way he was eyeballin' us?"

Taylor shrugged. "Don't rightly recollect."

"I do," Lea said with a strange look. "It was almost like he was studying you two for some reason. I wondered about it at the time."

"Lotta good it'll do him." Taylor chortled, pleased with himself. "Our faces never been on no wanted dodgers."

"Keep your voice down," Lea cautioned. "You two are cattle buyers, remember? Let's not talk out of school."

"Aw, quit worryin'," Taylor teased her. "So far as anybody knows, we're downright respectable. Aren't we, Earl?"

"Any worse and I'd feel like a church deacon."

The door swung open. Bat Masterson strode into the room with a look of high good humor. He saw Lea and veered toward the table, nodding as though delighted by his prospects for the night. His mustache lifted in a broad smile.

"Good evening," he said, his eyes fixed on Lea. "Would you mind if I join you?"

"Our pleasure," Lea said graciously. "We're celebrating Stony's victory in court. He was completely exonerated."

"Let me add my congratulations," Masterson said, taking a chair. "You acquitted yourself on all counts, Mr. Taylor. Not many men are so cool when guns are drawn."

"Well, thank you now," Taylor said, suddenly flustered. "That's a real fine compliment, comin' from you, Mr. Masterson. I hear you've been there yourself."

"On occasion," Masterson said with false modesty. "Like you, I lived to tell the tale."

Lea darted an imperceptible glance at Stovall. A silent message passed between them, and he understood she wanted to be alone with Masterson. "How about it, Stony?" he said, pushing back his chair. "I've got a taste for poker tonight. Want to try your luck?"

"You damn betcha!" Taylor said, jumping to his feet. "I'm on a winning streak."

"Behave yourselves," Lea admonished. "And please don't shoot any more cardsharps."

Taylor laughed. "I just doubt they'd try me after the other night."

The men walked toward the poker tables at the rear

of the room. A waiter materialized with a fresh glass, and Masterson poured himself champagne. Lea batted her lashes as they clinked glasses.

"Aren't you the stranger?" she said with a coquettish smile. "I wasn't sure I'd see you tonight."

"Business before pleasure," Masterson said importantly. "I've been playing ring-around-the-rosy with the Rangers. We had ourselves a fine game."

"Are you talking about the fight?"

"Nothing more, nothing less. We've put the Rangers off the scent for now. They're just the least bit befuddled."

"You make a girl's head spin," Lea said airily. "What does that mean . . . you put them off the scent?"

Masterson lowered his voice. "We've been shut out of Juarez, and everybody knows the fight's headed somewhere else. So we have to keep the Rangers guessing."

"Oh, how silly of me! You have to fool the Rangers because the fight will be held someplace in Texas. Isn't that what you're saying?"

"I think I've said too much already. You're too sharp for me, little lady."

"And you're just being gallant," Lea vamped him with a look. "But don't stop . . . I love a smooth talker."

"Well, now," Masterson said with a sly grin. "How long does your husband usually play poker? Do you think he'd miss us?"

"Whatever do you mean, Mr. Masterson?"

"Exactly what we've both been thinking since we met."

"Earl's an awfully jealous man."

"Then we'll have to be clever, won't we?"

"Let's see if he really gets involved in that game. Who knows what might happen?"

Masterson laughed jovially. "I'm willing to wait all night."

Lea thought he could wait till hell froze over. Yet she was pleased that she'd drawn him out, gulled him into a slip of the tongue. Men loved to brag about themselves, and now she knew. The fight would be held in Texas.

All that remained was to find out where.

NINETEEN

Stuart entered the office early the next morning. When he closed the door, he found Bates and Wheelock seated in glum silence. The expression on their faces somehow reminded him of stone gargoyles.

"We've got problems," Bates said. "Word's spreading that the fights have been canceled."

"Actually, I'm not all that surprised," Stuart noted. "Not after the newspaper reports about Juarez. The rumor-mill's at work."

Wheelock looked gloomy. "I'm afraid it gets worse. Over a hundred people have already demanded the money back on their tickets." He wagged his head. "They believe the rumor."

Late yesterday, Stuart had postponed the Fistic Carnival. With Juarez out of the picture, he'd secured agreement from Joe Walcott and the other fighters to revise the schedule. He now planned to hold all five fights, including the heavyweight championship, in one day. The announcement had apparently been greeted with skepticism; but he wasn't concerned. He was, instead, revitalized by the scope of it all.

No one would ever forget Valentine's Day!

"Tell you what," he said after pondering a moment. "Notify the reporters we'll have a press conference at one o'clock today."

Wheelock frowned. "What will you say?"

"Several things." Stuart ticked off the points on his fingers. "First, my personal guarantee that the Fistic Carnival will happen. Second, anyone who wants a refund will miss the fight of the century." He paused with a jaunty grin. "And lastly, John L. Sullivan would not travel a thousand miles for nothing. The fights will take place."

"Dammit, that's right!" Bates leapt to his feet. "I forgot all about Sullivan. What time does he arrive?"

"Three this afternoon."

"And two days before the fight!" Wheelock's gargoyle look vanished. "That's the very publicity we need. No one will want a refund."

Captain Bill McDonald walked through the door. His sober manner put a sudden damper on their enthusiasm. He nodded to Stuart.

"General Mabry wants to see you," he said. "I'm to bring you along to the hotel. Now."

Stuart arched an eyebrow. "That sounds vaguely like an imperial summons. Tell the *General* I'll be in my office all day. He's welcome anytime."

"Don't cause me any trouble. I'm ordered to arrest you if need be. Let's do it the easy way."

"Arrest me on what charge?"

McDonald tugged thoughtfully at his ear. "How about a public nuisance? That ought to do it."

"You'll never make it stick."

"Yeah, but you'd still get waltzed down to the hotel. Why make a fuss?"

"Your logic overwhelms me." Stuart shot a quick glance at Bates. "Don't worry, I won't be gone long.

Go ahead and set up the press conference."

He looked at McDonald. "Shall we, Captain?"

"I'm right behind you, Mr. Stuart."

Ten minutes later McDonald ushered him into a suite at the Pierson Hotel. Mabry was seated in an overstuffed easy chair beside the fireplace. Across from him, puffing a long cigar, was Governor Miguel Ahumada. McDonald took a position by the door.

"Have a seat, Mr. Stuart," Mabry said, waving to the sofa. "I believe you know Governor Ahumada."

"Only by reputation," Stuart said, settling himself opposite them. "What's all this about?"

"Valentine's Day," Mabry said in a satiric tone. "The governor and I have discussed it at length, and we agree on the central issue. You will attempt to hold your prizefight either in Texas or Mexico."

Stuart betrayed nothing. "Is that a statement or a question?"

"Interpret it any way you wish. We merely want to inform you of the consequences."

"Gentlemen, I'm all ears."

Mabry was not amused by his levity. "Whatever your destination—the location of the fight—you have no choice but to take a train. I intend to board that train, along with all my Rangers."

"Well, like I always say, the more the merrier."

"I have also spoken with Colonel Pritchard at Fort Bliss. He has placed a troop of cavalry at my disposal."

Fort Bliss was an army post located some miles north of El Paso. Until now, the cavalry had been patrolling the border with New Mexico. Mabry clearly had important contacts in Washington.

"I'm still listening," Stuart said. "You mentioned something about consequences. Could we get to it?"

"Very well," Mabry replied. "The stakes are now somewhat higher, Mr. Stuart. I have ordered the Rangers to open fire on the principals—Fitzsimmons and Maher—once the fight commences. You may be shot, as well."

"You'd fire on unarmed men?"

"That is correct."

"You're bluffing," Stuart said evenly. "That's against the law."

"*I am the law!*" Mabry's eyes burned with an evangelical fire. "Do not doubt my word, Mr. Stuart."

"So far as I'm concerned, it's a moot point. I have no intention of holding the fight in Texas."

"Then I suggest you listen closely to Governor Ahumada."

Ahumada idly waved his cigar. "General Mabry and I are in agreement," he said. "I have Rurales patrolling the border for fifty miles in either direction. They will fire on you and your fighters if you attempt to cross the Rio Grande."

"That too is a moot point," Stuart said with studied nonchalance. "You and I will never meet on the field of battle, Governor."

"Indeed?" Ahumada said skeptically. "Your choices are severely limited, Mr. Stuart. If not Texas or Mexico, then where?"

"You can read all about it in the newspapers."

"One last question," Mabry broke in. "Your associate, Enoch Rector, seems to have disappeared. Has he abandoned the film project?"

Stuart got to his feet. "Ask me no questions and I'll tell you no lies."

"Well, in any case, you've been warned. Given the slightest pretext, the Rangers and the Rurales will open fire."

"Good day, gentlemen."

Stuart walked to the door. As he went out, a telegraph messenger appeared and handed a telegram to McDonald. It was addressed to the Ranger captain, and he tore it open. He quickly scanned the contents.

Your inquiry E. Stovall and J. Taylor not productive. Known in Fort Worth as cattle buyers. No details available on business dealings or previous background. Drew a blank. Sorry.

> *Sheriff Orville Wilson*
> *Tarrant County*

McDonald squinted with concentration. From past investigations, he knew Wilson to be a good lawman. He thought it strange that the sheriff had unearthed no background information on Stovall or Taylor. All men, particularly legitimate businessmen, left a trail of some sort. Unless there was reason to cover the trail . . .

"Captain McDonald," Mabry called out. "Does that telegram concern me?"

"No, sir," McDonald said. "Just another case I was workin' on."

"For the moment, Captain, I want your attention focused on Dan Stuart and his cohorts."

"Don't concern yourself about that, General."

Mabry and Ahumada resumed their conversation. McDonald stuffed the telegram into his pocket, still puzzling over the message. What it meant, if anything, was unclear. But he was nonetheless bothered.

A fast gun with no traceable history would bear watching.

*   *   *

Upon returning to the office, Stuart stumbled into a heated debate. Fitzsimmons and Martin Julian were railing at his partner, and Bates seemed somehow on the defensive. They turned as he closed the door.

"There you are!" Julian said loudly. "Your Mr. Bates has been giving us the runaround. We want some straight answers."

Stuart nodded. "Answers to what?"

"We don't like what we're hearing in Juarez. The rumor is that Governor Ahumada and Mabry have made a pact. They intend to shoot the fighters!"

"I'm surprised you'd credit such nonsense. Do you really think the law goes around murdering people?"

"How should I know?" Julian shouted. "Does the law consider prizefighters to be *people*?"

Stuart took a grip on his temper. He collected himself, prepared to shade the truth without actually lying. His gaze shifted to Fitzsimmons.

"You've nothing to worry about," he said confidently. "I'd never put you in harm's way."

Fitzsimmons looked dubious. "I'm not so much concerned about the Mexicans. Governor Ahumada dropped by yesterday to watch me spar, and stayed to chat a while. He seemed a decent sort."

"So what concerns you?"

"The Rangers," Fitzsimmons said simply. "You set up the ring in Texas and I won't fight. I'd sooner forfeit than get myself shot."

"Nobody will be shot," Stuart said with conviction. "You have my solemn oath on it, Fitz."

Julian flung out his arms. "You haven't answered a thing!" he declared. "Where's the bout to take place? Texas, Mexico—or somewhere else?"

"I'll tell you tomorrow," Stuart said. "Just be prepared to board a train on an hour's notice."

"To where?"

"Wherever we stop."

"What a revelation!"

Julian whirled toward the door. Fitzsimmons followed along, then turned back at the last moment. "Don't you forget what I said about the Rangers."

"No, I won't forget, Fitz. You have my word on it."

Stuart drew a deep breath. He started to sit down, but then changed his mind. As Fitzsimmons and Julian emerged onto the street, Judge Townsend and Doc Albers came through the door. Their expressions were guarded, oddly distant.

"We need to have a talk," Townsend said without preamble. "With Juarez out of the picture, we have a problem. Our investors feel you haven't fulfilled your end of the bargain."

"Do they?" Stuart countered. "By rough count, I've brought twenty thousand people to El Paso for the fight. Have your investors profited?"

"That's not the point," Albers said crossly. "Our deal was for a fight in Juarez. You can't deliver."

"Gentlemen, I have a busy day ahead of me. What was your purpose in coming here?"

"We are withdrawing the prize purse," Townsend announced. "Under the circumstances, we have no other recourse."

"Well, what the hell, Judge. Another twenty-five thousand won't break me. Consider yourself off the hook."

"I must say, I admire your equanimity, Daniel."

"A gambler learns to take the bitter with the sweet."

"May I inquire where you plan to hold the fight?"

"You'll hear about it soon enough."

Stuart's tone signaled an end to the conversation. When Townsend and Albers went out the door, Bates rose from his chair with a quizzical expression. "You made it easy on them. Any particular reason?"

"A couple of reasons," Stuart said. "For openers, never waste your breath arguing with a welcher. As for the other, we need all the friends we can get in El Paso."

"What's that supposed to mean?"

"Why, Ed, it means we're not out of the woods yet."

"Are you talking about the Rangers?"

"The Rangers and the Rurales . . . and Valentine's Day."

The three o'clock train was on time. Stuart and Bates waited outside the stationhouse. A gaggle of reporters who had covered the afternoon press conference were in attendance as well. They were there to interview the Great John L.

Sullivan stepped off the lead passenger coach. Now thirty-seven years old and his waistline larded with fat, he was a vestige of his former self. Directly behind him was Paddy Ryan, his friend and sometime sparring partner and full-time attendant. The Great John L. was stumbling drunk.

"Welcome to El Paso," Stuart said cordially, his hand outstretched. "I'm Dan Stuart, Mr. Sullivan."

"And do they call you Danny Boy by any chance?"

Sullivan's speech was slurred and he listed slightly to starboard. He limped, favoring his left knee, and there was an ugly cut on his forehead. The reporters pushed forward, and he staggered toward them, supported by Paddy Ryan. He grinned a mushy grin.

"See this!" he crowed, rapping his split forehead.

"Four lads jumped me in a saloon and I laid 'em out colder'n a mackerel. As fine a donnybrook as ever you seen!"

The truth, as reported in yesterday's newspapers, was somewhat less heroic. A westbound train, with Sullivan on the observation platform, had pulled out of Dallas. He was drunk, and when the train lurched, he'd fallen onto the roadbed. The fall had knocked him unconscious, and he hadn't recovered for nearly an hour. But today, the reporters chose to accept his version of the incident. They were after larger headlines.

"John L.!" the sportswriter for the *Chicago Tribune* yelled. "Who do you pick to win the fight—Fitz or Maher?"

"Who the Christ cares?" Sullivan rumbled. "All I want is a crack at the winner."

"Are you serious?" asked Gabe Lawlor from the *New York World*. "You'd fight for the championship?"

Sullivan struck a fighting pose for the cameras. He leered over his meaty fists, his features contorted in a drunken scowl. He roared the boast he'd made famous in saloons from Boston to San Francisco.

"I can lick any son of a bitch in the house!"

Looking on, Stuart ruefully shook his head. He glanced sideways at Bates. "Whatever you're thinking, there will never be another like him. He's an original."

"What I'm thinking," Bates said, "is that we'll grab every headline in the country. A challenge from the Great John L.!"

Stuart smiled. "Too bad we can't put him in the moving picture."

"Enoch Rector would love it!"

"I suspect Sullivan would be one problem too many."

Stuart's wry tone belied his concern. His meeting with Mabry and Ahumada had left him deeply troubled. He knew the real fight had only just begun.

The Rangers and the Rurales were everywhere . . .

TWENTY

Early the next morning, the train from Las Cruces pulled into the depot. There were four coaches, all full, and passengers jammed the aisles. They slowly filed off the train.

Jack Quinn waited until the last of the passengers stepped off the lead coach. He moved out onto the platform, with Burns and Hall on either side of Peter Maher. They guided Maher along by his arms, leading him as they would a blind man. A thick gauze bandage covered the fighter's eyes.

Horace Wilcox, the stationmaster, saw them cross the platform. His features wrinkled with curiosity, but he couldn't bring himself to ask the question. He watched as they moved around the side of the depot at a hobbling gait, and assisted Maher into a hired carriage. He hurried back into the stationhouse.

A short while later the carriage stopped outside the Vendome Hotel. The men assisted Maher from the cab and led him into the lobby. The desk clerk and several men standing nearby stared at the fighter as though an apparition had appeared in their midst. Quinn engaged three rooms, ignoring the buzz of conversation from the onlookers. He sent a bellboy to fetch Stuart.

On the way upstairs, Quinn told himself it would be an unpleasant meeting. The original plan, worked out some time ago, was for Maher to arrive in El Paso today. Barring Juarez as the site, the fighters were to entrain this afternoon for a location as yet unannounced. But no one knew about Maher's eyes, and Quinn thought it unlikely the fight would come off tomorrow. He dreaded telling Stuart.

Some ten minutes later Stuart knocked on the door. When he came into the room, he found Maher stretched out on the bed, the bandage still in place. Burns and Hall gave him a sheepish look, hardly able to meet his gaze. Quinn tried to put the best face on things.

"You needn't worry," he said. "It's not as bad as it looks."

Stuart glowered at him. "What's going on here, Quinn? What's wrong?"

"Well, don't you see, there was a sandstorm. Peter got dust in his eyes and we thought—"

"When did this happen?"

"Day before yesterday," Quinn admitted. "We tried to treat it ourselves, but nothin' seemed to work. So we called in a doctor at Las Cruces."

"Wait a minute," Stuart interrupted again. "Are you saying Peter can't see?"

"Not just exactly. Things are sort of blurred, and he has trouble keepin' his eyes open. He's in a good deal of pain."

"Why the devil didn't you send me a wire? Why am I only hearing about this today?"

"We thought it was one of them temporary things. Never figured it'd go this far."

"Don't blame Jack," Maher interjected, raising himself up on the bed. "I'm the one that's at fault here. Shouldn't have gone runnin' in that sandstorm."

Stuart moved to the side of the bed. "Tell me the truth now, Peter. How bad is it?"

"Not near as bad as Jack makes out. I can still fight."

"The hell you will!" Tommy Burns blurted. "You fight and you'll end up blind. I'll not have it!"

"Nobody will force him to fight," Stuart assured the trainer. "What did the doctor in Las Cruces say?"

"Damn quack!" Burns fumed. "Gave us some ointment and told us not to worry. All his ointment done was make it worse."

Stuart let out a gusty sigh. "I think we'd better call in another doctor."

Summoned from his office, Dr. Alfred White arrived not quite an hour later. He was a portly man, with iron-gray hair and a take-charge attitude. After ordering a pan of fresh water, he dampened the bandage over Maher's eyes. Then, ever so gingerly, he peeled the gauze away. He muttered a curse under his breath.

"Doesn't look good," he said solemnly. "Not good at all."

Maher's eyes were puffy and inflamed, encrusted by dried mucus mixed with ointment. His left eye was almost swollen shut, and a latticework of fiery streaks veined his right eyeball. The doctor gently swabbed with a wet cloth, slowly clearing away the gummy film. Finished, he held his hand before Maher's face, fingers spread.

"Tell me now," he said. "What do you see?"

"Your hand," Maher said, trying to focus. "Though it's mostly a blur."

"Can you make out my fingers?"

"Not too good, Doc."

White got him seated on the edge of the bed, facing the window. In the strong sunlight, he then performed a closer examination of the right eye. Afterward, he pried open the left eyelid with his fingers and intently scrutinized the eyeball for a long while. Finally, clucking to himself, he lowered Maher back onto the bed. He turned to Stuart.

"Severe opthalmalia," he pronounced. "The alkali dust burned the surface of the eyeball, and there's some opacity of the cornea. We caught it just in time."

"How serious is it?" Stuart asked.

"Another few days and the damage would have been irreversible. Mr. Maher is a very fortunate man."

"So he'll still be able to fight?"

"Not tomorrow," White said sternly. "A week at the soonest, perhaps more. Depends on how he responds to treatment."

Stuart was visibly relieved. A postponement of the bout would result in all manner of problems. Apart from holding the crowds in town for another week, he would have to revise his strategy toward the Rangers. As well, he would need to reassure Enoch Rector that their moving picture was not in jeopardy. But the alternative—no fight at all—would have been a disaster. He felt a trickle of sweat roll down his backbone.

Dr. White ordered a rigid program of treatment. He prescribed eye drops, in the form of powdered cocaine diluted with water. The drops were to be administered once an hour, night and day, to relieve pain and speed the healing process. He promised to return the following morning and check on the patient.

"Don't dally around," he admonished Quinn on his

way out the door. "I'll leave the prescription at Tolland's Pharmacy. Start the drops within the hour."

There was a moment of strained silence when the door closed. Quinn finally turned to the bed. "Pete, you just rest easy. We'll have you good as new in no time. You've nothing to worry about."

Maher forced a smile. "Who's worryin'?" he said, a faint spark in his right eye. "I'd fight Fitz if I was blind as a bat."

Stuart preferred not to consider the possibility.

Lea came out of the bedroom. She was dressed for the day, her hair upswept and her eyes lightly shadowed with kohl. Stovall was slouched in a chair, the morning newspaper spread across his lap. He puckered his lips in a low whistle.

"I ever tell you you're a good-lookin' woman?"

"Now and then," she said with a dimpled smile. "Not often enough."

Stovall grinned. "Wouldn't want you to get swellheaded on me."

"I guess you're safe then. Where's Stony?"

"Went out to get some smokes. He'll be back directly."

Lea seated herself on the sofa. "I'm so excited I could bust a gusset. Tomorrow's the big day!"

"I'm a little antsy myself," Stovall said, dropping the paper on the floor. " 'Course, we've still got no idea where the fight's gonna be held. What happened to your magic spell on Masterson?"

"Oh, don't worry yourself about that, sugar. There's always tonight."

"What's that supposed to mean?"

"Tonight's the night I work the real magic."

"You just be damn—"

Taylor slammed through the door. He looked like he'd swallowed a horse apple and couldn't get his breath. His mouth worked in a strangled rasp.

"Peter Maher's done gone blind!"

Stovall straightened in his chair. "What the hell you talkin' about, Stony?"

"Heard it down on the street. His manager brought him in on the mornin' train. Got his eyes all bandaged up, and they have to lead him by the hand. Somebody spotted a sawbones over at his hotel."

Lea felt her heart stutter. "That doesn't mean he's blind. It could be anything."

"No, it's not, neither," Taylor said shakily. "The sawbones ordered some kind of special stuff from the drugstore. Word's all over town."

"I don't believe it," Lea said, her tone uncertain. "How in the world could he go blind . . . the day before the fight?"

"Who knows?" Taylor said. "But they're not leadin' him around by the hand for nothing. Sounds like a blind man to me."

"Christ A'mighty!" Stovall suddenly jackknifed to his feet. "There's not gonna be any fight tomorrow. The whole damn thing's off!"

"What d'you think I've been sayin'? 'Course the fight's off."

"That means we've got to rob Stuart's office today."

Taylor blinked. "How's that again, Earl?"

"Don't you see?" Stovall said, waving his arms. "Every sonofabitch and his dog will want his money back. The ticket money!"

"By God, I never thought of that. They'll have that safe cleaned out by sundown."

"Not if we beat 'em to it. We're gonna have to move fast."

"No."

Lea's sharp tone brought them around. She returned their stares with a determined look. "We're not pulling the job today. We can't."

"Why the hell not?" Stovall demanded. "We've been waitin' a long time to get our hands on that money. I don't aim to lose it now."

"Would you rather lose your life?"

"What're you talkin' about?"

"The Rangers," Lea said simply. "They'll figure Stuart's just pulling another fast one. Trying to gaff them into thinking Maher's blind. And knowing Stuart, they might be right."

"Yeah?" Stovall persisted. "So how's that put us at risk?"

"Think about it, sugar. Suppose Stuart's pulling some dodge to sneak his fighters out of town. The Rangers won't let him out of their sight, not for an instant! Do you want to walk into that?"

Taylor bobbed his head. "She's right, Earl. We'd get our butts shot off."

"Well, goddammit anyway," Stovall said irritably. "We come all this way to miss the boat? Stuart's gonna have to refund that ticket money."

"No he won't." Lea's voice brimmed with the conviction of a prophet. "I've told you before and I'll tell you again. Dan Stuart won't let us down."

"What kind of nonsense is that?"

"Trust me, it isn't nonsense. He'll pull off the fight."

"What makes you so sure?"

Lea smiled. "I know a winner when I see one. Stuart's our man."

"Christ on a crutch," Stovall grumped. "Let's just hope you're not wrong."

"Honey, I'm never wrong when it comes to men."

Stuart entered the suite shortly before noon. His features were drawn and he appeared somehow weary. He gave Julie a perfunctory kiss.

"What's wrong?" she said anxiously. "You look terrible."

"I've had better days."

"Has something happened with the fight?"

"Nothing good."

She listened quietly while he explained. He told her of Maher's eye condition, and the diagnosis by Dr. White. The Fistic Carnival would be postponed for at least a week.

"I closed the office for the noon hour," he concluded. "We were swamped with people demanding a refund on their tickets. It's turned into a madhouse."

"I can imagine," she said, seating herself beside him on the sofa. "Are you refunding their money?"

"Under the circumstances, we have no choice. But I've called a press conference for one o'clock. I'm hopeful that will turn things around."

"Are you talking about refunds?"

Stuart nodded. "I'll assure the press that it's only a temporary delay. The fight will take place."

"That's a marvelous idea," she said brightly. "Those reporters know you're a man of your word. They'll convince the public for you!"

"I think we'll be able to save most of the gate. Down deep, people want to believe the fight will happen."

"Well, of course they'll believe you. Peter Maher

will get better and everything will work out just fine. After all, what's another week?"

"Depends on who's talking," Stuart said soberly. "I managed to hold Fitz off till tomorrow morning. We're meeting at the office."

Julie appeared quizzical. "Why would he cause a problem?"

"Martin Julian worries me more than Fitz. Unless I miss my guess, he'll claim that Maher has forfeited the championship. He's always looking for an angle."

"Are you saying Fitzsimmons could win the championship without ever having fought?"

"Technically, he might have a case. From a practical standpoint, the public would never accept it. The whole thing would smell bogus."

"I should think so!"

Stuart's gaze drifted off into space. He was quiet a moment, lost in thought. Then, suddenly, he chuckled. "The Rangers are fit to be tied. They're dogging my every move."

"Whatever for?"

"Well, you know, lawmen are suspicious. They probably think Maher's illness is some new trick. And in a way, who could blame them?"

Julie laughed wickedly. "I think they may well have a point. You are definitely a trickster."

"Like I always say, life's one big jest."

"You've led them on such a chase. You ought to be ashamed of yourself."

Stuart chortled softly. "Not till after the fight."

TWENTY-ONE

Valentine's Day fell on a Friday. Everyone in El Paso was talking about the fight that almost was, and might yet be. The newspapers reported that Stuart now planned to hold the bout a week hence, the location still a mystery. Rumors flew like confetti in a high wind.

The public furor gradually lost steam. By all accounts, the newspapers were a persuasive factor, expressing confidence that the twenty thousand fight enthusiasts would indeed see a fight. The number of people demanding a refund on their tickets dropped off sharply early that morning. The public adopted an attitude of wait and see.

A few minutes before ten, Fitzsimmons and Martin Julian came into the office. Jack Quinn, representing Maher's interests, was seated in a chair beside the desk. Wheelock closed the door, barring entrance by anyone else, and Bates took a position blocking the streetside windows. Stuart rose from behind the desk.

"Gentlemen," he said pleasantly. "I appreciate everyone meeting here this morning." He nodded to

Fitzsimmons and Julian. "Peter Maher, for obvious reasons, will be unable to join us."

"Let's stop right there," Julian said curtly. "All kinds of stories are going around, and we'd like the truth of it. Is Maher blind, or isn't he?"

"Peter's condition is temporary. He's under the care of an excellent physician, Dr. Alfred White. There's no question he will recover."

"Is it true, what we read in the newspaper? He did his roadwork in a sandstorm?"

"Yes, that's how it happened."

Julian grunted. "Leave it to a thick-headed Mick."

"Watch your mouth," Quinn bridled. "I'll not have you talk about my man that way."

"You're the one at fault," Fitzsimmons broke in. "You shouldn't have let him run in such weather. I'd say it's you that's thick-headed."

"Gentlemen! Gentlemen!" Stuart silenced them with upraised palms. "There's nothing to be gained in a shouting match about who did what. We have serious matters to discuss."

"We came to listen," Julian said. "What's on your mind?"

"Well, first off, the fight will have to be postponed. We need to reach agreement on a new date."

"You have the cart before the horse," Julian informed him. "Are you stating for the record that Maher will not fight today?"

Stuart saw the trap. He had expected it, and earlier, he'd forewarned Bates that Julian would be a problem. Yet there was no way to skirt the issue.

"Why ask the question?" he said to Julian. "You've read the newspapers. You know the answer."

"So you're saying he won't fight today?"

"No, I'm saying he *can't* fight today."

"All the same thing," Julian stolidly remarked. "Maher has forfeited the match under the terms of the contract. We claim the championship for Fitz."

Stuart lit a cigar. "Technically, you're right," he said, snuffing the match in a wreath of smoke. "Of course, the public will never accept Fitz as champion. Not on some trumped-up technicality."

"Nice try, but it won't work," Julian said. "Jim Corbett *gave* the championship belt to Maher. Our claim is legitimate."

"You'll never convince the sportswriters of that. No one seriously believes Maher is the legitimate champion. He came here to win it by fighting Fitz."

"Yes, but he's not fighting, is he? So far as we're concerned, it's a forfeit and the title goes to Fitz. We'll take our chances with the sportswriters."

"I suppose you could," Stuart said with a casual puff on his cigar. "But if you do, that means you forfeit the purse. I won't pay for no fight."

Julian glared at him. "You owe us twenty-five thousand. I expect to be paid—today!"

"And I repeat, no fight, no purse. It's as simple as that."

"We'll take you to court."

"Go ahead," Stuart said, unconcerned. "No court in the land will award money on a prizefight. The political powers that be would never allow it."

"Come off it!" Julian snapped. "You're bluffing."

"You'd lose your shirt playing poker. I never bluff when I hold all the cards."

There was a profound moment of silence. Stuart took a puff on his cigar and blew a perfect smoke ring. He waited Julian out, confident that he did indeed hold the winning hand. Nothing talked louder than money.

"You're a cool one," Julian finally said. "After all Fitz has done for you, and now you'd put his feet to the fire. Not much gratitude there."

Stuart waved it off. "I think Fitz knows who owes what in this deal. Except for me, there wouldn't be a championship match. Am I right, Fitz?"

"I'll not deny you that," Fitzsimmons conceded. "But Martin's my manager, and I leave business matters to him. Whatever he says goes for me."

"We're not talking business here. The whole thing boils down to a matter of character, and pride as well. Do you want to win the championship in the ring . . . or steal it on a forfeit?"

"Steal it!" Julian blustered. "That's pure rubbish, and you know it. Fitz upheld his end to the very letter. He deserves the belt!"

Fitzsimmons nodded. "I'm here and I'm ready to fight. That was our deal."

"So you're ready to fight, are you?" Stuart kicked back his chair. "Well, good, you just come along with me. I'll give you your fight."

"Fight?" Fitzsimmons parroted dumbly. "Where are we going?"

"To see Peter Maher."

The shades were pulled down. A lamp, with the light turned low, cast umber shadows across the room. On the dresser, a newly purchased alarm clock ticked on toward the hour. The sound was like a mechanical metronome in the stillness.

Tommy Burns sat dozing in a chair. For the past twenty-four hours, he and Jim Hall had spelled one another, four hours on and four hours off. The alarm clock was reset each hour, and dutifully, following the doctor's orders, they administered the cocaine drops. Their routine was regulated by the clock.

Maher lay sprawled in the bed. The bedcovers were drawn over his chest, and his muscular arms were slack in fitful repose. He was worn out, forced from sleep every hour on the hour, alert only long enough to have drops placed in his eyes. His features were haggard in the silty light.

Burns awoke with a start as the door opened. Quinn led the way into the room, followed by Stuart and Fitzsimmons, with Julian a step behind. Blinking himself awake, Burns hurriedly got to his feet and moved forward with a look of surprise. The men crowded around the foot of the bed, and Quinn nodded to Burns. His voice was a sibilant whisper.

"How's he doing?"

"Not much change," Burns said. "He's still hurting, though he won't admit it. Never a word."

Fitzsimmons appeared stunned. He wasn't prepared for the swollen eyes and the inflamed discoloration, still fiery even in the dim light. He thought Maher looked helpless as a kitten.

Quinn cleared his throat. "Has Doc White been by?"

"Yeah, little while ago," Burns replied. "Told me it's not any worse, so that's a good sign. He said to keep up the drops like we—"

"Ummm." Maher groaned, stirring listlessly in the bed. "That you, Tommy?"

"Right here, Pete," Burns said, moving across the room. "You've got some company."

"Who's that?"

"Why, Dan Stuart and Ruby Rob Fitzsimmons himself. Come to pay their respects."

"Fitzsimmons?" Maher's voice was groggy. "Quit your jokin', Tommy."

"No, it's true," Stuart said, pulling Fitzsimmons forward. "Tell him yourself, Fitz."

"It's me, in the flesh," Fitzsimmons said awkwardly. "Didn't mean to bother you, Peter."

"Say, it's no bother at all."

Everyone jumped when the alarm clock jangled to life. Burns shut it off and gathered the bottle of cocaine drops from the dresser. He gave the men a lame smile.

"Time for his drops," he said. "Doc White's very particular about every hour on the hour. You lay back now, Pete."

Maher lowered his head into the pillow. He winced, gritting his teeth, when Burns pried his eyelids apart. Though he tried to hide it, the men looking on exchanged glances, all too aware of his pain. They watched as Burns worked the eyedropper, gently squeezing fluid into his blood-streaked eyes. He relaxed with the soothing effect of the cocaine.

"There now," Burns said, stepping back. "Wasn't so bad, was it?"

"Nothing to it," Maher said gamely, pushing himself upright in the bed. He squinted, trying to bring the men into focus with his right eye. "I'd know you anywhere, Fitz. Hard to miss that red hair."

Fitzsimmons looked embarrassed. "Are they taking good care of you, Peter? Anything you need?"

"Oh, I'm in fine hands. I'll be up and about before you know it. Are you ready for our little scrap?"

"Well, I suppose the question is . . . are you?"

"Don't you worry." Maher grinned, his one eye bright. "I promised you the fight of your life. And I'm a man who keeps my word."

Julian pushed forward, on the verge of speaking out. Fitzsimmons warned him off with a sharp gesture, and looked back at Maher. "Follow the doc's orders and get on your feet again, Peter. We'll have our scrap."

"I'll be there, Fitz. You can count on it."

Quinn ushered them out of the room a few minutes later. In the hallway, he assured them that Maher would be ready to fight the following Friday. A moment elapsed, then Julian turned on Stuart. His voice was thick with anger.

"Think you're clever, don't you?" he said hotly. "You sandbagged Fitz by bringing him here. Well, let me tell you—"

"That's enough!" Fitzsimmons interrupted, nodding slowly to Stuart. "I'll wait till next Friday and no longer. You got me?"

"That's a deal, Fitz," Stuart said earnestly. "I always knew you were a man of honor."

"And you fight dirty in the clinches, Daniel. I'm surprised at you."

"All I did was find your soft spot. You're not as tough as you make out."

Fitzsimmons couldn't argue the point. Nor would he try to excuse it. He was, instead, wryly impressed.

He thought Stuart had played him like a violin.

Later that afternoon Captain Bill McDonald marched into the office. His eyes were like ball bearings and his mouth was set in a hard line. He halted in front of Stuart.

"You're lookin' to get arrested," he said stiffly. "General Mabry and Governor Ahumada are on the warpath. They want your hide."

Stuart feigned shock. "What have I done now?"

"No need to put on an act. The Rurales found your boxing rings while they were patrolling the river. We just got the word."

The gambit was yet another diversion concocted by Stuart. Overnight, Bat Masterson and his men, in cooperation with the railroads, had secretly put out decoys. One boxing ring had been erected some ten miles north of El Paso, on the Texas side of the Rio Grande. The other ring had been constructed ten miles downriver, across the border on Mexican soil. Lumber for spectator stands had been unloaded at both sites.

"Let me get this straight," Stuart said at length. "Are you charging me with some offense?"

McDonald stared at him. "There's nothing illegal about building the rings. The law gets broke when you use them."

"Then I'm somewhat at a loss, Captain. What's the purpose of your call?"

"A word to the wise, Mr. Stuart. Don't try to finish construction on those spectator stands. Your men are liable to get shot."

"By the Rangers?"

"More likely the Rurales," McDonald said. "Justice tends to work a little quicker in Mexico."

"I'll certainly take that under advisement."

The door banged open. John L. Sullivan lumbered into the office with a zigzag step. He was reeling drunk, and Paddy Ryan, ever watchful, was only a pace behind. Grinning broadly, Sullivan lurched to a halt, weaving back and forth. He fixed on Stuart with a look of woozy good cheer.

"God bless all in this house," he said, apropos of nothing. "I've just come by to say hullo, Dan'l."

"John L. Sullivan," Stuart said with exaggerated

courtesy. "Allow me to introduce Captain McDonald, of the Texas Rangers."

"By all the Saints!" Sullivan bellowed. "And would you be tellin' me, Cap'n? Have you caught any desperadoes today?"

McDonald was not amused by happy drunks, famous or otherwise. "Nice meeting you, Mr. Sullivan," he said, glancing sideways at Stuart. "You remember what I told you about the Rurales."

"I won't forget," Stuart said. "And thanks for the warning."

"All part of the job."

McDonald went out the door. Sullivan tracked him with a bleary gaze. "Dan'l, m'boy," he said with boozy confidence. "You'd best watch yourself around that one."

"I thought so myself, John L., but now . . ."

The warning from McDonald seemed to Stuart somehow more personal than official. He told himself that it was a trick of the mind, wishful thinking. Yet he was forced to wonder.

Perhaps he'd found a friend in the enemy camp.

TWENTY-TWO

On Sunday afternoon Stuart took the Fistic Carnival to Juarez. With the event postponed, everyone was at loose ends and spirits were low. He decided to treat the pugilists to a bullfight.

At one o'clock they gathered outside the office. There were eight fighters in the group, and Julie planned to accompany them as far as Fitzsimmons's training quarters. She would spend the afternoon visiting with Rose Fitzsimmons and baby Rob. Neither she nor Rose cared to watch the gory spectacle of the bulls.

The Rangers trailed them across the bridge to Juarez. McDonald, along with his fellow captains and their men, outnumbered the fighters by five to one. From a distance, they observed as Julie was dropped off and Fitzsimmons and Julian joined Stuart's party. They were clearly under orders to stick close with the Fistic Carnival.

Stuart was amused by the tight surveillance. Over the past week he'd duped the Rangers with boxing rings up and down the Rio Grande, and the unsolved disappearance of Enoch Rector. They obviously suspicioned his every move, and they were alert now to the slightest trick. He thought they would be profoundly shocked by the last move in the game.

The amphitheater was overflowing with spectators. Stuart bought tickets for his group on the lower tier of boxes, directly overlooking the bullring. A few rows down, he saw Mabry seated with Governor Ahumada in the judge's stand. Their cordial manner indicated that they were now fast friends, united against the Fistic Carnival. Across the way, he saw the troop of Rangers crowd into the cheaper seats. The state of Texas apparently didn't splurge on its lawmen.

On the opposite side of the judge's stand, he spotted Bat Masterson. His security chief was seated with a woman and two men, all of them finely dressed. There was a familiarity to them, particularly the woman, and then it came to him. She was the attractive young lady who had studied him with such interest at Fitzsimmons's training gym some three weeks ago. Today, she seemed enthralled with Masterson, and while Stuart's interest was piqued, he was not surprised. Masterson had a way with the ladies.

The afternoon's entertainment opened with a colorful display of pageantry. The matadors, attired in their resplendent costumes, marched in stately procession around the ring. They were flanked by the picadors, mounted on horses armored with padding to protect them from the bulls' horns. The picadors carried steel-tipped lances, used to spear the bulls and weaken their shoulder muscles. The parade ended with the matadors doffing their caps in salute to Governor Ahumada.

The first *corrida* got under way with a trilling blast of trumpets. A massive black bull, horns glinting in the sunlight, charged out of a chute into the ring. The crowd cheered as the bull skidded to a halt, pawing the dirt, and glared contemptuously at those in the front rows. A picador rode out, circling the arena, and drove his lance into the bull's shoulder. The tip skidded off bone, tearing loose, and the enraged bull charged its tormentor. Head lowered, the bull thrust its horns beneath the padding and lifted the horse off the ground. The horse screamed, tossed aside like a doll, its stomach ripped open.

The picador hastily dismounted and ran for cover. A matador moved into the arena, distracting the bull with his cape, and lured it back into the chute. The disemboweled horse stumbled around the ring, its entrails dragging on the ground, and finally wobbled to a halt. Three workmen entered the arena from a gated portal opposite the judge's stand, leading a team of oxen. One of the men walked forward, drawing a long knife, and cut the horse's throat in a bright spray of blood. The horse shuddered, collapsing onto its rump, then rolled sideways into the dirt. A stillness settled over the onlookers as the oxen dragged the horse from the ring.

"Wonderful sport," Fitzsimmons mumbled. "You'd think the Mexicans would have no objection to prizefighting. They spill blood easily enough."

"We've made that argument many times," Stuart said. "The contradiction seems beyond them, or perhaps they simply ignore it. They take sport in killing animals."

Joe Walcott, who was seated on the other side of Stuart, looked queasy. He watched with morbid attentiveness as the horse was dragged through the archway. "Lord Jesus," he said in a small voice. "Horses ain't much in Mexico, is they?"

The other fighters muttered agreement. "Mebbe

we're lucky, Little Chocolate," George Dixon said, glancing at Walcott. "No tellin' what might've happened if we'd fought here. These folks got a taste for blood."

"There's some similarity to Roman times," Stuart added. "The gladiators fought to the death, and on occasion, they fought wild animals. A matador with a sword against a bull isn't all that different."

"Never thought of that," Walcott said, considering a moment. "Did they have colored gladiators in them days?"

"As a matter of fact, they did," Stuart said. "The Romans referred to them as Nigerians."

Walcott rolled his eyes. "You wouldn't have caught me fightin' no wild animals. I would've run for the hills."

"Amen to that," Dixon agreed. "Think I'll just stick to fightin' men."

Fitzsimmons nodded. "I'd not trade places with a matador. It's a dicey game they play."

The statement proved to be prophetic In the first *corrida,* the bull that had gutted the horse gored the matador in the leg. The next fight was a close call, with the matador escaping by a hairsbreadth after driving home the sword. The third *corrida* started with a picador being knocked off his horse and chased from the ring. The matador approached the bull with wary respect.

"¡Toro!" he shouted, jiggling his cape. *"¡Eh, toro!"*

"Toro, my black ass," Dixon said dubiously. "That boy oughta quit while the quittin's good."

Walcott shook his head, troubled by what he'd seen. A worrisome thought surfaced in his mind, an odd juxtaposition that scrambled bullfights with prizefights. He wondered whether the Fistic Carnival itself weren't hexed.

"Mistuh Dan," he said, looking around at Stuart. "I got myself to thinkin' about Peter Maher. Any chance he's not gonna fight?"

"The odds are in our favor," Stuart said confidently. "Dr. White assures me he'll be fit by next Friday."

"But just supposin' he ain't. What'll we do then?"

Stuart was all too aware that Fitzsimmons and Julian were listening. He chose his words carefully. "Maher will fight," he said with conviction. "I have no doubt of it whatever."

"Still sounds a little iffy to me," Walcott said doubtfully. "Have to ask you somethin' I know you don't want to answer, Mistuh Dan. Whereabouts these fights gonna be held?"

"Joe, you know the location's a secret. I wish I could tell you but I can't. You'll find out when we get there."

"Well, maybe you could just tell me this much. Does 'there' mean Texas or do it mean Mexico?"

"I really can't say."

"The boys and me"—Walcott motioned to the other fighters—"we been talkin' about it the last couple days. We figures the longer we hang around, the more chance we gonna get ourselves shot." He paused, lowering his voice. "The Mexicans on to you, Mistuh Dan."

"Oh?" Stuart said, deadpan. "What makes you think that?"

" 'Cause the Rangers is doggin' your heels. Way we see it, they'll force you across the border into Mexico. And them Rurale boys don't mess around. Shoot first and talk about it later."

"I understand your concern. But you have my word on it, Joe. No one will be shot."

"How you gonna guarantee us of that, Mistuh Dan?"

Stuart sensed he'd lost their trust. Yet to restore their confidence he would have to disclose the location of the fight. He simply couldn't risk alerting the Rangers, and jeopardizing his motion picture. There was too much at stake.

"Nothing in life is a hundred percent," he said. "All I can do is give you my word."

Walcott fell silent. He was the welterweight champion, respected by the other fighters, and they had clearly selected him as their spokesman. Stuart knew the situation had suddenly turned grave, but he felt helpless. The subject was dropped and everyone went back to watching the bullfights. Their silence seemed to Stuart an ominous note.

Later, after the last *corrida*, Walcott and the other fighters walked ahead. Stuart lagged behind with Fitzsimmons and Julian, and they reminded him that next Friday was the deadline. Unless Maher was prepared to fight, they would claim the championship belt, purse or no purse. The Rangers tailed along, watching as Stuart collected Julie at Fitzsimmons's house, and followed at a discreet distance. Julie sensed from Stuart's mood that something had gone terribly wrong.

Joe Walcott waited with Dixon and the other fighters on the Texas side of the bridge. He tipped his hat to Julie and then explained to Stuart that all of the fighters were in agreement. They appreciated his efforts on their behalf, and they wished him well with the Fitzsimmons–Maher bout. But to a man, they were no longer convinced that Stuart could protect them

from the Rurales. They were forced to withdraw from
the Fistic Carnival.

"Sorry, Mistuh Dan," Walcott ended with a rueful
shrug. "Me and the boys just don't see no other way."
He nodded to the Rangers, who stood watching from
the opposite side of the bridge. "Them folks mean to
do you some powerful harm. We never signed on for
that."

"Joe—" Stuart hesitated, torn between confiding in
Walcott and the need for secrecy. "Is there anything
I could say that would change your mind?"

"Wish there was, Mistuh Dan. Guess it's just one
of them things."

"What are your plans?"

"Why, I suppose we'll be catchin' the evening
train. We done seen enough of Texas."

Walcott rejoined the other fighters. As they turned
downtown, Julie took Stuart's arm. "Dan, it's just terrible," she said in a wavering voice. "What will you
do now?"

"I think I'd better call a press conference. Fast."

"Judas Priest!" Bates exploded. "How could those
bastards pull out at the last minute?"

Stuart seemed resigned. "Some men are easier
frightened than others. They feared for their lives."

"What the hell brought it on so sudden?"

"I gather they've been talking among themselves
for days. They're convinced we'll have no choice but
to hold the fight in Mexico. I couldn't persuade them
otherwise without tipping our hand."

Stuart and Bates were sequestered in the office with
Wheelock. A hurried press conference had been put
together by Wheelock, and he only now finished the

last of his calls. He replaced the phone receiver on the hook.

"I told them six o'clock," he said. "We'll still make the morning editions."

"God," Bates huffed sullenly. "Once this hits the papers, anyone with a ticket will be pounding on the door. We've lost the gate."

Wheelock groaned. "It's the straw that broke the camel's back. They'll all want a refund."

"Cheer up," Stuart said, trying to lighten the mood. "We still have Fitz and Maher—and the motion picture."

"Let's hope you're right." Bates stared at the massive safe against the rear wall. "Tomorrow, we'll probably be cleaned out by noon. Four hundred twenty-three thousand by last count."

"So we'll only make a million. We knew all along the motion picture was our money machine."

"How are you going to handle the press?"

"I plan to tap-dance . . . quickly."

The reporters began pouring in shortly before six. Within minutes, the office was packed to capacity, cameramen jockeying for position. Stuart waited behind the desk until everyone was in place. He raised his arms for silence.

"I have an announcement," he said. "Due to the tyrannical actions of the authorities, we have been forced to cancel the Fistic Carnival. There will now be one fight—the most important fight!—Fitzsimmons and Maher."

"Authorities?" asked the reporter for the *Dallas Morning News*. "Are you talking about Texas or Mexico?"

"All of them," Stuart responded. "Texas, Mexico, and the United States government. Our fighters have been coerced and threatened and hounded beyond endurance. Discretion being the better part of valor, they elected to fight another day—somewhere else."

Gabe Lawlor of the *New York World* outshouted the others. "What makes Fitz and Maher so brave? Why didn't they quit?"

"Ruby Rob Fitzsimmons and Peter Maher are undaunted in the face of adversity. They came here to fight for the heavyweight championship of the world—and they will not flinch!"

"What about Maher?" yelled the sportswriter for the *San Francisco Chronicle*. "Will he be in shape to fight?"

"Indeed he will," Stuart reaffirmed. "Peter Maher has the constitution of an ox. He will take the fight to Fitzsimmons."

"Who do you blame most?" the correspondent for the *Chicago Tribune* called out. "Texas, Mexico, or the White House?"

"Gentlemen, what we have witnessed is a shameful attempt to gain political currency under the pretext of enforcing the law. I blame them one and all—the lot—an insidious alliance!"

Stuart thrust his arm in the air. Cameramen crowded closer and flash-pans popped, and he gave them a square-jawed look of outrage. His visage was that of a man determined to prevail against all odds.

He thought John Q. Public would strongly support the underdog.

TWENTY-THREE

FISTIC CARNIVAL CALLED OFF!
STUART DENOUNCES FIGHT FOES

The headlines sent shock waves through El Paso. On Monday, when the morning editions hit the streets, everything stopped while people hovered over their newspapers. A pall settled on the town, and a collective groan swept through the thousands who had traveled there from far places. They were at first appalled by the news. Then disbelief turned to wholesale panic.

The newspapers reported that Joe Walcott and the lesser fighters had already departed El Paso. The stories went on to relate that the Fitzsimmons–Maher bout was still scheduled for February 21. But while the public endorsed Stuart's attack on government leaders, their attitude about the championship match was hardly what he'd expected. They no longer believed he could pull it off.

By late morning, the fight headquarters at the Sheldon Building was mobbed. Thousands of people blocked the street, all clamoring for a refund on their tickets. The city police and the Rangers were called in to restore order, and quickly took charge of what threatened to become a riot. The crowds were formed into lines on the sidewalk, stretching the length of the block, and curled around the corner onto a side street. Two people at a time were allowed into the office.

Bates and Wheelock, seated at desks, exchanged money for tickets. Stuart stood at the rear of the room with Bat Masterson, watching as stacks of cash were rapidly depleted from the safe. One of Masterson's men scurried back and forth, assigned to keep Bates and Wheelock supplied with funds. The others were ranged along the walls, there to provide security in the event of trouble. Masterson slowly shook his head.

"What a pitiful sight," he said. "Never saw money disappear so fast."

Stuart nodded. "There's a herd mentality when people panic. No one wants to be last in line."

"You'd think they might give you the benefit of the doubt. I mean, what really brought them here was Fitzsimmons and Maher. The other fights were icing on the cake."

"Bat, I sadly miscalculated their reaction. When the other fights were canceled, they lost faith altogether. They don't believe the championship bout will ever happen."

"What's the latest on Maher?"

"I saw Jack Quinn on the way out of the hotel. He said they're planning on returning to Las Cruces today. Maher's recovered far better than anyone expected."

"I'll be switched," Masterson said, clearly astounded. "Two days sure as hell worked wonders. Sounds almost miraculous."

"Dr. White was of the same opinion," Stuart remarked. "He attributed it to Divine intervention and the strength of Maher's willpower. He says he never saw a man so determined to get well."

"Are you saying he's back to normal? Has he recovered his sight?"

"Quinn told me he's halfway there. They plan to resume his training program in earnest."

"You ought to announce that out on the street. Maybe it'd put the slow-down on these refunds."

"Too late now," Stuart said in a regretful tone. "Once people lose faith, there's little to be done. They'd write it off as more hyperbole—same song, second verse."

"Damn shame," Masterson said, watching his men take another stack of cash from the safe. "Do you think they'll clean you out?"

"No, as a matter of fact, I don't. Some people stick to the very last, hoping against hope. I'd bet four or five thousand hold on to their tickets."

"So maybe you'll wind up with a hundred thousand in the kitty. That's a damnsight better than nothing."

"Anything's better than nothing, Bat."

Captain Bill McDonald walked through the door. He glanced at Bates and Wheelock, shelling out money for tickets, and moved on toward the rear of the room. The safe caught his attention a moment, and then he looked around, nodding impassively to Masterson. His gaze shifted to Stuart.

"Helluva mess out there," he said. "Must be ten thousand people waitin' to get paid off."

"And more on the way," Stuart observed. "What can I do for you, Captain?"

"Word got around that Maher's on the mend. Anything to it?"

"I'm delighted to say that Peter Maher has improved quite nicely. Why do you ask?"

"Just curious," McDonald said. "General Mabry figured it for another one of your tricks. Guess he was wrong."

Stuart forced a smile. "The general is wrong more often than not. Wouldn't you agree?"

"I reckon that's not for me to say. 'Course, you got his bowels in an uproar with them newspaper stories. Don't recollect he's ever been called a tyrant."

"Well, I'm not responsible for his bowels, Captain. Was there something more?"

McDonald lowered his voice. "Mabry's gonna drop by Fitz's training gym this afternoon. He's fixin' to invite all the press boys." His mouth quirked in a faint smile. "Thought you might want to be there."

"I appreciate the tip," Stuart said, openly surprised. "But I'm not sure I understand. Why do me any favors?"

"Who said I done you a favor? I was just passing the time of day."

McDonald turned away, walked toward the door. The men blocking the entrance parted to let him through, and he crossed the sidewalk. A moment later he disappeared into the crowd.

"I'll be damned," Masterson said, flabbergasted. "What the hell was that all about?"

"Bat, I'm not altogether sure. Perhaps McDonald doesn't care for the tactics of his sterling leader."

"Or maybe it's a setup to get you over to Fitz's gym."

"No, I don't believe so."

Stuart reminded himself that it wasn't the first favor. Once before, the Ranger captain had shown ambivalence about Woodford Mabry's tactics. And now again today.

He thought McDonald operated by an older code.

A code unknown to those within the political arena. Or those who did their dirty work.

There was honor even in the heat of battle.

The train station was in a state of chaos. Some three thousand people milled around the depot, waiting to depart El Paso. The crowd swelled by the moment, as disenchanted fight enthusiasts rushed to buy a train ticket. The Southern Pacific and the Texas & Pacific sent frantic telegrams to their respective headquarters, requesting additional trains. By one o'clock, the depot was under siege.

John L. Sullivan and his traveling companion, Paddy Ryan, stood on the platform. They were preparing to board an eastbound train, already running an hour late. Several reporters, looking for a twist on the story, surrounded the former champion. Sullivan was only moderately drunk, and the newsmen found him somewhat more coherent than normal. He was enjoying a final moment in the limelight.

The jostling crowd eddied and swirled around them. The reporters were forced to shout over the constant din of noise. "Mr. Sullivan!" hollered the correspondent for the *Saint Louis Post-Dispatch*. "Do you believe the Fitzsimmons–Maher bout will take place?"

"I do not," Sullivan rumbled. "Why else do you think I'm leavin' town? It's naught but a pipe dream now."

The reporter for the *Chicago Record* waved his notepad. "John L., are you aware that Peter Maher returned to his training camp at Las Cruces? He caught the morning train."

Sullivan waved him off. "You've seen the last of

Maher. He'll not toe the line come Friday. And more's the pity."

"What makes you so certain?"

"Why, it's all tommyrot about him regainin' his sight. The man's so blind he needs a cane."

"What if he doesn't fight?" demanded the reporter for the *El Paso Evening Telegram.* "Do you think Fitzsimmons deserves the championship?"

Sullivan grimaced. "Nobody deserves the belt unless he wins it in the ring. Otherwise, he's no champion at all."

"What's your opinion of how Dan Stuart's been treated? Do you think the government played fair?"

"Are you serious now? All these do-gooders are nothin' but hooligans in disguise. They ganged up on Stuart like a bunch of wharf rats. He never had a fightin' chance."

The train whistle sounded. Paddy Ryan pulled Sullivan into the vestibule of the passenger coach. The sportswriter for the *San Francisco Examiner* pushed forward. "What if there's no fight here?" he yelled. "Would you come out of retirement, John L.?"

"I'll fight any man alive!" Sullivan said in a booming voice. "Fitzsimmons or Corbett, or anybody else. Anytime, anywhere!"

The cars lurched forward. Sullivan leaned out of the vestibule and shook his fist in the air. His trumpeted shout drifted back over the train station.

"I can lick any son of a bitch in the world!"

Stuart walked into the gym at three that afternoon. A small crowd watched as Fitzsimmons pounded the speed bag with a flurry of punches. His shoulders were knotted with muscle.

Woodford Mabry stood near the ring. He was accompanied by Captain Jim Brooks and four Rangers. His mouth pursed with irritation as he glanced at Stuart, and he quickly looked away. He went back to watching the workout.

Some fifty reporters were gathered on the opposite side of the ring. Their heads swiveled in unison, their eyes fixing on Stuart, and they suddenly seemed more alert. Seldom were they all in the same spot at the same time, and Stuart realized that the tip from McDonald was in earnest. Mabry had summoned the entire press corps.

Fitzsimmons finished with a drumming *rat-a-tat-tat* on the speed bag. The crowd applauded politely as he turned away, and Charlie White handed him a towel. He crossed the room, mopping sweat off his forehead, warily glancing at the Rangers. He stopped beside Stuart, and the reporters moved forward in a tight phalanx. They waited for someone to fire the opening salvo.

"Very impressive, Mr. Fitzsimmons," Mabry said with a bogus smile. "Too bad all your hard work has been in vain."

"You're mistaken there," Fitzsimmons said, refusing to take the bait. "Peter Maher will need a shamrock when he steps into the ring."

"Well, don't you see, that's my point. Mr. Maher will never enter the ring. Nor will you."

Stuart appeared unruffled by the statement. He waited, resisting the urge to speak out, content to pick his spot. Mabry turned to the newsmen.

"You gentlemen of the press are perhaps more observant than Mr. Fitzsimmons. Today, you have witnessed what amounts to an exodus from the city of El Paso. The people boarding those trains are at last convinced of what I told you from the start—there will be no prizefight."

Fred Martin of the *New York Times* spoke out. "General Mabry, there's no question you nixed the Fistic Carnival. How can you be so certain about the Fitzsimmons–Maher bout?"

"Consider the facts," Mabry said sharply. "The Rurales all along the Rio Grande. The U.S. Cavalry on the New Mexico border. And the Texas Rangers here in El Paso." He waved dismissively. "Where would this prizefight be held?"

"That's old news," said the reporter for the *Chicago Tribune*. "We all know you have Stuart and his fighters surrounded. Why bring us here to say it again?"

Mabry gave him a crafty smile. "Governor Culberson has authorized me to make an announcement. He is prepared to declare martial law at the slightest hint the fight will be held on Texas soil. In short, the suspension of habeas corpus."

"What does that mean, exactly?"

"Quite simply, it means we would be empowered to arrest and detain anyone merely on suspicion. No actual crime would be required for the Rangers to take action."

A brittle silence descended on the gym. The reporters turned en masse, watching Stuart for a reaction. His expression revealed nothing, and yet he felt a cold admiration for Mabry. He thought the adjutant general was running a monumental bluff, one designed to frighten fighters and fight enthusiasts alike. The purpose was to scare everyone into hopping aboard the next train out of El Paso.

"What do you think, Mr. Stuart?" asked the reporter for the *Dallas Morning News.* "Will the threat of martial law alter your plans?"

"Not in the least," Stuart said brashly. "But I feel obliged to alter my press statement of yesterday. I withdraw the allegations of tyranny." He paused with a wry smile. "Actually, I owe the governor and General Mabry a debt of gratitude."

"Gratitude?" the reporter echoed. "How do you figure that?"

"I see now that the best way to promote something is to prohibit it. No amount of money could have bought such favorable publicity for our motion picture."

"So the fight will go on as scheduled?"

"Indeed it will."

"Any word on where?"

Stuart grinned. "Ask me on Thursday."

"Goddammit!"

"Will you please calm down?"

"I told you we should've robbed 'em last week."

"Do you want everybody in the hotel to hear you?"

"I don't give a gnat's ass who hears me!"

Earl Stovall stalked back and forth across the sitting room. Lea, who was seated in a chair, watched him with growing anxiety. Taylor was slumped back on the sofa, his eyes on the ceiling. The atmosphere in the room was electric.

Their squabbling had begun with the morning newspapers. The cancellation of the Fistic Carnival had left them stunned and on edge. All day, from the windows of the suite, they had watched as thousands joined the line for ticket refunds. Stovall had contained his simmering anger with muttered curses, pacing from room to room. But now, unable to suppress it any longer, he'd exploded in a dark rage.

"I shouldn't have listened," he said, turning on Lea. "Last week was the time to pull the job, and I knew it. I just flat knew it!"

"Think back a minute," Lea said patiently. "We agreed it wasn't the right time. Not with all these Rangers in town."

"We didn't agree on nothin'. I let you talk me into it. The way I always do."

"Leave her be," Taylor said, twisting around on the sofa. "She was right then and she's right now. We would've got our butts shot off."

Stovall glowered at him. "This here's between me and Lea. You stay the hell outta it."

"Let's all take it easy," Lea counseled. "Fighting among ourselves won't help. We've still got a job to do."

"Yeah?" Stovall barked. "Who says so?"

"Bat Masterson."

Earlier that afternoon Lea had gone out for a walk. She felt the need to escape the oppressive atmosphere of the suite, and she'd insisted on going alone. On the street, across from Stuart's office, she had encountered Masterson outside a café. He was on his way back from a late dinner, and he'd taken a moment to talk with her. Their brief conversation had been revealing.

"You lost me," Stovall said, staring at her. "What's Masterson got to do with anything?"

"I talked with him," Lea replied. "When I went out, we just happened to meet on the street. He told me something very interesting."

"Lemme guess," Stovall grumped. "The fight's been called off between Fitzsimmons and Maher."

"As a matter of fact, the fight's still on for Friday.

What he told me had to do with the gate."

"Haven't you looked out the window lately? There's not gonna be any gate. Everybody's leavin' town."

"Nooo," Lea said slowly. "Dan Stuart thinks four or five thousand will stick around. And I believe he's right."

"So he's right?" Stovall persisted. "What's your point?"

"A hundred thousand dollars."

"For chrissakes! Damn near a year and a half ago we started out with our eye on a million. Now you're talkin' about a lousy hundred grand?"

"Well, sugar, it's not chickenfeed," Lea said. "Any way you count it, it's at least triple what we ever got on our best bank job. And it certainly beats no payday at all."

A moment slipped past in strained silence. Then, suddenly, Taylor burst out in laughter. "She's got you there, Earl. Any payday's better'n no payday."

"I suppose," Stovall mumbled. "Let's just hope the fight comes off."

Lea winked at him. "Dan Stuart won't let us down."

"Seems like I've heard that song before."

"Sugar, it's not a song, it's a hymn."

"You pray to Stuart, do you?"

"No," Lea said quietly. "I pray for him."

TWENTY-FOUR

On Wednesday circulars were posted throughout town. The notices advised the public that special trains would depart for the Fitzsimmons–Maher bout on Thursday evening. The fight was still scheduled for Friday, February 21.

Stuart had spent a good part of Tuesday in conference with representatives of the railroads. The Southern Pacific and the Texas & Pacific were virtual conspirators in Stuart's scheme. Their lines had already profited immensely, and the final stage would further enhance their balance sheets. The plan was a tightly guarded secret among railroad executives.

Early Wednesday morning Stuart reviewed the logistics of the plan with Edward Bates and Bat Masterson. The timetable for each step was critical, and he stressed the need for the various elements to come off as scheduled. To no small degree, they were discussing a battle plan, and the tactics revolved around deception and disinformation. Their objective was to thoroughly confound the Texas Rangers.

Late that morning Stuart emerged from the office. On the opposite side of the street, Captain Bill

McDonald stood talking with two Rangers, who were assigned to watch the fight headquarters. Stuart waited for the trolley car to trundle past, and then crossed the street, aware that his sudden appearance had caught the Rangers' attention. He nodded pleasantly to McDonald.

"Good morning, Captain."

"Mr. Stuart," McDonald said. "What can I do for you?"

"I would like to talk with General Mabry. Perhaps you would be kind enough to escort me to the hotel."

"Is the general expecting you?"

"No, he isn't," Stuart replied. "But I think he'll agree to see me. We have matters to discuss."

McDonald shrugged. "Guess there's one way to find out. Let's go ask him."

Stuart fell in beside the Ranger captain. As they turned downtown, McDonald pointed to a circular attached to a lamppost. "Everybody's talkin' about these posters you put out. They're wonderin' where you aim to hold the fight."

"Their wondering will end on Friday. I'm not at liberty to say anything more."

"Seems like your ticket refunds have slowed down. How many people you expectin' to show up at the train station tomorrow?"

"On the order of five thousand," Stuart commented. "Not what we originally envisioned, but still a respectable number."

"True believers, huh?" McDonald said. "Figured you'd pull it off, no matter what."

"How about you, Captain? I get the feeling you would like to see the fight yourself."

"I'm as partial to a fight as the next man. 'Course,

that's just between you and me. I'm sworn to uphold
the law."

Stuart looked at him. "Even when you don't agree
with the methods used to enforce the law?"

"That's part of wearin' a badge," McDonald said.
"Orders are orders, whether you agree or not."

They walked along in silence a moment. "I'm curious," Stuart finally said. "Could I ask you something
in strictest confidence?"

"Fire away."

"I have a hunch you think Mabry's gone too far.
Am I right or wrong?"

"You never heard me say it?" McDonald waited
for him to nod agreement. "Your prizefight's a matter
of morality squeezed into law, and the Rangers
weren't meant to police morals. We ought to be out
catchin' bank robbers and such."

"I endorse the sentiment," Stuart said. "So what's
your opinion of Mabry as a lawman?"

McDonald snorted. "I think he's a damn fine politician. Not that you heard me say that, either."

"Captain, I'm as deaf as a stone."

A short while later they entered the suite at the
Pierson Hotel. Mabry was seated in an easy chair beside the fireplace, his features stern. Across from him,
hat in hand, Captain John Hughes occupied the sofa.
McDonald ushered Stuart forward.

"General," he said, halting by the sofa. "Mr. Stuart
wanted a word with you. I brought him along."

"So I see," Mabry said, clearly annoyed by the in-
trusion. "Well, what is it, Mr. Stuart?"

"A matter of courtesy," Stuart said with some
irony. "Tonight, three freight cars of lumber will depart El Paso by different trains. I thought you should
be advised."

"I gather you're up to your old tricks. And where are these trains bound?"

"New Mexico, Fort Hancock, and points east."

Fort Hancock was located some fifty miles southeast of El Paso. The army post was situated along the banks of the Rio Grande. Directly across the river was an uninhabited stretch of Mexico.

"That's all very interesting," Mabry said skeptically. "Why the sudden rush to inform me of your plans?"

"Two reasons," Stuart noted. "First, to advise you that the fight will not be held in Texas. Nothing has changed in that regard."

"And the second reason?"

"You have no justification for asking the governor to declare martial law. Captain Hughes and Captain McDonald will bear witness to this conversation. The fight will not take place on Texas soil."

"I don't need you to tell me my business, Mr. Stuart. Anything else?"

"I believe that's all."

"Good day to you, then."

Stuart turned back across the room. When the door closed, Mabry smacked a fist into his palm. "The gall of the man!" he said angrily. "What do you make of that, Captain McDonald?"

"Well, sir—" McDonald knuckled his mustache. "I think two of them trains are likely meant as decoys. The third's probably headed for the fight location."

"Why would he need more lumber?"

"Walkin' over here, he told me he expects five thousand people at the fight. Sounds like he aims to build more spectator stands."

"Stuart and his damnable games," Mabry growled.

"But we're still faced with a critical question—where is the third train headed?"

"No tellin'," McDonald said. " 'Course, Fort Hancock would be mighty handy. Just a short run from here to there."

"Notify Governor Ahumada to station a Rurale patrol across from the fort."

"Yes, sir."

"Captain Hughes," Mabry said in a commanding voice. "I want one of your men aboard each of those three trains. They're to telegraph me upon arriving at the final destination."

Hughes got to his feet. "Good as done, General. Don't you worry about a thing. Stuart won't give us the slip this time."

"You had better make sure of that, Captain. Very sure."

McDonald was on the verge of speaking out. But then, upon reflection, he saw no reason to further anger Mabry. The odds, based on past experience, were not in their favor. The game with trains seemed to him a losing proposition.

He thought it likely Dan Stuart would snooker them again.

A starry sky shone down on the rail yards. Three trains stood chuffing steam on sidings south of the depot. One locomotive was positioned for a northern run, toward the New Mexico border. The other two were headed south.

All three trains were hauling a flatbed stacked high with lumber. One of the southbound freights would be switched onto a siding upon arriving at Fort Hancock. The second would continue on and follow the eastward route of the Texas & Pacific. The termination point was San Antonio.

Bat Masterson and Ed Bates were concealed in the shadows at the south end of the rail yards. Masterson's assignment was to spirit Bates aboard the eastbound freight, without alerting the Rangers. The train would stop briefly in Langtry, some three hundred ninety miles down the line. There the flatcar with the lumber would be unloaded.

Captain John Hughes walked along the tracks. He was accompanied by three Rangers, Marvin Hart, Dave Posey, and Fred Aten. They stopped first at the northbound freight, where the engineer refused to answer any questions about the flatbed loaded with lumber. After considerable argument, Ranger Hart was allowed to climb aboard the cab of the locomotive. From there, Hughes and his men crossed the tracks to the trains waiting in line on the southern route. A heated debate resulted in Ranger Posey stepping aboard the lead train.

The engineer of the second southbound freight was even more obstinate. A headstrong man, thick through the shoulders, his name was Olaf Gunderson. When Hughes and Aten stopped beside the engine, he moved to block the steps. He stared down at them.

"You've got no business on my train. Stand clear with you."

"Stand clear yourself," Hughes ordered. "We're Texas Rangers and we're on official business. Let my man aboard."

Gunderson grabbed a broad-bladed scoop shovel from the coal bin. He brandished it with both hands. "Your badge ain't no good with me. Try boarding and I'll flatten your ass."

Hughes pulled his pistol. "Drop that shovel and get

he hell out of the way. I won't tell you again."

"Don't make me laugh," Gunderson scoffed. "You ain't gonna shoot anybody."

"That's what you think." Hughes thumbed the hammer on his six-gun. "You're threatening an officer of the law and that's all the excuse I need. Stand aside or I'll fire."

Gunderson muttered a sharp curse. He tossed the shovel into the coal bin and moved back inside the cab. Aten clambered up the steps, drawing his pistol, and covered the engineer. The whistle sounded on the northbound freight.

"Stick with him," Hughes yelled to Aten. "We'll wait for your wire."

Aten nodded. "You'll be hearin' from me, Cap'n."

Hughes hurried off toward the depot. As he disappeared into the silty darkness, the northbound let loose another blast on the whistle, and got under way. The engineer on the lead southbound, as though awaiting a signal, throttled up and slowly pulled out of the rail yards. The second southbound freight lagged behind by about five minutes.

By then, Hughes was standing on the depot platform. Masterson and Bates emerged from the shadows at the far end of the rail yards, cloaked in darkness. They quickly moved across the tracks as the last train got up steam and began rolling. Bates hopped onto the observation platform of the caboose and Masterson flung his suitcase aboard. With a final wave, Bates hefted his bag and pushed through the door of the caboose. The train rumbled off into the night.

Masterson turned to check on Hughes. He saw the Ranger captain round the corner of the depot and walk toward town. As he moved across the tracks, he chuckled softly to himself, wagging his head with amusement. The shell game had worked yet again.

Bates was on his way to join Enoch Rector.

A short while later Masterson completed his report to Stuart. He expressed confidence that the Rangers were no wiser for their evening's sojourn into the rail yards. Stuart walked him to the door, commending him on a job well done. They were one step closer to the fight.

Julie came out of the bedroom. The hour was late, and she had already changed into a nightgown and a filmy peignoir. From the bedroom, she'd overheard most of the conversation, and she saw that Stuart was pleased that everything had gone smoothly. He briskly rubbed his hands together.

"Went off like clockwork," he said jubilantly. "Ed made his getaway without a hitch."

"I'm not in the least surprised," she said, seating herself on the sofa. "I mean, after all, you've kept the Rangers guessing from the very start."

Stuart joined her on the sofa. "Ed and Enoch will be all set when we get there. The ring, the stands, the whole works."

"You're like a little boy with his first Christmas tree. I've never seen you so excited."

"Well, stop and think about it! Nearly a year and a half and we're finally going to pull it off. Finally!"

She touched his arm. "I'm so happy for you, and so proud, too. You've worked so hard."

"You're a trouper yourself," Stuart said, taking her hand. "I know it's been difficult on you at times. Especially the last month or so."

"Oh, I think it was worth it in the end. You promised me a trip to Paris—remember?"

"I always deliver on a promise. We'll do up gay Paree in style."

Stuart's gaze seemed to turn inward. He was silent for a long moment, and then he squeezed her hand. "We'll go to Paris, but I have to disappoint you on the fight. I've decided you should stay here."

"Why?" she said in a hurt voice. "I had my heart set on seeing your motion picture get made. You can't just leave me behind!"

"I've thought about it and I don't see any other choice. There's liable to be trouble at the fight."

"What kind of trouble?"

"The Rangers," Stuart said soberly. "There's no way to predict how they'll react. Mabry is capable of anything."

She searched his eyes. "Are you saying he might arrest you? Or something worse?"

"Come on now, don't start imagining things. I'll be busy enough without worrying about you. I'll feel better knowing you're waiting for me here. There's nothing more to it than that."

She knew he was tempering the truth. He wanted her safe in El Paso, even though he was willing to put himself at risk. Yet she knew as well that no amount of argument would change his mind. He was determined that she would stay behind.

"You're just maddening," she said, snuggling closer. "I won't sleep a wink while you're gone."

Stuart put his arm around her. "I'll bet you have sweet dreams thinking about Paris. We'll have ourselves a whale of a time."

She suppressed the urge to correct him. Their trip to Paris would be the least of her thoughts. Nor would she have sweet dreams.

She would dwell instead on fear, her worst fear. The Texas Rangers.

TWENTY-FIVE

Peter Maher returned from Las Cruces on Thursday. The noon train was on time, and he stepped off the passenger coach with his entourage. A carriage was waiting to take them to the Vendome Hotel.

A wire from Stuart had directed them to arrive no later than early afternoon. At the depot, reading the handbills tacked to the walls, they discovered that ten fight trains would depart that evening. No time had as yet been announced, and the destination was still unknown. The stationmaster told them Stuart planned to make an announcement that afternoon.

Gabe Lawlor, the *New York World* sportswriter, spotted them through the window of the telegraph office. He rushed outside as they moved across the platform. "Mr. Maher!" he yelled. "Could you spare a minute?"

Maher turned at the sound of his name. Three days in Las Cruces appeared to have worked wonders on his physical condition. His eyes were clear, with no visible signs of infection, and he looked in fighting trim. Jack Quinn, Tommy Burns, and Jim Hall surrounded him as though forming a protective barrier. He nodded brusquely to the reporter.

"I'll give you a minute but no more. What is it you want?"

"Your eyes!" Lawlor exclaimed, peering at him. "You're healed!"

"Indeed I am," Maher said. "I told anyone who would listen I'd be up for the fight. And here I am."

"What do you attribute your recovery to?"

"Good clean living, proper training—and no sandstorms."

"That's incredible," Lawlor marveled. "Have you heard the fight's to be held at Fort Hancock?"

"Fort Hancock?" Quinn interrupted. "Where the hell's that?"

"Fifty miles south of here. Actually, the fight will take place across the river in Mexico. The word leaked out a little while ago and it's all over town. I just telegraphed our New York office."

"Did you?" Quinn said. "Have you checked that with Dan Stuart?"

Lawlor brushed it off. "Stuart refuses to make any announcement until this afternoon." His gaze swung back to Maher. "How do you feel about the fight? Are you ready for Fitzsimmons?"

Maher laughed out loud. "I'll put him down for the count. You can bet the bank on it."

Lawlor followed them to the carriage. When they pulled away, he was still scribbling in his notepad. On the ride uptown, Quinn was unusually silent, his brow furrowed in thought. He finally turned to Maher.

"I don't like it," he said. "Fifty miles is too close for comfort."

"Are you talkin' about this Fort Hancock?"

"Yeah, and it don't make sense. Why would Stuart pick a spot so close to Juarez? We'll have those damn Rurales swarmin' all over us."

Maher shrugged. "Jack, I'll not argue the time or the place. All I want is a crack at Fitzsimmons."

"You might have to fight the Rurales to get at him. I've no wish to tangle with the likes of them."

"That goes for me, too," Burns added. "The dirty bastards are quick with a gun, and Stuart promised us nobody'd get shot. What's the deal here?"

"Good question," Quinn said. "I think I'll have a word with Stuart. Let's just see what's what."

Quinn ordered the driver to stop outside the Sheldon Building. He walked into the fight headquarters as the carriage proceeded on to the hotel. Maher seemed unperturbed, idly staring at the crowds jamming the sidewalks. He shook his head.

"I never knew a man to fret on things the way Jack does."

"Well, he gets my vote," Burns said doggedly. "We've got cause to worry, and then some."

Maher grunted. "All I'm worried about is deckin' that bloody Aussie."

"Then you can rest easy, Pete. You're the next champion."

"Tommy, like I told that reporter—take it to the bank."

The freight train rocked to a halt before a windswept depot. Ranger Fred Aten leaned out the side of the cab, staring at a weathered sign over the stationhouse door. He turned to the engineer.

"Why the hell we stoppin' in Langtry?"

"End of the line," Olaf Gunderson said. "Leastways for that load of lumber."

"Langtry?"

"Ain't that what the sign says? Looks like Langtry to me."

Aten jumped off the locomotive. He pulled out his pocketwatch and checked the time, noting that it was almost four in the afternoon. The train had traveled across the barrens of western Texas throughout the night and all day, pausing occasionally to take on water for the boilers. Still groggy from the sixteen-hour ride, Aten labored with a rough mental calculation. They were almost four hundred miles east of El Paso.

A hazy sun dropped steadily toward the horizon. Off to the north, Aten saw endless miles of scrubland, flat as a billiard table. To the south, the terrain dropped off into a steep canyon, and he heard the muted roar of water. His mind suddenly snapped to attention, and he realized that the sound was the rush of the Rio Grande, not five hundred yards away. Across the river was Mexico, the state of Coahuila, and a thousand miles of desert. And not a Rurale within a three-day ride.

To his rear, he heard the babble of voices. He turned and saw forty Mexican laborers scrambling aboard the flatcar. One of them, clearly the *jefe,* was shouting orders and windmilling his arms in wild gestures. Off to the side, Aten saw a man in a business suit, watching with studied interest as the laborers began unloading the lumber. He blinked, then blinked again, hardly able to credit his eyes. He rushed forward.

"You're Edward Bates," he said in a tone of strangled disbelief. "Where the hell'd you come from?"

"Off the caboose," Bates said with a chipper smile. "I hitched a ride."

Bates was brimming with vigor, rested from a

night's sleep in one of the bunks in the caboose. By contrast, Ranger Aten, who had dozed fitfully in the rattling locomotive, was tarred with coal soot and wobbly with fatigue. He scowled at Bates with an addled frown.

"Why you unloadin' this lumber in Langtry?"

"I'll give you three guesses," Bates said with a jaunty grin, "and the first two don't count."

"Gawddamn!" Aten croaked. "You tellin' me this here's it? *Langtry!*"

"Ranger, I have to say, you're a mighty fine guesser."

"You're gonna hold the gawddamn fight here?"

"That's your second guess," Bates quipped. "One more and you've got it."

"I'll be a ring-tailed sonovabitch."

The news seemed to stagger Aten. He wiped soot off his face, and his gaze was abruptly drawn to a ramshackle building west of the depot. He saw an older man, with a snow-white beard and craggy features, standing on a shaded porch. A sign affixed to the roof of the building glinted in the sunlight.

JUDGE ROY BEAN
JUSTICE OF THE PEACE—LAW WEST OF THE PECOS

"Kiss my dusty butt," Aten groaned. "You shore picked the middle of nowhere."

Bates chuckled. "I'll have to admit, it's not El Paso."

"Gen'ral Mabry's gonna shit his pants."

"I wouldn't be at all surprised."

Aten ambled off toward the depot. He tried to phrase the telegram in his mind, and warned himself to keep it simple. Anything clever might get him busted out of the Rangers.

General Woodford Mabry was not a man noted for his humor.

The depot was chaos in motion. By eight that night nearly five thousand people were ganged around the stationhouse, some still waiting to buy tickets. Ten trains were scheduled to depart El Paso at nine o'clock.

Late that afternoon Stuart had posted a notice in the window of the office. The notice informed the public of the train departures that evening, and the destination. Word swept through town and mobs of people descended on the train station, clamoring for tickets. They were dismayed to learn that Langtry was four hundred miles down the line, a fourteen-hour train ride. Thousands nonetheless queued up before the ticket windows.

There were five passenger coaches on each of the trains. The first three trains had one or two Pullman coaches, and some had a limited number of private compartments. Stuart arranged compartments for Fitzsimmons and Maher in separate coaches on the lead train, as well as a compartment for himself, and one for Bat Masterson and George Siler, the referee. On his own, Masterson secured a compartment for Lea and Stovall, with a day-coach seat for Taylor. Seats were reserved for the press corps on the same coach. The trains began boarding shortly after eight o'clock.

Adjutant General Woodford Mabry commandeered a private compartment on the lead train. Three of the Ranger detachments accompanied him, with the men and their captains seated in a day coach. The fourth detachment, under the command of Captain John

Hughes, was ordered to remain behind in El Paso. Mabry was not wholly convinced that Langtry was the final destination, and he was wary of trains being switched or rerouted somewhere down the line. He left behind a reserve unit in the event of further trickery by Stuart.

On the depot platform, as they were boarding, Captain McDonald saw Stovall and his wife, accompanied by Taylor. He watched as they entered the vestibule of the second passenger coach, the same coach occupied by Maher and his entourage. Once again he was reminded of the report on Taylor and Stovall from the sheriff in Fort Worth. Since then, nothing had occurred to further arouse his suspicion of the men. Yet his instincts still told him that all was not as it appeared with the two cattle buyers. Taylor was just too fast with a gun.

All around the depot thousands of people began a mad scramble to board the trains. A wild melee broke out as men jammed the doors, pushing and shoving, and rushed to claim seats. The Rangers bulled a path through the crowd, with Mabry in the center, and escorted him to his compartment. There, the men were instructed to find seats on the coach, and the three captains were ordered to stay behind. When the door closed, Mabry moved to the window, looking out at the mob surging around the long line of trains. He finally turned to Brooks, McDonald, and Rogers.

"I still find it hard to believe," he said. "Why in God's name would Stuart pick Langtry? I'm convinced it's a ruse of some sort."

"What about the telegram?" Brooks commented. "Ranger Aten was pretty clear about Stuart's partner. Why else would Bates get off at Langtry?"

"Captain, we've learned to expect the unexpected

from Stuart. Bates might be nothing more than a decoy."

"I'm not so sure, General," McDonald said. "Once these trains are headed east, Stuart would have a helluva time diverting them anywhere else. And he couldn't turn 'em around this side of Del Rio."

"Maybe so," Rogers ventured. "But there's fifty miles of border between Langtry and Del Rio. He could have another fight location set up anywhere along the way."

"So Governor Ahumada pointed out," Mabry said. "He shares my belief that this might be more of Stuart's subterfuge."

Late that afternoon, Mabry had met with Ahumada in Juarez. When informed of the telegram, Ahumada voiced strong suspicion that Stuart had so openly announced the site of the prizefight. Though he wired the governor of Coahuila, he noted that Rurale patrols would never reach Langtry by tomorrow. Even so, he was not overly concerned that it mattered either way. He thought Stuart's final ploy was yet to be revealed.

"Funny thing about that telegram," Brooks reflected out loud. "Aten didn't say anything about seein' that motion-picture feller, Enoch Rector. Wherever he is, that's where the fight's gonna be."

"Tell you one thing," McDonald said. "Stuart's not fool enough to hold it in Langtry, or anywhere else in Texas. I'm bettin' it'll be somewheres in Mexico."

Mabry appeared unconvinced. "I want guards posted throughout this train. I'm to be advised at the first sign of anything suspicious. That will be all for now, gentlemen."

The Ranger captains filed out of the compartment. In the companionway, they passed Masterson as a woman admitted him to a compartment toward the front of the coach. McDonald got a quick glance before the door closed, noting that the woman was Stovall's wife. He wondered again what business Masterson had with Fort Worth cattle buyers.

"How can we ever thank you?" Lea said as Masterson entered the compartment. "You're such a sweetheart to arrange all this! I dreaded the thought of riding in the day cars."

Masterson grinned like a schoolboy. He nodded to Stovall and Taylor, who were seated across from one another by the window. "Glad to be of service," he said. "No reason you folks shouldn't travel in comfort."

Lea simpered. "Well, it was very considerate of you. Is it true, what people say about Langtry? Four hundred miles?"

"Yeah, I'm afraid so," Masterson affirmed. "We're in for a *long* ride."

"And after the prizefight?" Lea asked. "Will everyone return to El Paso?"

"Everyone connected with the fight will. Whoever wins—Fitzsimmons or Maher—that's where they get paid off. The purse won't be awarded at the fight."

"Why not?"

"Langtry's rough country," Masterson said. "Dan Stuart wouldn't travel with twenty-five thousand in cash. Not even with me and my boys along for security."

"We have to go back, too," Lea said. "We left all our things at the hotel."

"Then we ought to plan a celebration. Maybe we could get together at the Gem. How's that sound?"

"Oh, I think it sounds simply wonderful!"

The train lurched with a jolt. "Got to go," Masterson said, ducking out the door. "This show's about to get on the road."

Lea turned to Stovall and Taylor as the door closed. "Did you hear that?" she said with a gloating smile. "I told you Stuart wouldn't carry all that money on this train. Our hundred thousand will be waiting right here when we come back."

"Tell you the truth," Stovall said, "I'm tickled pink to hear it. I'd hate to pull a job with all these Rangers on board."

Taylor chuckled. "I wanted to see the fight, anyway. I put a bundle on Fitzsimmons."

Outside, Masterson hurried forward in the companionway. As the train gathered speed, he crossed the vestibule into the lead coach. Through the window, he saw that the depot platform was now deserted, and he imagined five thousand people shoehorned onto ten trains. He rapped on the door of Stuart's compartment.

"There you are, Bat," Stuart said, admitting him with a broad smile. "We're finally on our way, my friend. Have you ever seen anything like it?"

"Nobody has," Masterson said sportily. "Not since Moses parted the Red Sea."

Stuart laughed. "I'll settle for the fight of the century."

Their train cleared the edge of the rail yards. Behind, strung out in a caravan, the other trains pulled out at intervals of ten minutes. The last train steamed past the depot shortly before midnight.

The lights of El Paso faded into the distance.

TWENTY-SIX

The landscape was desolate. To the cardinal points of the compass, the terrain was bleak and hostile, filled with sand, rattlesnakes, and thorny chaparral. A brassy sun stood lodged in a sky barren of clouds.

Stuart sat staring out the window of his compartment. During the night, the train had stopped twice to take on water, and they were now some sixty miles west of Langtry. He felt infused with vigor, for he was nearing the end of a long, arduous road. All his efforts had brought him at last to Friday, February 21. The day he would stage the championship match.

The arid countryside whipped past in a blur. His thoughts were on the fight and the motion picture, and what awaited him in Langtry. He felt confident Bates and Rector would have everything in order, but he was still concerned about the Rangers. He knew Woodford Mabry was on the train, and he considered the Ranger leader to be the joker in the deck. No man, particularly a politician, liked to be outsmarted. Or made to look the fool.

There was a knock at the door. When Stuart opened it, the conductor stood waiting in the companionway.

He knuckled the brim of his hat in a salute.

"We're pulling into Sanderson, Mr. Stuart. The trains will stop there to take on water. I'd recommend you let everybody grab a bite to eat. It's the last stop before Langtry."

Stuart consulted his pocketwatch. "One o'clock now," he said. "What time do you estimate we'll arrive?"

"Another two hours, anyway," the conductor informed him. "I'd judge right about three."

"That's cutting it close. We have a lot to accomplish before the sun goes down."

"Yes, sir, I know what you mean. You want to skip the meal break?"

"No, we'd better not," Stuart said. "Give it thirty minutes and then have the engineer blast his whistle. Anybody not on board gets left behind."

"Whatever you say," the conductor acknowledged. "Just a word about the return trip, Mr. Stuart. There's siding for one train at Langtry. What about the others?"

"I understand the nearest turnaround is Del Rio?"

"Yes, sir, that's a fact."

"After the fight, take the other trains there. I suspect most of these people will go on the San Antonio and make connections. Anyone returning to El Paso can catch a later train."

"I'll take care of it, Mr. Stuart."

The train jarred to a halt. Sanderson was a small whistle-stop, with a population of less than a thousand. As Stuart stepped off the coach, he thought the town was about to be overrun. He wondered if there was enough food to feed five thousand people.

Beyond the depot, there was a crude collection of shops and stores along the main street. The merchants, somewhat awestruck, watched from their doorways as ten trains slowly ground to a stop and began disgorging passengers. A floodtide of hungry fight enthusiasts suddenly swarmed over the town.

Fitzsimmons paused at the edge of the business district. A large black bear was chained to the corner of a feed store, warily alert as people rushed along the street. For a man who routinely sparred with an African lion, the temptation was too much to resist. Martin Julian tried to dissuade him, but it was a losing argument. Fitzsimmons approached the bear with his fists cocked.

A crowd stopped to watch the impromptu bout. The bear ran to the end of his chain, then turned with a snarl, fangs bared. Fitzsimmons kept his distance, flicking jabs, and thumped the bear on the nose. The bear roared in outrage, swiping angrily with a massive paw, and Fitzsimmons nimbly dodged the blow. He stung the bear with another jab, playing to the crowd, and stepped back. He raised his arms in victory.

"I'll give Peter Maher even worse before the day's out."

The crowd cheered with delight. Someone at the rear yelled as the laughter dropped off, and pointed toward the depot. They all turned and saw Maher jogging along the railroad tracks, arms pumping, snapping punches in the air as he ran. Jack Quinn and his entourage watched with approval from the shade of the stationhouse. Fitzsimmons looked singularly unimpressed.

"Wait till we get to Langtry," he said with a cocky grin. "He'll have nowhere to run then."

The gibe brought another cheer from the crowd. Fitzsimmons feinted a jab at the bear, and took a bow when the bewildered beast backed up against the wall of the feed store. Julian finally pulled him away, and with Charlie White trailing along, they walked off up the street. A café on the corner was mobbed, but the people waiting outside waved the fighter to the front of the line. He readily shook outstretched hands as he moved through the throng.

On the opposite corner, a milling crowd was gathered outside a Chinese café. Bat Masterson, who was among the first off the train, was seated inside with Lea and Stovall, and Taylor. Woodford Mabry and his Rangers, who had managed to beat the crowd uptown, were seated at nearby tables. Waiters scurried back and forth from the kitchen, trays loaded with steaming dishes, their pigtails flying. The din of noise was constant as customers clamored for attention.

"Good grub," Taylor said around a mouthful of fried rice. "Chinamen know how to cook."

"Yes, but where is the tea?" Lea said, glancing at her empty teacup. "Who ever heard of Chinese food without tea?"

"I'll take care of it." Masterson signaled a waiter who kept on going. "Anyone remember which one waited on us?"

Stovall shook his head. "Damn Chinamen all look alike."

"*Waiter!*"

Masterson flagged a waiter headed for the kitchen with an empty tray. The man rushed on with a harried expression, scarcely glancing at them. Unaccustomed to being ignored, Masterson lunged out of his chair and grabbed the waiter's pigtail. Brought up short, the man was jerked backward and the tray clattered to the floor. The waiter yelped with surprise.

Captain Bill McDonald, who was seated at the next table, rose from his chair. He seized Masterson's arm in an iron grip. "Mind your manners," he ordered. "Let the man go."

Masterson scowled at him. "Would you like to take it up, Captain?"

"I've done took it up," McDonald said in a hard voice.

Mabry and the other Rangers watched with amused interest. Stovall and Taylor froze with their forks in midair, and Lea seemed to hold her breath. Masterson laughed without mirth, and let go of the waiter's pigtail. McDonald released his arm.

"You're the law in Texas," Masterson said with a cold smile. "Come see me sometime in Colorado."

McDonald grinned. "First time I'm there, I'll look you up."

The shrill blast of a train whistle sounded in the distance. Everyone in the café bolted from their chairs, tossing money on the tables, and started for the door. On the street, the Rangers followed along as Masterson and his friends hurried toward the depot. Despite the harsh words with Masterson, McDonald's gaze was drawn to Stovall and Taylor, and the woman. A haunting sense again came over him that something was out of kilter.

He felt deep in his gut that he knew them . . . from somewhere.

The caravan of trains ground to a halt before Langtry. Stuart checked his watch and anxiously marked the time at three-thirty. Through the window, he saw Bates and Rector, waiting outside the depot with Judge Roy Bean. He moved quickly into the companionway.

Langtry lay in squalid isolation beneath a muslin sky. Apart from the depot, there was a general store and eight houses, several constructed from adobe. There were no streets, no electric lights, and the population hovered around fifty. The town's focal point was the Jersey Lilly Saloon.

Enoch Rector rushed forward as Stuart stepped off the train. "Thank God you're here," the film producer said, clasping his hand. "I'd practically lost hope this day would ever come."

"You worry too much," Stuart said genially. "I told you we'd pull it off."

"Yes, yes," Rector agreed. "But now we must hurry, Daniel." He flung an arm toward the sun, slowly retreating westward. "I need the light for my camera. No light, no motion picture!"

"I understand," Stuart said, his gaze shifting to Bates. "Everything in order, Ed?"

"We're ready to go," Bates acknowledged. "Finished the last of the bleachers this morning. All we need are the fighters."

Stuart turned to Roy Bean. "Good to see you again, Judge," he said, offering the older man a warm handshake. "I appreciate all you've done, especially keeping it a secret. You're a man of your word."

" 'Course I am," Bean said in a raspy voice. "You pay me right, I do the job right. One hand washes the other."

"Well, you've certainly kept the lid on Langtry."

"Nobody takes a shat around here 'lessen I say so."

The statement was no idle boast. Judge Roy Bean was a legend along the border, to Texicans as well as Mexicans. A man of cantankerous nature, he had traveled the lower Rio Grande as a trader for some twenty years. In the early 1880's, during the railroad expansion, he followed the tracks westward, operating a tent saloon for rail crews. He finally settled in Langtry in 1882.

The town was then known as Vinegaroon. Bean took it upon himself to rename it Langtry, in homage to Lillie Langtry, a curvaceous English singer he worshiped from afar. His saloon, the Jersey Lilly, was named for her as well, though the spelling was somehow twisted in the process. Soon afterward, he got himself appointed justice of the peace, and the saloon served as his courtroom. He dispensed justice with the whimsical hand of a buccaneer.

On one occasion, when a valued customer of the saloon killed a former Chinese railroad worker, Bean frivolously dismissed the case. He justified the ruling on the grounds that shooting a Chinaman was not specified as illegal under Texas statutes. Everyone in Langtry lived in fear of his capricious mandates, and though he was now seventy years old, he still ruled the town as though it were his personal fiefdom. By his own pronouncement, he was universally known as the Law West of the Pecos.

Mabry, followed by his troop of Rangers, approached the depot. "Judge Bean," he called out, "I am Woodford H. Mabry, Adjutant General of the state of Texas. I demand an explanation for this travesty."

"Simmer down," Bean said in a vociferous tone. "What the hell's a travesty, anyway? You accusin' me of something?"

"I refer to this prizefight," Mabry announced. "You are an officer of the court, and I will not countenance duplicity. How dare you hold this unlawful affair in Langtry!"

Bean leered at him. "You oughta get your head out of your ass, sonny. I ain't holdin' nothin' in Langtry."

"You're not—"Mabry sputtered, thrown off by the

old man's feisty manner. "Explain yourself, sir."

"Let me explain," Stuart interrupted. "I've told you any number of times that the fight will not be held in Texas. You chose to question my word."

"Then why is Judge Bean involved? Explain that, if you will!"

"Follow me."

By now, all the railroad cars were empty and thousands of people were converging on Langtry. Stuart instructed Bat Masterson and his men to form the crowd into orderly lines, and hold them at the edge of town. He then led Mabry and the Rangers across an open plot of ground and past the Jersey Lilly Saloon. Bates and Rector, followed by Judge Roy Bean, trailed along behind.

Beyond the saloon, the terrain abruptly dropped off into an abyss. The ground simply stopped, and the men found themselves staring over the rim of a steep bluff. The wall of the sheer precipice was some two hundred feet high, studded with outcroppings and craggy ledges. Off in the distance, the waters of the Rio Grande snaked through an expanse of flatland. Beyond that was an infinite sea of desert.

Stuart motioned the men forward. He led them down a winding trail, carved from the rocky palisade by generations of Mexicans leading pack animals. The descent was broad and gradual, tramped flat and smooth by the hooves of burros loaded with trade goods. At the bottom of the cliff, in the shadow of the looming rim, was a beach that fronted the river. And farther along, a bridge.

The bridge itself was a feat of engineering. Small boats had been butted together to form pontoons, and over the top a wide walkway had been constructed, secured by heavy timbers. The purpose of the trainloads of lumber rolling out of El Paso was now evident; the bridge was solid and sturdy, and looked like it would last a century. The men trooped across the planked walkway in bemused silence, the rushing waters of the river beneath their feet. Their eyes were fixed on the spectacle directly ahead.

The bridge ended on a broad sandbar near the opposite shore. The patch of ground was some five hundred yards in length and roughly half that in width. In the center of the sandbar stood a boxing ring and spectator stands suitable for seating upwards of five thousand people. Off to one side, west of the ring, a boxlike shelter housed the bulky camera equipment. Enoch Rector's technical assistants watched as the men stepped off the the bridge.

"General Mabry," Stuart said, spreading his arms. "You are now standing in the state of Coahuila— Mexico."

"Are we?" Mabry said skeptically. "The Rio Grande has many twists and turns, Mr. Stuart. For all I know, we're still in Texas."

"Judge Bean," Stuart beamed. "Would you mind clarifying that point for the General?"

Bean swiped at his snow-white beard. "Survey was done more'n twenty years ago," he cackled. "Got an official signed-and-sealed copy up at the saloon. You've been outslicked, Gen'ral. This here's Mexico."

Mabry's features went beet-red, his eyes angry slits. The Rangers looked from him to Stuart, their mouths agape with consternation. McDonald quickly turned away, smothering a laugh with a thorny hand. He thought he'd been right all along.

Dan Stuart had led them on a merry chase. All the way to hell and gone. A sandbar in Mexico.

TWENTY-SEVEN

The last of the crowd filed down the rocky bluff. Masterson's men kept them moving along in orderly fashion, herding them across the bridge that spanned the Rio Grande. By five o'clock, the stands were packed with eager spectators.

Mabry refused to be a part of the spectacle. The Ranger captains knew better than to argue, and led their men back up the steep trail. At the top, after a brief conference with McDonald, Mabry was persuaded that their legal position would not be compromised on the Texas side of the river. He allowed the men to watch from the rim of the cliff.

Masterson stationed men around the four sides of the ring. They stood facing the spectator stands, their holstered pistols in plain view, prepared to quell any disturbance. He arranged seats in the front row for Lea, Stovall, and Taylor, close beside Judge Roy Bean. Lea was excited, having never seen a prizefight, and watched the preparations with rapt interest. Judge Bean, despite his years, still had an eye for the ladies.

"Mighty big day," he said in his most engaging manner. "Who you bettin' on, missy?"

All around them men were placing personal wagers. Lea shook her head. "I'm afraid this is my first prizefight," she said. "But if I bet, I think I would have to favor Fitzsimmons."

"I'm for Maher, myself," Bean said, fluffing his snowy beard. "Any man's got a score to settle, that's the man for me. He's gonna walk away with it."

"Perhaps you're right," Lea conceded. "I really don't know that much about the sport."

"Looka there!" Bean pointed toward the opposite side of the ring. "We're fixin' to see history made here today. A goldurn motion picture right in my own back yard. Don't that beat all?"

Enoch Rector's film operation was situated west of the boxing ring. The wooden structure was raised above the stands, and afforded a clear view of the action. The westerly sun, flooding across the sandbar, provided ample light for the Kinetoscope camera. Rector and his assistants were visible through a large opening in the front of the structure. He peered out, searching for Stuart, and raised his arm overhead. His signal indicated that the Kinetoscope was ready to roll.

Stuart, who was standing at ringside, acknowledged the signal with a wave. He turned to George Siler, the referee. "Time to get on with it, George. Everything set?"

"Dan, I'm nervous as a whore in church," Siler said with a fleeting smile. "I just hope I don't embarrass anybody . . . especially myself."

"All you have to remember is that you're the boss once the fight starts. You'll do fine."

Siler mounted the steps to the ring. Stuart walked to a table by the apron, where Bert Sneed of the *New Orleans Times-Democrat* was seated in a chair. Sneed was to act as the official timekeeper, controlling the flow of the bout with the second-hand on his pocket-watch and a large gong. Stuart spoke with him briefly, then looked off toward the southern edge of the sand-bar. He pumped his arm in a rapid motion.

Ed Bates was waiting beside a large, conical tent. He threw back the flap and Fitzsimmons emerged, fol-lowed by Martin Julian and his handlers. The fighter was attired in blue boxing tights and a red and blue belt, embroidered with a kangaroo on the traditional shield of Australia. The crowd welcomed him with a spontaneous roar as he strode across the sandbar and climbed into the ring. He raised his arms high over-head with a broad smile.

To the north, the flap on another tent whipped open. Maher stepped into the sunlight, trailed by Jack Quinn and his cornermen. He wore the Irish colors, green tights and a white belt, emblazoned with a silver harp on a green shamrock. The spectators greeted him with a rousing ovation, cheering while he made his way forward and ducked through the ropes. He shuf-fled around the ring with a look of stoic intensity.

Stuart took a seat at the timekeeper's table. In the ring, Siler supervised as the fighters were fitted with lightly padded leather gloves. After Julian and Quinn inspected the gloves, nodding their satisfaction, Siler moved to the center of the ring. Bert Sneed clanged the bell for silence.

"Your attention pul-eez?" Siler's voice carried over the sandbar. "A fight to the finish between Ruby Rob Fitzsimmons and Peter Maher for the heavyweight championship of the world. May the best man win!"

Enoch Rector rolled the camera as Siler brought the fighters and their handlers to the center of the ring. Fitzsimmons and Maher, their features impassive, stood locked in a staring contest. Siler looked from one to the other.

"You're to obey my instructions at all times," he said in a forceful tone. "This bout will be conducted under the Marquis of Queensberry rules. Either man who violates those rules will be disqualified and declared the loser. Let's have a fair fight, gentlemen. Good luck to you both."

The fighters touched gloves and Siler motioned them back to their corners. He glanced quickly at Stuart, then nodded to the timekeeper. A hush settled over the spectators as the cornermen crawled through the ropes. Sneed rang the bell.

Fitzsimmons sprang from his corner. He rushed forward eager for the scrap, his pale blue eyes glinting in the sun. Maher lumbered out, head tucked low behind cocked fists, his arms rippling with muscle. There was no hesitation, no sparring to feel the other man out. Maher launched a roundhouse right and Fitzsimmons slipped the blow, countering with a sharp left-right combination. They clinched, wrestling about with brute strength, and Siler ordered them to break. Before he could separate them, Maher delivered a hard right to the jaw.

"Foul!" Julian screamed from the corner. "Hitting in a clinch. Foul!"

Siler stepped between the fighters. He wagged a finger at Maher. "Do that again and you're disqualified. Keep it clean."

"Leave it be," Fitzsimmons declared, thumping his gloves together. "I'll lay him out anyhow."

They again squared off, and Fitzsimmons flicked a jab. Maher bobbed low, stepping inside, and planted a hard right to the ribs. Fitzsimmons grappled him into a clinch, and the referee hastily broke them apart.

Before Fitzsimmons could retreat, Maher waded in, landing a right to the body and a sizzling left hook to the mouth. For an instant, Fitzsimmons appeared dazed, blood spurting from a split lip, and he fell into a clinch. Siler moved to separate them.

From ringside, Stuart saw the determination on Maher's face and heard the pulsing chant of the spectators. Fitzsimmons seemed to recover, and Stuart watched as the fighters went toe-to-toe in the middle of the ring. Maher pounded away, his arms a blur of motion, driving Fitzsimmons across the mat and into the ropes. The crowd smelled blood, sensed that Fitzsimmons was on the verge of going down, and urged Maher to finish it. Then, with a nifty sidestep, Fitzsimmons slid off the ropes and dodged a murderous right cross. He backpedaled into the open ring.

Maher came after him. Fitzsimmons bobbed and weaved, slipping blows, rolling with the punches, evading damage with nimble footwork. He circled, forcing Maher to chase him, deftly avoiding being drawn into a clinch. As they moved again to the center of the ring, Maher closed the gap, feinting with his right, and fired a splintering left hook. Fitzsimmons stepped aside, leaving Maher off balance, and planted his feet. He loosed a sledgehammer right cross.

Maher went down as though clubbed by a pickaxe. He rolled onto his side as Siler began the count, his eyes vacant. Quinn and Burns bellowed at him from the corner, exhorting him to get up. The count went on, Siler's arm rising and falling, and Maher levered himself onto his hands and knees. On the count of eight, he stared into the fireball of the sun, struggling to rise, and then the last thread of consciousness slipped away. He dropped headlong to the canvas.

"Ten!" Siler shouted. *"And you're out!"*

The fight of the century was over in one minute
and forty-three seconds of the first round. Fitzsimmons danced around the ring as though on springs,
jubilantly waving his arms in victory. Five thousand
spectators rose to their feet in a thunderous roar, their
cheers reverberating off the walls of the craggy bluff.
The sound echoed for miles along the waters of the
Rio Grande.

Stuart sat stunned, unable to credit it. His eyes went
from Fitzsimmons to Maher and then back again. He
realized he was watching the new heavyweight champion of the world.

He wondered if Enoch Rector had got the knockout
on film.

Langtry was a scene of bedlam. After the fight, the
spectators ascended the twisting path up the rocky es-
carpment overlooking the river. Thousands of people
milled about the town, awaiting trains that would arrive later that night. Their talk centered on the sud-
denness of the championship bout.

Some of them were disgruntled, carping to anyone
who would listen. They had traveled from far places,
and waited weeks for the fight, only to have it end in
the first round. To a large extent, they felt cheated,
robbed of seeing the usual brawl that lasted twenty or
thirty rounds. But in the main, the crowd was awestruck, ecstatic that they had witnessed a moment in
history. They knew the fight was one for the record
books. A piece of boxing legend.

Stuart was no less elated. The bloody slugfest had
been captured in its entirety by Enoch Rector on Kinetoscope. Though truncated, less than four minutes
from the referee's instructions to Fitzsimmons's victory dance, the fight would be celebrated in the annals

of the ring. The knockout, an instant of dramatic ferocity, would play to packed houses in vaudeville theaters across the country. America would wait in line to watch the first motion picture of a championship bout.

The Jersey Lilly Saloon was mobbed with thirsty fight enthusiasts. Roy Bean was charging two dollars a shot, and fast depleting the inventory in his stockroom. Some of the locals had been pressed into service as bartenders, and Bean excused himself when Stuart signaled to him from the door. Outside, they walked to the rear of the saloon, the only vacant spot in town. Stuart extended an envelope.

"Five thousand," he said with a cordial smile. "Your last payment, and well earned, Judge. We couldn't have done it without you."

"Damn tootin', you couldn't," Bean said, quickly counting the money. "Nobody 'sides me would've had the brass to hornswoggle them Rangers."

Stuart had developed a fondness for the old reprobate. "Judge, you're one of a kind," he said, offering a handshake. "It's been a pleasure doing business with you."

Bean grinned slyly. "You ever get the notion to put on another prizefight, come see me. We'll do 'er all over again."

"I'll certainly keep it in mind, Judge."

Twilight was settling over the land as they parted. Stuart walked across to the depot, where his train for El Paso stood waiting on the tracks. Mabry and the Ranger captains were huddled in conversation, and they looked around as he stepped onto the platform. Mabry motioned to him, moving forward with McDonald.

"Very cleverly done," Mabry said in a grudging

manner. "You have a knack for duplicity, Mr. Stuart."

Stuart ignored the gibe. "Will you be returning to El Paso with us?"

"No, as a matter of fact, I'll await the next train to Austin. I plan to take the Rangers with me. All, that is, except Captain McDonald."

"Oh?"

"I'm not through with you yet," Mabry said. "Captain McDonald carries a personal letter from me to Governor Ahumada. I've asked the governor to press charges, and request your extradition to Mexico. I suggest you obtain legal counsel."

"Perhaps I will," Stuart remarked. "Although I have no plans to visit Juarez, and I'll be leaving El Paso within the week. So it's probably a moot point."

"A week is more than enough time, Mr. Stuart. I've instructed Captain McDonald to arrest you the moment Governor Ahumada prefers charges."

Stuart glanced at McDonald. The Ranger turned his head slightly, lowering one eyelid in an imperceptible wink. Mabry was unaware of the byplay, but Stuart got the message. McDonald considered it dirty pool, and he intended to ignore the order. He was, in the end, a friend in the enemy camp.

"Are you a betting man, General?" Stuart asked, looking back at Mabry. "I'll wager I never see the inside of a Mexican jail. Governor Ahumada knows the game's over—even if you don't."

"We'll see about that, Mr. Stuart."

"Have a good trip home, General."

Stuart walked toward the train. Fitzsimmons and Maher stood talking with Bat Masterson beside the lead passenger coach. Quinn and Julian, who normally stared daggers at one another, were engaged in lighthearted conversation. From the looks of things, the fight had healed many old wounds.

"You pack a solid punch," Fitzsimmons was saying to Maher. "Three or four times, you had me on my heels. I thought I was a goner."

"Turns out I was the goner," Maher said with a rueful smile. "You're a slick one, Fitz, and there's the God's honest truth. I never knew what hit me."

Fitzsimmons, magnanimous in victory, waved it off. "And a lucky punch it was, Peter. I got you before you got me."

All ears, the reporters gathered around them busily jotted down their words for posterity. The train whistle tooted three long blasts, and the conductor yelled, *"All aboard!"* The fighters and their managers, the newshounds and Masterson's gunmen, separated and hurried to their respective cars. Bates waited for Stuart in the vestibule of the lead coach. Stuart took a last look at Langtry.

"I doubt we'll ever forget this place, Ed. We wrote a piece of history today."

Lea Osburn would have endorsed the sentiment. Yet her mind had already skipped ahead to tomorrow, and a safe stuffed with cash in El Paso. She was seated with Stovall and Taylor in their private compartment. As the train got under way, her eyes suddenly brightened, and she clapped her hands. She pointed to the Rangers on the depot platform.

"Look! Look!" she squealed. "The Rangers are staying behind. We're rid of them!"

Stovall and Taylor stared back as the train chugged out of Langtry. The Rangers stood bunched behind Woodford Mabry, throngs of people swirling around them. Taylor brayed a wild laugh.

"Goddamn, it's our lucky day! Did you ever see such a pretty sight?"

"Never," Lea said, bubbling with excitement. "What a load off my mind."

Stovall grinned. "Get your hundred thousand out, Dan Stuart. Here we come."

"Yes," Lea added happily. "With bells on."

The train rolled westward into deepening night.

TWENTY-EIGHT

Rose Fitzsimmons and baby Rob were waiting outside the stationhouse. With them were Julie and Walt Wheelock, and a crowd gathered to welcome the new heavyweight champion. The train pulled into El Paso shortly after ten on Saturday morning.

Stuart and Fitzsimmons were the first to step off the train. Julie hurried across the platform and threw herself into Stuart's arms. Fitzsimmons gathered baby Rob and Rose in a bear bug, and she planted a kiss full on his mouth. The reporters ganged around, their cameramen jostling for position. They began shouting questions.

"Mrs. Fitzsimmons!" yelled the correspondent from the *San Francisco Examiner*. "How do you feel about Ruby Rob winning the championship?"

"Why, I feel wonderful," Rose said happily. "I knew he'd bring home the crown in fine fashion. My Bob's the best there is."

"Do you think he would have fared as well against Gentleman Jim Corbett?"

"Mr. Corbett didn't act like a *gentleman* toward my husband. Not with all those nasty things he said to you boys in the papers. I want Bob to knock his block off."

"How about it, Fitz?" asked Gabe Lawlor of the *New York World*. "Would you take on Gentleman Jim?"

"Tell Corbett to get a reputation," Fitzsimmons declared with a broad grin. "He's an actor these days, too high-and-mighty for the ring. He'll have to earn a shot at the title."

Peter Maher slipped around the edge of the crowd. He was old news, and the reporters were no longer interested in his opinion. With Quinn and his handlers, he rounded the corner of the depot and headed toward the hotel. Captain McDonald watched him slink away, and thought there was nothing sadder than a pug who had been drubbed so soundly. He wondered if Maher would ever fight again.

Ferris Johnson, the telegrapher, appeared with a wire for McDonald. The message was from Mabry, stressing the urgency of an immediate conference with Governor Ahumada. In the wire, Mabry noted that he had also telegraphed Captain John Hughes, relieving him of further duty in El Paso. Johnson confirmed that Hughes and his troop of Rangers had ridden out earlier that morning, bound for their regular post in Ysleta, ten miles south of town. McDonald considered it a good omen, for he was now the only Ranger responsible for Dan Stuart. He walked toward the bridge to Juarez.

The press was still eager for quotes. "Mr. Stuart!" called out the sportswriter for the *Dallas Morning News*. "Will you promote another prizefight?"

"I think not," Stuart said with a wry smile. "From now on, I'll stick with poker. The cards are more predictable."

There was an appreciative burst of laughter. Fred Martin of the *New York Times* waved his notepad. "What about a Fitzsimmons–Corbett match?" he inquired. "Would that change your mind?"

Stuart looked intrigued. "I might consider that at some point in time. Assuming we could get Gentleman Jim off the stage and into a ring."

"You'd need a miracle," Fitzsimmons scoffed loudly. "The bugger's afraid I'll spoil his matinee-idol looks. And I would!"

The cameramen got the new champion to pose for a photo with Rose and baby Rob. Afterward, Stuart made arrangements with Fitzsimmons to meet at the office at one o'clock. There, with the appropriate ceremony and the press in attendance, he would present the prize purse of $25,000. As the reporters followed Fitzsimmons to a waiting carriage, he then turned to Bat Masterson. Julie clung to his arm as though she might never let go.

"Bat, you've done a fine job," he said cordially. "Come by the office a little before one and we'll settle accounts. I think you deserve a bonus."

"Well, now, that's mighty good of you, Dan. I'm obliged." Masterson motioned to his men, who were standing nearby. "Any need to bring the boys along when you pay off Fitz? We'll be glad to look after things."

"No, let them get some rest," Stuart said. "With the press there, we won't require security. I expect quite a crowd."

Lea walked past with Stovall and Taylor. She caught Masterson's eye and silently mouthed the words, "See you later." He nodded with a sly grin, and watched them cross the depot platform. As they disappeared into the crowd, he turned to his men, wondering how he could get her alone tonight. He thought there had to be a way to ditch her husband.

On the street, Lea bypassed the carriages for hire. She led Stovall and Taylor uptown at a brisk pace. "Did you hear that?" she said. "Stuart's paying off Fitzsimmons at one o'clock. We'll have to move fast."

"Why?" Taylor said quizzically. "What's the big rush?"

"Get your ears unplugged," Stovall muttered. "You want Fitzsimmons to walk away with twenty-five thousand of *our* money? Not on your life!"

"We'll hit them at noon," Lea interjected, glancing at Taylor. "Stony, find a livery stable and hire their three best horses. Bring them around back of the hotel."

"What are you two gonna do?"

"I have to change clothes," Lea told him. "I've never yet pulled a job wearing a dress. Today's not the day to start."

Stovall nodded. "Stony and me have got to change duds, too. A suit and tie don't work for the trail."

"All the more reason to hurry."

They marched off in the direction of town.

Stuart emerged from the Vendome Hotel shortly before noon. He was bathed and shaved, wearing a fresh suit for the press conference. On the way out the door, he'd promised Julie that the steady diet of all work and no play was about to end. A party was planned that night to celebrate Fitzsimmons's victory, and the completion of the motion picture. After that, he was all hers.

Outside, he crossed the street and walked toward the Sheldon Building. As he entered the office, three riders reined their horses in at the curb. Stovall and Taylor dismounted, leaving their horses snubbed to a hitch rack. Lea stepped out of the saddle, still holding her reins, and pretended to check the cinch on her horse. She wore a long duster, with pants and boots, her hair stuffed inside a low-crowned hat. Her eyes swept the street.

Stovall and Taylor crossed the sidewalk. They were dressed in range gear, and as they came through the door, they pulled their guns. Wheelock's features blanched, and he rose from behind his desk, staring at them. Stuart and Bates saw the look on his face, and turned to find themselves covered by two armed men. Stovall wagged the snout of his pistol.

"This here's a holdup," he said. "Don't try anything foolish."

Stuart sensed a familiarity about the men. But he was so astounded that he couldn't place them. "We're not armed," he said, fanning his jacket aside. "What do you want?"

Stovall nodded toward the rear of the room. "Let's get that safe open."

"You're out of luck," Stuart said, running a bluff. "We deposited the fight proceeds in the bank."

"Bullshit!" Taylor thumbed the hammer on his Colt. "Open 'er up and be damn fast about it. No more monkey business."

"You can't blame a man for trying. Just take it easy with those guns."

Stovall followed him to the safe. Stuart spun the combination knob left, then right, then left again. He cranked the handle and swung open the massive doors. The top shelf was piled high with stacks of cash.

"Well, looky here!" Stovall fished two gunnysacks

from inside his coat, and tossed them to Stuart. "Fill 'em up, and move it right along. We haven't got all day."

Stuart began filling the gunnysacks.

Captain Bill McDonald crossed to the north side of the street. As he approached the Gem Variety Theater, Masterson came through the door. They exchanged a glance, and Masterson started to turn away. Neither of them had forgotten the incident with the Chinese waiter.

"Hold on," McDonald said. "I'm on my way to see Stuart. You'll be interested in the news."

Masterson looked around. "I'm headed there myself. What's your news?"

"I've just come from talking with Governor Ahumada. He's not going to press charges against Stuart."

"Why not?"

"The governor's a reasonable man," McDonald said. "I explained the situation to him, and he finally saw the light. It'd take a year in court to get Stuart extradited to Mexico."

"I must have heard wrong," Masterson said with a strange expression. "Sounds like you talked him out of it."

"Why would I do a thing like that? I just explained the facts."

"General Mabry's liable to roast you over the coals."

"I suspect we've heard the last of it. Him and Ahumada don't talk too regular."

Masterson appeared bemused. "Maybe I've misjudged you, Captain. Why go out on a limb for Dan Stuart?"

"Those are your words, not mine. I was just doing my duty."

The door to the fight headquarters flew open. Two men stepped out, their guns drawn, each of them carrying a bulky gunnysack. Masterson recognized Stovall and Taylor, and he stopped, too startled to speak. McDonald recognized them as well, and suddenly it all came together in his mind. He saw another man, slighter in build, vault into the saddle of a horse at curbside. The duster the man wore triggered the memory that had eluded him the past few weeks. They were the bank robbers known to every peace officer in Texas. The gang that had outwitted the Rangers for over two years.

A chair exploded through the window of the office. *"Robbers!"* Stuart bellowed from inside. *"Police! Police!"*

"Halt!" McDonald commanded. "Drop your guns!"

All in an instant, McDonald and Masterson drew their pistols. Stovall leaped the curb, but Taylor twisted around, firing on the run. The shot went wild, and McDonald returned fire, with Masterson only a beat behind. Taylor howled, a bloody furrow seared over the top of his left hand, and dropped the gunnysack. He jumped off the sidewalk as Stovall swung aboard his horse. McDonald extended his six-gun for an aimed shot.

Lea opened fire. She held her horse steady, pistol at arm's length, and thumbed off five shots in a staccato roar. A slug pocked the sleeve of McDonald's coat, and another sent Masterson's hat spinning in the air. The third buzzed past Masterson's ear, and the fourth nicked McDonald high on his right arm. Even as the last shot was fired, they dove for cover and flattened themselves on the sidewalk. The slug dusted them with powdered concrete.

The gang reined their horses hard away from the curb. As Lea spun around, her hat flew off and her long, flaxen hair tumbled down over her shoulders. For a moment, her face framed in the noonday sun, there was no mistaking her features. Then she switched hands, winging a final shot with her other pistol, and gigged her horse after Stovall and Taylor. The gang clattered off west along the street.

McDonald and Masterson slowly got to their feet. They stared after the retreating horses in dumb silence, their jaws unhinged with disbelief. A moment elapsed before McDonald collected his wits. "Tell me," he said hollowly, "wasn't that your lady friend?"

Masterson rolled his eyes. "I wouldn't believe it if she hadn't almost killed me."

"Helluva note," McDonald mumbled. "Got ourselves outshot by a woman."

"Captain, I won't tell anybody if you don't."

"Bat, you've got yourself a deal."

They agreed never to speak of it again.

Ten miles west of town Lea reined to a halt. Stovall and Taylor skidded to a stop beside her. Their horses were breathing hard from the long gallop.

Before them, a lazy bend in the Rio Grande led northward. To the south, directly across the river, lay the barrens of Mexico. On the opposite shore to the west was New Mexico Territory.

"Thought all them Rangers was gone," Taylor said, his left hand crusted with blood. "Where the hell'd that McDonald come from?"

"How about Masterson?" Stovall chimed in hotly. "The sorry bastard tried to shoot us."

"Yeah," Taylor added. "And after all we done for him."

Stovall glowered around at Lea. "Why didn't you kill him? You had the chance."

"Don't push it, Earl," Lea warned. "We got away with our skins and the money. Let's leave it at that."

"Some big payday!" Stovall whacked the gunnysack tied to his saddlehorn. "We're lucky if there's fifty thousand in there."

Lea shrugged. "That's enough to hold us for a while. We'll get along."

"What about the Rangers?" Taylor asked. "You reckon they'll sniff out our trail?"

" 'Course they will," Stovall said. "We can't never go back to Fort Worth. They'll look there first thing."

"So where do we go?"

"Mexico," Lea said, staring across the river. "We've worn out our welcome in Texas. Time for a change of scenery."

Stovall groaned. "Nothin' in Mexico but chili peppers and scorpions. How about someplace else?"

"The Rangers aren't allowed to operate south of the border. We'll be safe there."

"How long you plannin' to stay?"

"Until we're in the clear. You let me worry about that, sugar."

"Lea's got the right idea," Taylor said, nodding to himself. "Fifty thousand ought to go a long way in Mexico. We could live high on the hog."

"Yeah, I suppose," Stovall agreed with a heavy sigh. "Tell you one thing for damn sure. From now on, let's stick to banks. Lots easier to earn a livin'."

"Don't worry," Lea said with a quick smile. "We've robbed our last prizefight."

They forded the river into Mexico. As they rode

south, Lea thought back over their time in El Paso. There were many things she regretted, particularly missing the payday of a lifetime. But she was none-theless gladdened by her faith in Dan Stuart.

In the end, he hadn't let her down.

The victory party was held in the hotel ballroom. There was a lavish buffet supper and tubs of iced champagne. A quartet of musicians played sprightly tunes.

By seven that evening, the ballroom was packed with boisterous well-wishers. The press corps turned out en masse, along with the mayor and members of the city council. Bates and Wheelock were there, chat-ting with Enoch Rector and his assistants about the motion picture. Bat Masterson delivered apologies for his new friend and fellow shootist, Bill McDonald. The Ranger captain was off organizing pursuit of the robbers.

Ruby Rob Fitzsimmons, the guest of honor, arrived with Rose shortly after seven. They were greeted by Stuart, the host of the affair, and Julie, who looked radiant in a mauve silk gown and pearl choker. Fitz-simmons commiserated with Stuart about the holdup, though he'd been paid in full from the sack of cash dropped by the robbers. Stuart was relatively sanguine about the loss of $50,000, happy to have escaped with his life. The motion picture, he quipped, would ade-quately compensate for the inconvenience.

The room hummed with talk of the fight. The guests sought out Fitzsimmons, congratulating him all over again for the remarkable first-round knockout. There was conversation as well about the robbery, what seemed a finale to the most bizarre chapter in the annals of the ring. The sportswriters were as intrigued with Masterson as they were the new champion, for he had acquitted himself well in the shootout with the bandits. For his part, Masterson feigned modesty and studiously kept his pact with Captain Bill McDonald. He made no mention of the latest Annie Oakley, the woman otherwise known as Lea.

After everyone had sampled the buffet, Stuart signaled the musicians. They segued into an overture as he halted before them and turned to face the crowd. He raised his champagne glass.

"A toast," he said with a proud smile. "To the man of the hour and the new heavyweight champion of the world—Bob Fitzsimmons!"

"Speech! Speech!" the crowd chanted. "Let's hear from Fitz!"

"I've a toast of my own," Fitzsimmons announced, hoisting his champagne glass. "Here's to a sporting man who pulled it off when the Texas Rangers and the Mexican Rurales—and even the United States government—stood against him. Here's to Dan Stuart!"

The crowd broke out in wild applause. Stuart clinked glasses with Fitzsimmons, and they quaffed their champagne to cheers of mutual admiration. After the hubbub abated, Stuart left Fitzsimmons and Rose surrounded by sportswriters. He collected Julie, who gave him a dazzling smile and quick kiss on the cheek. They crossed the room to Enoch Rector.

"We've done it," Stuart said vigorously. "The fight of the century, and we got it on film. I think we should congratulate ourselves."

Rector uttered a jolly laugh. "A glorious day, Daniel. We're going to be rich and famous. Imagine!"

"Enoch, I see a whole new career—motion pictures."

"Yes, yes, there's no end to the possibilities. Do you have another project in mind?"

Stuart grinned. "We've only just begun."

EPILOGUE

Captain Bill McDonald was frustrated in his quest. The gang of robbers so ably led by a woman seemingly vanished on February 22, 1896. He searched Texas from the Rio Grande to the Red, and worked with an artist to create wanted dodgers that were plastered across the state. Yet the robbers never pulled another job, and for all practical purposes, he was chasing a phantom. In later years, among old friends and always in confidence, he spoke of the woman who could shoot the wings off a horsefly, in flight. He considered her the deadliest *pistolero* of all the outlaws he'd known in a long and distinguished career as a peace officer. In private moments, he often thought she would have made a helluva Texas Ranger.

Lea Osburn never returned from Mexico. She convinced Earl Stovall and Stony Taylor to invest their loot from the prizefight robbery in a cattle ranch. They bought a spread in the state of Chihuahua, and settled down to make a life for themselves. With Lea's canny gift for business and finance, and the men's savvy for cows, they soon became cattle barons. Lea and Earl were married in the fall of 1896, and raised a family of four girls and three boys. Stony Taylor ultimately found a hot-blooded señorita who thought he was brilliant, and sired ten children. Their hacienda on the Rio Corralitos became a showplace, and Governor Miguel Ahumada was their frequent guest. No one ever suspected that the *noter americano* ranchers were once the bane of the Texas Rangers.

Bat Masterson never forgot the woman who had so thoroughly duped him in El Paso. For years, she was the subject of sweet dreams, and an occasional nightmare, and either way, he invariably awoke in a lathered sweat. From his experience with the Fitzsimmons–Maher bout, he became intrigued by the sports world in general, and began to dabble in newspaper writing. In 1902, he moved to New York City, where he quickly caught on as the lead sportswriter for the *Morning Telegraph.* President Theodore Roosevelt appointed him a deputy U.S. Marshal, and over the next two decades he was showered with honors for his role in winning the West. He died of a heart attack in 1921, working at his desk on an article that used sports as a metaphor for life. The last words out of his typewriter were: "I have observed that we all get about the same amount of ice. The rich get it in the summer and the poor get it in the winter."

Dan Stuart went on to usher boxing into the modern era. In 1896, shortly after the Fitzsimmons–Maher bout, he mounted a lobbying campaign with officials in Nevada. Late that year, the state legislature voted into law a bill that legalized prizefighting. Stuart traveled to New York where he signed Gentleman Jim Corbett and Ruby Rob Fitzsimmons for a championship match, to be held St. Patrick's Day, 1897. Corbett was lured off the Broadway stage and into the ring by pride and vanity, and accusations in the press that he feared Fitzsimmons. He accepted the challenge to his manhood.

In early 1897, Stuart selected Carson City, Nevada, as the site for the match. He brought in a hundred carpenters and a half-million feet of lumber, and built an outdoor amphitheater based on ancient Rome's Colosseum. On March 17, St. Patrick's Day, twenty thousand people filled the stands, with gate receipts of $400,000. Enoch Rector staged a far more sophisticated motion picture production, with *three* Kinetoscope cameras and film exposed at twenty-four frames a second. Bat Masterson was chief of security, and George Siler again served as referee. For the first time in boxing history, a wife worked her husband's corner. Rose Fitzsimmons acted as one of Ruby Rob's seconds.

The opening bell for the long-awaited battle sounded at the stroke of noon. For the first five rounds, Corbett gave Fitzsimmons a lesson in the art of "scientific" boxing. In the sixth Corbett landed a smashing left hook and dropped the champion to the canvas. Fitzsimmons got to his feet at the count of nine, groggy but game, and displayed remarkable recuperative powers. Corbett's failure to put him away proved the turning point of the fight, and Fitzsimmons launched an assault to the body. By the fourteenth round, Corbett was weary, his reflexes slowed by the body blows, and Fitzsimmons hammered him with a left just below the heart. Corbett went down, his face ashen, gulping for air and crawling about the ring on his knees. Then, his strength sapped, he collapsed to the floor and Siler counted him out. A bloodied Fitzsimmons was declared the undisputed champion of the world.

The blow that finished the fight became a piece of

boxing lore. A short, ripping left, delivered to the sternum, the punch all but paralyzed Corbett's lungs and resulted in the first knockout of his career. Sportswriters promptly dubbed it the "solar plexus punch," and it became one of the most legendary knockouts of all time. Enoch Rector captured the "solar plexus punch" on film and the motion picture grossed more than a million dollars at theaters across the country. Dan Stuart, widely acclaimed as the reigning impresario of the sport, declared it "the greatest contest in ring history." Then, with no worlds left to conquer, he retired from the fight game. He devoted the balance of his life to development of the motion picture industry.

Professional boxing ultimately achieved legitimate status with the onset of World War I. In 1917, the government adopted boxing as a means of quickly conditioning untrained civilians for the rigorous life of a soldier. Religious organizations, in a spirit of national solidarity, supported the effort and withdrew their objections to prizefighting. A war, brutality at its worst, brought about the acceptance of boxing as a reputable sport.

Dan Stuart would have appreciated the irony.

THE TRAIL DRIVE SERIES
by Ralph Compton

From St. Martin's Paperbacks

The only riches Texas had left after the Civil War were five million maverick longhorns and the brains, brawn and boldness to drive them north to where the money was. Now, Ralph Compton brings this violent and magnificent time to life in an extraordinary epic series based on the history-blazing trail drives.

THE GOODNIGHT TRAIL (BOOK 1)
_____ 92815-7 $5.99 U.S./$7.99 Can.

THE WESTERN TRAIL (BOOK 2)
_____ 92901-3 $5.99 U.S./$7.99 Can.

THE CHISOLM TRAIL (BOOK 3)
_____ 92953-6 $5.99 U.S./$7.99 Can.

THE BANDERA TRAIL (BOOK 4)
_____ 95143-4 $5.99 U.S./$7.99 Can.

THE CALIFORNIA TRAIL (BOOK 5)
_____ 95169-8 $5.99 U.S./$7.99 Can.

THE SHAWNEE TRAIL (BOOK 6)
_____ 95241-4 $5.99 U.S./$7.99 Can.

THE VIRGINIA CITY TRAIL (BOOK 7)
_____ 95306-2 $5.99 U.S./$7.99 Can.

THE DODGE CITY TRAIL (BOOK 8)
_____ 95380-1 $5.99 U.S./$7.99 Can.

THE OREGON TRAIL (BOOK 9)
_____ 95547-2 $5.99 U.S./$7.99 Can.

THE SANTA FE TRAIL (BOOK 10)
_____ 96296-7 $5.99 U.S./$7.99 Can.

THE OLD SPANISH TRAIL (BOOK 11)
_____ 96408-0 $5.99 U.S./$7.99 Can.

THE DEADWOOD TRAIL (BOOK 12)
_____ 96816-7 $5.99 U.S./$7.99 Can.